Sandison, Janet
Jean at noon; or, Summer's treasure.
St. Martin's Press [c1971]
252 p.

I. Title.

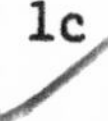

JEAN AT NOON

JEAN AT NOON
is the second of a four-novel sequence
under the general title of
'AN APOLOGY FOR THE LIFE OF
JEAN ROBERTSON'
the first of which, JEAN IN THE MORNING,
appeared in 1969.
Janet Sandison is the pseudonym of Jane Duncan,
author of the 'My Friend' sequence of novels

JEAN AT NOON

or

SUMMER'S TREASURE

JANET SANDISON

ST MARTIN'S PRESS
NEW YORK

Printed in Great Britain
Library of Congress Catalog Card Number: 76-166479
First published in the United States of America in 1972

AFFILIATED PUBLISHERS: Macmillan & Company,
Limited, London – also at Bombay, Calcutta, Madras and
Melbourne – The Macmillan Company of Canada,
Limited, Toronto

The author and publisher wish to thank the copyright holders of the verses quoted in the text

CHAPTER ONE

There's a one-eyed yellow idol to the north of Khatmandu,
There's a little marble cross below the town;
There's a broken-hearted woman tends the grave of Mad Carew,
And the Yellow God forever gazes down.

'The Green Eye of The Yellow God,' by J. Milton Hayes.

As I turned the key in the lock, the question uncoiled like a reptile in my mind: 'When I go in, will he be dead?' The question arose every time I went into our rooms and every time it was followed, as now, by the shamed glance downwards at my shabby shoes on the shabbier linoleum while I wondered whether the question were fathered by the wish for his death. Did I wish he were dead? I was never sure and I glanced over my shoulder and round the dim hall, feeling that if I wished my father to be dead, the guilt of this wish must stand behind me in physical form, ready to strike me down.

I picked up the letter that lay at my feet and let myself into the room, to be overtaken now, as always, by the uncertainty as to whether I was grieved or relieved that he was still alive when I found him sitting, as always, in his red plush armchair, his swollen feet and ankles on his red plush footstool, his eye-glass in his right eye, his red carnation made of stiffened cotton in his button-hole.

His sunken eyes looked at me over the bags that trembled on his cheeks; looked at me over the massive bag of his swollen paunch as he asked, as he did every evening: 'Good house, tonight, old boy?'

My father never called me by my name, Charles. He did not call anybody by name. He addressed men as 'old boy', 'old top', 'old thing' or 'old chap', and those that he considered to be of inferior rank as 'my good man' or 'my dear fellow'. When the man from the wine shop insisted on a payment on account, my father became very stern and said: 'Look here, my good man—'

'Do you want anything to eat?' I asked him.

'No, thankee, old chap. Just a little drink, I think,' and his pudgy yellow hand reached for the bottle of cheap red wine that stood on the cheap gilt table beside his chair.

Everything in this room of his was red plush and cheap gilt so that all about him was the aura of the music-halls in which he had spent most of his life. In November of 1923, the room was already a period piece with its heavy red plush draperies, its ornate gilt-framed mirrors and the red plush shawl, fringed with red silk, that draped the piano. From behind the red plush curtains and yellowed lace that screened the window, it was difficult to believe that, beyond the glass, lay a dank but fecund back street in Islington, greasy under the London fog, but, seen in the context of the street and the city, the room took on the air of a backwater into which had been washed the debris of a life and of a way of life that were in decay. The piano and the double bed, with its gilt headboard adorned with a figure of Eros, whose gilt bow was broken, were the main pieces of furniture and stacked along the walls were a number of battered trunks and hampers which contained what my father called 'my papers'. These were music-hall bills of performances in which he and my mother had appeared and newspaper cuttings which mentioned their names, Charles and Kitty Carew. My mother had died two years before, in November of 1921, after falling and breaking her thigh on the slippery steps that rose from the street to the door of the flats in which we had then lived. I did not know the details of her dying. I was at school at the time and my father did not let me know of her death or send for me until after she was buried and he had moved our household from Fulham to these cheaper rooms in Islington that we now occupied.

I was neither astonished, shocked nor hurt by what my father had done. I was only angry when he told me that, at sixteen, my schooldays were over and that I must turn to and earn my living. I begged him to let me transfer from the cheap boarding-school in Sussex to one of the free schools in London but he would not hear of this. 'These places are not fit for gentlemen,' he said but he did not object when, as a gentleman, I began to earn my living as an assistant in the grocery shop round the corner and, a little later, to earn a little more by playing the piano in the local cinema in the evenings. He ignored the grocery and approved of the cinema because it was tenuously connected with the 'business' and my mother had occupied such a position in a cinema in Fulham until she died. This was how my father lived, by a complex illogical system of ignoring all that displeased him and which could not be romanticised into pleasing him. The grocery was beyond romance but my chair at the piano in the pit of the sleazy cinema, which he had never entered, could be given something of the glamorous aura that surrounded the theatre in his mind. I suspected that the death of my mother was akin to the grocery in being beyond romanticisation. It seemed that she had fallen on the steps at about eleven-thirty at night and had lain there until about four in the morning, when she was found, unconscious and half-frozen, by a policeman who had had difficulty in waking my father. I had no doubt that he had retired to bed drunk, for there was no reason that that night when my mother had happened to fall should be different from any of his other nights, but I had never tried to discuss the matter with him because it would have been pointless. I accepted the death of my mother as a fact and my father quickly incorporated it into this scheme of things under the title of 'the tragedy'. It was a tragedy that he, a sick man, should have been so suddenly and terribly bereaved and it was because of the tragedy that I had to leave school and earn my living. The tragedy too necessitated our move to these cheaper rooms in Islington which were cluttered with the red plush, cheap gilt and old trunks of the splendid days before the tragedy, days which daily became more splendid in my father's mind but which I could remember as always having been on the sleazy edge of the shabby-genteel.

These rooms which we now occupied had originally been one room, probably a drawing-room on the left of the front door of the original house. A door in the corner of my father's room gave access to my own smaller apartment and we shared with two other lodgers a kitchen and a lavatory at the back of the hall. My own room contained no red plush or gilt although I had to give some of its space to three hampers of papers because my father's room could not contain them and it was always a relief to me to go through the doorway and shut out the plush and gilt and clutter.

The clutter was watched over by an enormous gilt-framed painting of my father which hung above the hearth where the gas fire sputtered day and night. The portrait depicted him in what had been his favourite role, as Charles Carew, Master of the Musical Monologue, as he was described in the play-bills, the role of Mad Carew in 'The Green Eye of the Yellow God'. It was a poorly executed work, yet it might have been good as a portrait, for it gave the impression that this handsome man, in army officer's mess dress, against a background of a romantically imagined Khatmandu, was mortally in love with himself. This seemed to me to be the most important truth about my father. He loved the romantic vision of himself that he had created. He loved himself as Mad Carew, as 'Rake' Windermere, as the handsome singer of sentimental songs who, according to himself, had rocked all the music-halls of Britain and North America and reality no longer came between him and this image. He saw himself still as the handsome Mad Carew and was unaware that as he sat, flabby and grossly swollen in his red plush chair, he looked more like a grotesque gigantic parody of the Little Yellow God.

When I looked at the portrait above the hearth, I was grimly aware of my own likeness to my father as a young man and when I looked at the figure in the red plush chair, I would hope to die before I became old.

I went round behind his chair to perform my first duty on each of my returns to the room, to take away and empty the urine bottle that lay on the floor between his right hand and the wall and I discovered now that in this corner there was a fresh crate containing eleven bottles of wine. The twelfth was on the table beside his chair and for perhaps the hundred-thousandth time, I wondered how much money he had left and whether he would die before he had spent it all on cheap wine, cheaper cigars and dark red cotton carnations. And on my way across the hall to the lavatory I wondered, too, why I did not abandon him and strike out on my own.

The answer to this question was the answer common to every question that had risen during the eighteen years of my life – money. This was the only constant in the shifting sands of life as I knew it. Money. If I abandoned my father, left this shabby dirty house, I would be no better off. Indeed, I would be considerably worse off. If he did nothing else for me, my father did pay the rent of this sleazy den of ours. I had a little over a hundred pounds in the bank, saved over the two years since my mother died and I had left school. Most of my life from the ages of six to sixteen had been spent at school, a school shabby-genteel like the rest of my background which, at the end of ten years, sent me home in a state of near-perfect non-education. I knew how to use a knife and fork and how to address a Dame of Empire in the unlikely event of my meeting one, but in my case the school had failed in the only thing it really tried to teach. It had failed to give me the illusion that I was a 'gentleman'. I came home from it for the last time with the knowledge that in five years I would be a twenty-one-year-old man and that I had no qualifications of any kind and worse, that I had, as far as I could see, no prospect of obtaining any. It was useless to yearn for contact with what I saw as the real world of real people by becoming a doctor, when a university where I might qualify was as remote as the stars and it was forlorn to think how long it might take to save enough to go to university out of my present earnings, which were four pounds, five shillings a week. I earned three pounds working in the grocery and I earned twenty-five shillings playing the piano in the cinema from six till ten-thirty six evenings a week. To learn to play the piano quite badly and mostly by ear had been part of my gentleman's education, the only part that could be turned into money.

I stared at the spattered wall behind the smelly lavatory bowl. How much money did the old man have left? How long would it be before he died? The dank smell of the bowl made me remember the smell of the chapel at school, the long sermons in which Christ and cricket seemed to mean the same thing, a sort of 'Play up! Play up and play the game!' Chapel had indicated that it was bad form to wish for somebody to be dead, especially your father, just as it was bad form to say that you wished to beat your opponents at cricket. Somewhere, outside in the real world of the streets, London and England, I knew that there were real things like right and wrong, good and evil, but inside this half-world where I was trapped there were only good and bad form, cricket and not cricket. Well, it might not be cricket to think of the old man dying but, still, would he do it before he had smoked and drunk all the money?

My father had always been inclined to drink too much but it was only after the death of my mother that his degeneration had become so rapid. He romanticised and excused his self-indulgence by claiming that the tragedy had been more than he could bear but I believed that, in actual fact, his present state of alcoholism was merely the logical progression of his former way of life.

The relationship between my mother and himself had been a curious one, but it was only after her death and I myself became a little older that I had begun to think about it and try to analyse it. Outwardly, they maintained a continuous love affair, a sickening demonstration of flirtatious gestures and coy endearments but, after my mother died and my father began to drink so heavily, I realised that she, although she publicly lived up to his pet-name for her which was 'Kitten-puss', had been able privately to exercise a control over him which no kitten could have exercised.

As he drank his wine, sighing and shedding maudlin tears over 'the tragedy', I began to feel that, under the tears and sighs, there lay a thankfulness that she was dead and he was free at last to indulge his appetite for alcohol, in the form of the cheap red wine which was genteel and also the best he could afford. During the last six months, he had never been out of his room. He could no longer walk, but shuffled on his swollen feet from his bed to the chair by the gas fire. Our life for me had been reduced to that single question: would he die before he had drunk and smoked all the money?

The few play-bills and press-cuttings from the past that I had troubled to read seemed to indicate that the double act of Charles Carew, Master of the Musical Monologue, supported by Kitty Carew at the pianoforte had earned a considerable amount of money in its time but that time was long ago. According to my father, the Great War and the cinema had been the double-murderers of artists like himself but he was well over fifty in 1914, I thought, and I knew that he was already drinking heavily and losing his flamboyant good looks.

During the war, I could remember him and my mother performing in some of the seedier suburban halls but during the five years between 1918 and 1923 he had earned nothing. It was during this period that my mother had become a cinema pianist.

When I returned to his room with the urine bottle, the level of the wine in the bottle on the table had sunk considerably and my father was staring dully ahead of him. I sent a glancing imprecation towards the thought of Mrs Hartley down in the basement who had, no doubt, fetched him this new case of wine. As I bent by the chair to place the urine bottle where he could reach it, he sighed out: 'Dear little Kittenpuss' in a maudlin whisper. This meant that he was lapsing into the drunken rose-flushed dream of the past that overtook him at this stage of wine and the evening. It meant too that he wanted an audience but I was not going to stay and listen to his maunderings. Kittenpuss. The name had always irritated me. My mother's name had been Catherine and this coy corruption of it by my father had been part of the spell of unreality that he had cast about her, just as the women who came to the grocery made me belie myself in a curious way when they addressed me as 'Handsome', which was their pet-name for me. I did not want to be petted by them, even to the slight extent of being given a pet-name but in this I was different from my mother, who had wanted to be petted by my father and had willingly behaved like a kittenpuss in order to please him. As I grew older, I had come to understand that no woman can be a kittenpuss and a mother at the same time and I began to recognise that my parents lived inside a cocoon of what they called 'Romance', which formed a screen between them and the rest of the world, including myself. They saw themselves not as parents but as lovers and I had grown accustomed to their regarding me as a strange encumbrance that had been wished upon them, but the word 'Kittenpuss' had brought back, momentarily, the resentment that had haunted my childhood, a resentment and a defiance set up to conceal my loneliness and my instinctive awareness that my mother was not really a kittenpuss. I did not know what the truth of her character was but I knew that the coy gambols of the kittenpuss were not the reality, whose hard edges showed fitfully through the veil of Romance, as when she brought in a small but regular wage as a cinema pianist while my father sat dreaming of the past, as when she flirtatiously placed a new red cotton carnation in his button-hole but remarked that they now cost threepence instead of the former twopence.

'There was once a day,' he had remarked on one such occasion, 'when I wore real ones, a fresh one each morning and each evening. Those were the days, my Kittenpuss,' and they were off, their ship of romance in full sail into the dream of the glorious past, removing them from reality, placing a clouded distance between them and myself.

I knew very little of my antecedents and most of what I had heard of them I was uncertain whether to believe. In this realm of romance in which my mother and father lived, truth was a rare bird that seldom found a resting-place and for as long as I could remember, I had been wary of the gilt over the grey plaster, the pink light reflected by the discreetly placed mirror. My father was, I believed, of Irish origin but I doubted the reality of the 'great house by the broad Atlantic', with its parchment of the Carew descent from Brian Boru, which he had left, cast off for ever by his family, to follow the star of his art as Master of the Musical Monologue. In a similar cautious way, I believed that Kittenpuss had originated in Glasgow but I doubted whether her father had been 'rolling in it, old boy and she gave it all up for her Carlo', as my father so often said. In the realm of romance, all frogs were princes once and all goose-girls princesses but the truth was never vouchsafed to me.

My bedroom was cold and stale-smelling as I drew from my pocket my week's money, prior to budgeting it into so much for food, so much for gas, so much for this, so much for that and a little left over to put into the bank. Why did I want so passionately to study medicine, to be a doctor? Had Kittenpuss's father, my grandfather, been a doctor, perhaps? This ambition had been with me for a long time, causing me to study in an ungentlemanly way that had made me very unpopular at school. Looking back, school had been a nightmare. Bad as things were now, they were better than then. Even to think of it made my right hand move towards my hair, an urge I repressed at once, knowing that I must ignore the horrible hair that had caused me to be known first as 'Bubbles', then as 'Beauty' before the two nicknames were run together into 'Bubbly-beauty' in recognition of my ready tears. I had cried a lot in the early days at school but not later on. In time, I became accustomed to the bullying, to having parents who hardly ever visited me and caused me agonies when they did because they were so different from all the other parents. I even became accustomed to being left at school during the holidays, came to prefer that, indeed, to coming home. Batsy, as we called our headmaster, Mr Batsford and his wife Mrs Batsy were old and stuffy but blessedly ordinary and there was no romance in their rooms on the attic floor where I lived with them above the empty echoing classrooms during the school holidays.

I remembered having pneumonia up there one Christmastime and how the doctor had brought me a present, the only real present I had ever had because my parents always gave me for Christmas clothes and football boots and cricket pads and things I had to have for school but did not want. The doctor gave me a cardboard box which had a book inside that told the story of a waggon train going across the American prairie and being attacked by Indians but in the box as well were cardboard models of all the people and animals and things in the story. There were white people and Indians and horses and the waggons, even wigwams and bushes and trees and I could sit in bed and act out the whole story of the battle.

The doctor told me that, one day, I might go to America

and see the real prairie for myself but I was doubtful. America was a place where my father and mother had been on tours but I seldom went where they went and the places they went to did not seem to be real. I was very doubtful about it indeed but then the doctor said: 'You will be a man some day and a man can go where he likes and do what he likes. You can go to America if you want to.'

'Could I be a doctor?' I asked him.

'Why not? If you are determined about it, you can be a doctor, Charles.'

Charles. I was happy to be called Charles and not Carew or Bubbly-beauty.

I stared down at the few notes and coins on the table. Why was I thinking of all this now? I sat down on my bed and stared at the wall, feeling that I was back in the attic room at school. I had been ten years old at that time when I had pneumonia and that doctor, whose name I had never known, had been the first real person, as I described him in my mind, that I had ever met. He was tall and thin, with dark eyes and a wooden leg which replaced the real one that he had lost in France in 1914, but although he had an artificial leg, the rest of him, the part that mattered, was real. He stayed the same, stayed his real self, no matter who he was talking to and did not change as Mr and Mrs Batsy did when they were in the presence of the only pair of titled parents who came to the school. He called people by their real names, like Charles and all the things he said sounded like real true things, as when he had said: 'If you are determined about it, you can be a doctor, Charles.' And because he was real, he was important, with an importance you could feel, an importance that made even Mr and Mrs Batsy a little afraid of him, afraid even to change in that queer way and suck up to him, as they sucked up to the titled parents. He was so real that, while they were in the room with him, Mr and Mrs Batsy became real too. They stopped being the 'Head and his good lady' and became a scared old couple who were afraid that a boy would die of pneumonia and get their school a bad name and damage their livelihood. The doctor had been so real, as I recalled it, that my ambition to be a doctor like him had persisted down the eight years from that time in the face of all the improbabilities of its realisation. 'If you are determined about it—' he had said. I was determined and I still believed him.

I sorted out the money slowly, putting off the moment when I would have to go back to my father's room, while all the time my duty to go there and try to persuade him into bed weighed on my conscience. My room was as cold and dank as the November rain that dripped out-of-doors but it was better than the plush and gilt cavern where the gas-fire popped its fumes into the miasma of cigar-smoke and the smell of urine.

All day, while I was out, my father used the urine bottle and he was careless with it, making drips on his clothes, on the plush chair, on the carpet, on his bed clothes and the stale smell had taken a permanent hold on the hot airless room.

When I had put my money away, I noticed on the table the envelope I had picked up from the hall floor when I entered the house. I must have pushed it into my pocket, escaping from it for a little while, as I always did with anything that came to us through the post. If he has run up another bill, I thought as I stared at the envelope, if he has not paid the rent again, I shall kill him, but I knew even as I thought it that I would not do it, not because it would not be cricket to kill your father but mainly because it would be stupid. Given a little time and a little more wine, he would kill himself. Perhaps the latest case of wine in the corner would be enough to do it. I picked up the envelope and turned it over. It was addressed to Charles Carew Esquire and on the flap at the back there was an embossed circle enclosing the embossed words: 'Moore, Donovan & Co., Solicitors, Dublin'. Suddenly, the shadowy fine old house by the broad Atlantic took on substance in my mind. Perhaps, after all, it existed and perhaps, too, the family had 'had a change of heart', as my father so often hoped might happen. I took the letter through to his room.

His eye-glass in his eye, he held the sheet of paper at arm's length and squinted at it, while I stood rigid with impatience. The eye-glass, a circle of plain glass on the end of a black cord, was mere decoration and he ought long ago to have had the spectacles that vanity would not let him wear. I doubted whether he could read the letter at all. He certainly read little of the text in the film and theatre magazines that Mrs Hartley in the basement lent to him and concentrated mainly on the illustrations.

At last, he allowed his right hand, which held the letter, to droop limply and dramatically over the arm of his chair while his left hand reached for his glass of wine. The pouches on his face and under his jowls quivered while the ready tears rose to his eyes.

'Alas,' he said, 'poor Lucy's dead,' and he took a sad sip from his glass.

'Lucy? Who is Lucy?'

He shook his bald yellowish head from side to side. 'She was me wife, old man,' he said, keeping a stiff upper lip.

It had happened at last, I thought. That red rot-gut has poisoned his brain, poor old bastard.

'Listen, old chap,' I said, standing beside his chair with my hand on his shoulder, 'your wife was Kitty, your little Kittenpuss and she died two years ago.'

'Kittenpuss, ah Kittenpuss,' he said and heaved a long sigh. 'Kittenpuss was m' love but not m'wife, old boy. No. Lucy was m'wife – the Honourable Lucy O'Shaughnessy, God rest 'er soul.'

'You are mad,' I shouted at him, 'mad, I tell you!'

I shook his shoulder violently, causing the wine in the glass to slop over on to his already stained trousers and he looked up at me, his face heavy with hurt and reproach before a senile leer spread outwards from his eyes over the folds of yellow flesh. In that moment, I knew that he was ugly, depraved, degenerate and many other things but that he was not mad.

'You didn't know that I once bedded down with an Honourable, old man?' he asked, as if he were having a cosy man-to-man chat with an acquaintance in a theatre bar.

'Look here, think what you are saying.' I was trying not to shout at him. 'If the Honourable Lucy whoever-she-was was your wife, what about my mother?'

'Your mother?' He looked up at me with drunken solemnity. 'She was m' little Kittenpuss, the love of m' life.' He set down his empty glass, moved his body in the chair a little, became very much the man of the world for a moment. 'So Lucy's dead. Very sad. A hard woman, a woman of little understanding but I am sorry she is gone. Poor Lucy.'

He swayed in his chair towards the nearly empty wine bottle and I took it up, refilling the glass but, before I handed it to him, I held on to it firmly for a moment and said: 'You were married to this Lucy? You and my mother were – lovers only?'

'Only? You say *only*?' He reached for the glass but I drew it away and he now became maudlin, tears welling over to be lost among the puffs and pouches of flesh on his face. 'What a love that was! We lived only for each other. My Kittenpuss was my true wife in the eyes of Heaven and now she is gone and Lucy is gone too and I, who have given so much to the world, am poor and sick and alone.'

'But this means that *I* am a bastard,' I said and dropped the full glass of wine on to the chipped tiles of the hearth where the gas-fire sputtered behind its row of white skeletons.

'Oh, come now, old boy,' my father said in outraged protest, whether at my language or at the loss of the wine I did not know, until he added: 'Kittenpuss and I did not intend –

after all, old chap, she was forty-five when you were born. I mean, who'd have thought it at forty-five, after all these years, don'tcherknow? Open another bottle of wine for me, there's a good chap.'

I did as he asked, set the bottle and a fresh glass on the table beside him and retired to my own room.

Sitting on my bed again, I felt a constriction of my throat and chest as if I were bound about with rope but when my brain cleared, I realised that the bonds were mental and not physical. The genteel schooling to which I had been subjected, which I had despised and had thought to have left me unaffected, now held my mind in its grip. I was a bastard, a manifestation of something that happened only in the 'lower' classes, among the 'skivvies' as the school maidservants were called. For what seemed to be a long time, I was suspended in a state of shock but it could not have been very long before full consciousness returned to me and, along with it, reason. Bastard I might be but, in my real self, I was no different from what I had been before. If anything, I was a little more real, in that I was aware of one more fact about myself and facts carry with them their overtones and implications. I had never been fond of my parents but this new fact removed by one flash of light much of the black guilt that my lack of affection had carried with it. 'Kittenpuss and I did not intend – I mean, who'd have thought it at forty-five, after all these years, don'tcherknow?' my father had said. The words explained a great deal, in particular those concealed considering glances that my parents had bent on me down the years, glances that implied that I was something that they could not account for, like a live squawking cuckoo in the red plush nest. Our abodes had always been called 'little nests' by my parents. Nests! Suddenly, a practical thought rose out of the chaos in my mind. That envelope had come straight from Dublin, to this address in Islington without being re-directed. How had that firm of solicitors known where my father was to be found? We had had many addresses in my lifetime, as we moved from one little nest to another, all in the seedier streets of London and all alike, for just as some birds line their nests with clay, my parents lined every nest with their gilt, plush, play-bills and photographs. Nevertheless, from the point of view of the post office, a nest in Islington is very different from a similar nest in Fulham.

I went back to my father's room and without asking for permission took up the letter from the table by his side.

'Dear Sir, We are instructed to inform you that the Honourable Mrs Lucy Mary Carew died on 25th November, 1922. Yours faithfully,' the letter said baldly above the scribbled signature of a clerk.

'How did these people know where to find you?' I asked my father. 'It is a year since she died. Why didn't they let you know before?'

'I wrote to Lucy, old man,' he said, looking down into his wine glass. He then added in his most hurt and peevish tones: 'Dead. Just think of it. And never left me a penny.'

I was accustomed to his inability to see anything except from his own point of view but this was so outrageous that I protested: 'Why should she leave you anything, for God's sake? She was your wife and you left her for another woman. Why should she leave you anything?'

He did not answer me, of course. This sort of logic was no part of his manner of thinking. 'A cold hard woman, Lucy. Always was. Rolling in it, that family.' He shook his head sadly. 'Not a penny,' he repeated. He was growing very drunk.

'Did you write to her asking her for money?' I asked.

Looking indignant, he made a vain attempt to raise himself in his chair, to take on the role of the last stanza of 'Rake' Windermere. At his failure, his indignation lapsed into peevishness. 'Certainly not,' he said. 'Thought the time had come t' let bygones be bygones. Felt that Lucy and I could be a comfort to one another in'r old age. After all—' his voice quavered ' – 's a lonely life for a man here alone day after day, night after night.'

And especially the nights, I thought, you dirty old brute, but there was no sense in quarrelling with him, no sense in expecting reason from him. What I wanted was information about how much money he had left and information about my mother.

'Where did you meet Kittenpuss?' I asked.

He looked pleased, took another sip of wine. 'Ah, what a night that was! June and the moon sailing above the trees, old boy and Kittenpuss like a flower in her blue satin dress.'

'Where was this?'

'At this castle.'

We were off into the realm of romance again. He had probably picked my mother up on some street corner.

'What castle?' I persisted.

'Scotland. Place called Loch-something. Near Glasgow. Lochbottom. No. Lochfoot. Had a singing engagement for this soirée this duke was giving at this castle. Gave them "Mary of Argyll" an' "Lost Chord", I remember. Could always get them with the Chord. Never a dry eye. Was only a singer in those days. Came to the monologues later on. By Jove, those were the days. "The Green Eye of the Yellow God". That was the one.

There's a one-eyed yellow idol to the north of Khatmandu,
There's a little marble cross below the town,
There's a broken-hearted woman tends the grave of Mad Carew—'

His wine glass was empty and taking the bottle from the table, I moved away from him. 'What was the name of this castle?' I asked.

'Castle?' He looked at the bottle in my hand. 'Windsor.

Ah, yes, I was engaged for Windsor once but they cancelled. Pour out a little drink, old boy.'

'The castle in Scotland,' I said, 'and Kittenpuss in a blue satin dress.'

'Mrs Simpson,' he boomed suddenly, in the voice of a major-domo or butler, 'Mr Simpson, Miss Simpson, Miss Jessie Simpson, Miss Catherine Simpson and there was my Kittenpuss.'

'Her name was Simpson?'

'Cer'ainly, old boy.' He made an impatient gesture at the bottle and I filled his glass. 'Queer thing. Two sisters like big scraggy crows and then Kittenpuss. She came away with me that night, old man. I can see it now, the moon above the trees as the carriage carried us down the drive to the station. 'snot given to everybody t'love as my little kitten and I loved.'

He maundered on for a long time but I received no more concrete information and when he was at last in bed, I turned the gas-fire and the gaslight low and went across the hall to the kitchen.

Simpson. It seemed fairly certain that my mother's name and therefore my own name was Simpson. What's in a name? Bubbly-beauty, Carew or Simpson. Did it matter? It did. When I left this place, I would leave it as Charles Simpson and take on my own real identity. Could bastards enter universities? There was some famous Scottish divine who had been born a bastard. Scottish universities took bastards anyhow. Scotland. Simpson. I looked round the kitchen with its tangle of pipes, gas pipes, water pipes, drain pipes, the tortured plumbing of an old house converted into flats that looked like a nest of serpents. First things first. It was useless to think of universities with only one pound, seven and ninepence left out of my week's money to put into the bank. How much money had the old man left? That letter to his wife Lucy had the smell of a desperate throw.

Later, lying in bed while the rain drip-dripped in the outer dark, it felt strange to be aware of knowing my father so intimately and to be aware at the same time that he did not know me at all. Neither he nor my mother had ever known me, had ever wanted to know me, for they had never allowed me to become a reality for themselves. I had always been the cuckoo in their nest, the accident, the 'who'd have thought it after all those years' that my father had spoken of tonight. I was not part of the Romance, the Carlo-Kittenpuss story. I had always been the encumbrance in my short periods at home before my mother died, the unwanted presence that made the twittering love-making on the red plush sofa slightly ludicrous.

'And has my Kittenpuss a little kiss for her Carlo?'

'Darling one!— Little poppety, run through and play with your soldiers, there's a love.'

My flesh crawled between the sheets when I thought of them, she already grown blowsy, he already showing the degeneration that was now so pronounced, still carrying on their legend among the chipped gilt and dusty red plush. If only I could be on my own, knowing nobody and being known by nobody.

How much money was left? Should I stay or should I go? Even if I went, the money that was left would surely come to me when he died if I kept in touch with the bank at the end of the street. Money and its filthy importance in this money world! Still, recognise its importance. Do not pretend like Carlo and Kittenpuss that it did not matter, that the world was well lost for love.

Perhaps their pretence about money had been the worst pretence of all, the pretence about it not mattering while, at the same time, they conserved what they had, spending it only for their own pleasure, as my father was doing with his wine and cigars. I remembered the 'little musicales', the cheap wine and sandwiches dispensed to a few music-hall artists less successful in former days than themselves, hospitality scantily given that Carlo and Kittenpuss might wallow in a little sycophantic admiration that would revive in memory the applause that had once rung out for Mad Carew.

Between the sheets, my body was cold and rigid with loathing for their entire second-rate world. And how much money was left? It was the most terrible thing of all to me that this was the vital question, that the only thing in the world that mattered to me that night was how much money still remained.

CHAPTER TWO

Each looked at each as he rode away.
Grim silence reigned supreme.
The sun went down and the moon held sway,
Flooding all with a silver stream.
Then a muffled form crept down the mound,
With a wistful glance about,
Then with head erect, but without a sound,
'Rake' Windermere stepped out.

'"Rake" Windermere,' by Leonard Pounds.

IN the days that followed, I hammered at the flabby pudgy yet defeating resistance of my father's mind, trying to discover the truth about our financial situation while his moods ranged from reproach to peevishness, from self-pity to ludicrous attempts at dignity but I learned nothing.

'University! Medicine! Disgusting profession. Sordid, really sordid, old boy,' he assured me. 'You should enter the real profession. After all, I have given you my looks, my flair for music. You may never have my presence on the stage but you could go quite a little way, yes indeed, with my name behind you.'

'My name is Simpson,' I reminded him.

He looked hurt, then became defiant as he said: 'It would have been Carew if it had been possible. Simpson would never do in the profession, never, especially these days.' He tapped the film magazine on the table by his chair. 'Italian names – that's the thing, old boy. Rudolph Valentino. Ramon Novarro. Even the British ones use Italian names. Look at Ivor Novello. That fellow Valentino is making a fortune out there in America. Pity your hair is yellow and curly. Took after little Kittenpuss there, you did. I was dark, almost black.

Dark's better for a man, more manly, don'tcherknow. You could dye it, of course.'

'All right,' I said. 'Give me the fare to America and I'll dye my hair and go.' I found it impossible to be serious all the time.

My father looked up at me, deeply hurt. 'The fare to America! D'ye know what you are saying, old top? I have hardly enough to keep body and soul together and *you* expect me to send you to varsity and pay your fare to America. You must look facts in the face, m'boy.'

I was more than willing to look facts in the face. 'How much money *have* we got?' I asked.

'My wants are simple and few,' he said sadly, 'simple and few.'

After a crazy claustrophobic few minutes of such conversation in the stuffy room, I was glad to escape to the grocery along the street or even to the piano chair in the picture house.

But despite all his advice to me to go to America, dye my hair and turn myself into Carlo Carova, I am quite sure that my father never visualised my leaving him. He lived in his world of dreams, ignoring the real world of the fuggy room and our sleazy way of life, yet he was confident that these basic realities of ours were immutable and permanent. He accepted that I would always be there to provide the water biscuits and cheese which were the only food he ate, to clean his room, to persuade him to change his linen and then help him to do so. He seemed to regard me as an automaton that supplied the sordid necessities of life, that performed the squalid duties such as emptying the urine bottle, thus leaving his mind free to dream his dreams, indulge his nostalgia for the past and think sadly of the harshness of Lucy, who had not left him a 'single brass farthing for the sake of auld lang syne'.

I did not want to stay with him and yet I could not go. I went on from day to day, wondering how long he would live, what we would do when his money was finished, wondering, even, how many bottles of wine I could provide for him each week when we came to live entirely on what I could earn. And this was in the face of my knowledge that he should not have wine at all. I spent all my spare time reading books which I drew from the public library, one literary classic and two or three medical books each week. My reading in the medical text-books had taught me enough to recognise my father's condition as of heart and liver origin, to recognise the asthmatic character of his breathing and the dropsy that caused the swelling of his belly, legs and feet. In my own way, I think I fled from reality as my father did. I think I knew that he could never grow better and I think I wanted to provide for him, if I could, the comfort of the cheap wine that was killing him, but these things I did not admit to myself. 'Christmas,' he said one evening about mid-December. 'Ah, Christmas. In the old days, my boy, Kittenpuss and I celebrated Christmas at the Café Royal every year. Those were the days *and* the nights.' He burst into breathy song:

'Or ever the knightly years were gone
With the old world to the grave,
I was a king in Babylon
And you were a Christian slave.

Ah, the poetry of those days and those nights,' he continued. 'We must have a little party at Christmas, dear boy, a little party, a little bird and a little bottle as Kittenpuss used to say.'

Yes, while I had pneumonia in the attic at school, I thought, but, even against my will and in the teeth of my own self-pity, I provided the bird and the bottle for Christmas. I have been glad, since, that I did. I found him dead in bed on the morning of Boxing Day, 'Rake' Windermere finally stepped out at last and I am glad that he had his final party, although it was probably instrumental in killing him.

The doctor was sympathetic, as were the managers of the

grocery and the picture house and the people from the other rooms in the house but, after the cheap funeral, when I came back to the red plush room out of the rain in the street, I felt very lonely, a little frightened and curiously bereft. He had been impossible, a monstrosity both in mind and body, but he had needed me. He had been someone to serve and it was this giving of service that I missed most. The outside world which, when he had been with me, had beckoned so enticingly, now seemed vast and hostile, with no need for someone called Charles Simpson.

The manager of the bank at the end of the street, try as he would, looked more relieved than sad when I told him my news. The letter to Lucy had been, as I had thought, a desperate throw, one of my father's wilder dreams of romance-to-the-rescue for, when the funeral expenses had been paid, there remained to my credit the sum of ninety-eight pounds, three shillings and twopence.

'You might as well say it,' I told the bank manager. 'My father died just in time.'

Like most people, the banker was averse to bringing into the light what could be left under the carpet and he made a deprecating little noise before venturing a gentle rebuke of my raw youth.

'Mr Carew was not to know, any more than it is given to the rest of us to know, what life holds for us. Mrs Carew's death was most tragic and unexpected.'

'My mother's death? What – why – how is that connected – ?' I stopped in confusion.

'Her income died with her. Mr Carew was not to know this would happen,' he told me a shade impatiently.

'She had an income? How much?'

He looked regretful at having spoken, nervous, gave a dyspeptic little burp. 'I am not sure that this is relevant.' He frowned, moved the blotter on his table by half-an-inch. 'Bank business is highly confidential, you know, young man.'

'I am my father's sole heir as you yourself have told me. His will was left in your hands. Surely it is no breach of confidence to inform *me* about my family's affairs. What was the nature of my mother's income? Did it come from an investment?'

'I do not know, Mr Carew.'

'Then what *do* you know?' I had a sudden certainty that I could bully him, that there was something in me that he feared. He was a nervous, rabbity little man, the sort of man born to a lifetime of petty importance, treading thin ice spread over a pit of fear of bigger men and bigger importances. What he feared in me could only be the aura of wealth, the only importance that he recognised.

'Mrs Carew died in November. At 1st December, the sum of two hundred pounds was drafted to the credit of her account at this bank. I had to inform Mr Carew that it was my duty to inform the drafting bank of Mrs Carew's decease.'

I wanted to laugh for I seemed to hear the voice of my father in this office along with us: 'Come, come, my good fellow, is that necessary?' Instead of laughing, however, I gave a long sigh and rose from the chair. For a glorious moment, life had seemed to be taking a better turn but I came bumping back from the realm of romance into winter in Islington. Then, with my hand on the doorknob, a thought struck me.

'This money that was drafted – where was it sent from?'

'Sent from? It was forwarded from our Fulham branch where—'

'Where did the draft come from originally?'

'Originally? It is a long time since I had to inform the drafting bank with regret of the decease of Mrs—'

'You must have some record,' I interrupted his pomp and circumlocution. 'It is only two years and one month since my mother died.'

He looked frightened, then took on a look of desperate

determination to satisfy me and be rid of me at any cost. 'One moment, please,' he said, went away and was gone for a long time. When he returned, he was carrying a dusty buff-covered file of papers which he began to thumb through slowly, clumsily and with a furtive air as if my prying eyes might catch some glimpse of the holy-of-holies in the Temple of Mammon, but at last he gave a satisfied little snort and closed the file with the index finger of his right hand between the pages. Hugging the papers against his breast, he said: 'The drafting bank was the Bank of Scotland, Lochfoot by Glasgow, and that is all I can tell you, Mr Carew.'

His voice was hurried, low and shaking as he summoned all his courage to defend to the last drop of his blood the inner secrets of his temple.

'That will do,' I said. 'Thank you. Good afternoon.'

I walked back to the rooms through the cold rain in a dream state that made me afraid, afraid that I had inherited enough of my father's nature to make me a victim of romance. Still, as I brewed a pot of tea in the kitchen, it seemed incontrovertible that, until twenty-five months ago, there had been somebody in Lochfoot by Glasgow who had enough money and enough interest in my mother to send her the sum of two hundred pounds a year. My grandfather? An uncle? Who? By the time I had drunk my tea, my plans were made. I was going to Lochfoot to find my relatives but first I had to get rid of the last debris of my parents' lives.

Having informed the landlord of my intention to leave the rooms at the end of January and having resigned from my post at the piano in the cinema, I gave my evenings to the examination and disposal of the contents of all the trunks and hampers. I hoped to find some further information about my antecedents, something that would place me more definitely in the vast world about me but as I emptied hamper after trunk and carried the contents down to the dustbin in the basement, I found nothing. Every music-hall programme and news-cutting that carried the names of Charles and Kitty Carew had been hoarded; there were photographs by the hundred, photographs of my father in his various roles, photographs of my mother, seated in evening dress at a piano, photographs of both in theatre foyers and by ships' rails but there was nothing that was relevant to the one incident in their lives that was not utterly ephemeral, myself.

My mother had had a few old-fashioned pieces of jewellery, I remembered and also some furs, but my father must have sold these things during the two years since her death for they were nowhere to be found now. Still, as I turned out trunk after hamper, the hope remained with me that I would find something informative or something of value but it was not until the last trunk of all that I found the last of my inheritance. Among yet another welter of Mad Carew in his mess dress and 'Rake' Windermere in his pith helmet, there was a faded photograph of three young women, two tall and dark, one short and fair, grouped about a potted palm and wearing evening dresses of about the year 1880. Under the picture, which was glued to an oblong of cardboard, was printed: 'John Shaw, Sauchiehall Street, Glasgow.' Looking at the faded ghosts of the young women, I heard my father's voice: 'Queer thing. Two sisters like big scraggy crows and then Kittenpuss', and when I turned the cardboard over between my hands, I found on the back, in faded ink, the words: 'Bessie, Jessie and me in our dresses for the soirée at the Castle.' The capital letter of the last word had been written with a bold proud flourish as if the writer had had some foreknowledge of how the soirée was to change the course of her life, I thought fancifully but I knew that what the capital letter more probably indicated was the social importance of this event for which these grand new dresses had been purchased. My mother had always had a high respect for rank and wealth, especially for wealth.

I laid the photograph carefully aside and went on with

renewed hope through the contents of the trunk but I found nothing more of interest until I came upon a book at the bottom, a book in a faded red cover that bore the title in black letters: *A Garland of Gems for Drawing-room Performance.* Between my hands, it fell open at a page headed: '"Rake" Windermere by Leonard Pounds. (Best suited for performance by Gentlemen).'

I threw the book at the heap of photographs for the dustbin and now it fell open at the fly-leaf, making me pick it up to read what was written there. 'To Cathie on her eighteenth birthday with love from Mama.' I closed the cover and laid the book carefully beside the photograph of Kittenpuss and the two scraggy crows.

Nothing now remained in the trunk except a few scraps of paper at the bottom but it was there between a torn theatre programme and a card inscribed: 'Roses for my rose of all the world with love from Carlo' that I found my birth certificate. It informed me that I was born in Edinburgh on the tenth of June, 1905, a male, named Charles Simpson. There was a column headed 'Name, Surname, and Rank or Profession of Father, Name and maiden Surname of Mother, Date and Place of Marriage', but it contained the words 'Catherine Isabella Simpson' and nothing more. It confirmed, I thought somewhat wryly, that I was not only a bastard but a Scottish bastard of Irish extraction, a mixture which my genteel school would have considered unseemly and ungentlemanly.

Towards the end of January, the entire contents of my home realised the sum of one hundred and three pounds and some shillings, the best-selling items being, to my amazement, the many framed play-bills which covered the many cracks and stains on the wallpaper. The large painting of my father as Mad Carew was sold for five shillings.

With my bank-book in my pocket, along with ten pounds in cash and all my other belongings in one suitcase, I made my way to Euston Station, filled with a tremulous sense of life just beginning, of the past being a nightmare from which I had just awakened into a free and wonderful world. I had little faith in the outcome of this journey I was making and no belief that, even if I found any Simpsons in this place called Lochfoot, they would take any interest in me or my story. In my experience, people were interested only in themselves and their own stories but I was young, it was mid-February and in the air there was a sense of spring lurking in the wings, waiting to take the stage in the first shaft of sunshine, at the chirp of the first sparrow. I still had less than four hundred pounds and medical school was as far away as ever but, by some means, the great day might come. On that confident morning, in that new freedom, everything seemed possible. I suppose that I had inherited some of my father's outrageous optimism, the optimism that made him hope that Lucy would leave him 'something for auld lang syne'.

As the train rattled northwards through Crewe, on through Cumberland and into the Scottish Lowlands, I amused myself with the *Garland of Gems for Drawing-room Performance*. Here they all were, 'The Green Eye of the Yellow God', '"Rake" Windermere' and all those other nightmares of my childhood which had always stood like masks between me and my parents, between my parents and reality, but now the verses were rendered harmless and ludicrous, pathetic on the printed page in their falseness as poetry, pathetic as my father had been pathetic in the end in his falseness as a man.

The book also contained 'The Orphan Boy's Tale' which had often been 'given' by my father to pianoforte obbligato by my mother at the little musicales which they often staged for their own amusement. I remembered how I used to hide in the hall cupboard of the Fulham flat, stopping my ears as it began. It turned me into Bubbly-beauty, not because of its own content, rendered with hideous sentimentality by my father and mother, but because it made me aware of my own orphaned feeling, brought to the surface the terrifying sense of being an outsider from which I was always hiding. But as I read it now it made me smile.

Look down, dear parents! Look and see
Your happy, happy orphan boy

it ended on a note of pathos and I had a wild desire to shout my own orphan happiness to the Heavens.

At the station in Glasgow, about six in the cold dark of the evening, I asked a kindly policeman about Lochfoot and how far it was from the city.

'Up the line – forty minutes or so the train takes.'

'Is it a big place? Shall I be able to find a hotel or lodgings there?'

'Och, aye. Enquire at the police station when ye get there, lad.'

He went on to direct me to another railway station from which the trains to Lochfoot left and I thanked him and went on my way through the soft, cold grey rain, feeling that I was in a strange land where people spoke in an unfamiliar tongue. My memories of that time are keen and clear, as if my mind had been a new clean sheet, receiving the first impressions of a new life.

As the policeman had said, the train took only about forty minutes, although it stopped some six times before a voice called 'Lochfoot!' through the dark and I got out. I found the police station, a cosy place with a warm fire of bright coal in the office. The policeman told me of a small hotel called the Lochfoot Arms near at hand and as I was turning away, I said: 'By the way, I am looking for some friends I have lost touch with. The name is Simpson.'

He was a large fat man with a heavy belly and I was predisposed to dislike and distrust men of this aspect but he was helpful enough. 'There's two or three of the name of Simpson in the town,' he said, coming round from behind the high wooden barrier and looking at me downwards from face to feet, then looking up at my face again. 'There's Simpson the gravedigger up at the cemetery – ' he considered me ' – but *you* wouldna be looking for *him*.' Why was he so sure about this?

'There was a Miss Bessie Simpson and a Miss Jessie Simpson—' I began, wondering what more I could say about my lost friends, having now already said all I knew.

'Och, *now* I know where you're at, sir,' he interrupted me, his manner becoming deferential. 'That will be the Misses Simpson o' Laurelbank, sir, up in the Crescent.'

After this, I had some difficulty in getting out of the police station, so anxious was the man to help me, so profuse was he in the detail of his directions as to how I would find Lochview Crescent and then Laurelbank, so inquisitive was he about my connection with what he called 'the ladies' there. But at last I was able to bid him an unenlightened goodnight and find myself a room at the Lochfoot Arms.

Having had a meal, I went straight up to bed but I could not sleep in spite of my long strange day. It was so difficult to absorb the fact that these women in the photograph, Bessie and Jessie, were real people of flesh and blood and not figures of romance like all the Mad Carews and 'Rake' Windermeres. The photograph beside my bed must have been taken in the 1880's, judging from the dresses on which I had become fairly experienced on my way through those trunkfuls of photographs and this was the year 1924. It was difficult to believe that Bessie and Jessie were still here after forty years, still here and recognised immediately and with deference by the police sergeant. Cold as it was, I got out of bed and examined my face in the glass, smiling at myself. My hair had curled with the rain, as it always did, but women admired it as a rule. Yes. As the old man had said, he had given me his looks and maybe the hated 'beauty' that had been the derision of my school-fellows might be of some service after all. I returned to bed and now examined the faded photograph. My little jet of confidence seeped away. The two scraggy crows did not look susceptible, as I had found teashop waitresses and shop assistants susceptible. The charm that had worked upon Kittenpuss would have no effect on those two who, it seemed, had failed to charm or be charmed during forty long years.

Perhaps it would be as well, I comforted myself, if they were not susceptible, for I had always promised myself that I would never use such sleazy means as physical charm in any situation of importance, that I would never get 'round' people as my father had got 'round' our fellow lodger Mrs Hartley or any other person who could be useful to him. I wanted very much to study medicine and was prepared to go to some lengths in order to do so but even more than this I wanted a life that was real, without pink lampshades and distorting mirrors, a life free of flattering and being flattered, a life that was open, clear and free of shams.

Maybe, I thought now in my uncertainty, I had wasted some of my precious money on the new suit and shirt that hung in the wardrobe, on this long journey of forlorn hope but I felt no regret for, for the first time in my life, I felt that I was my own man, a person with a clearly outlined identity. And there was just a chance that these women who seemed to be 'people of substance' as the phrase went, might lend me the money for a university training, for the sake of auld lang syne, in the words of my father. People of substance. That is what I was now, I told myself. I was not, as is commonly meant by the cliché, a rich man but, for the first time in my life, I felt secure in the substance of my own identity.

CHAPTER THREE

Look down, dear parents! Look and see
Your happy, happy orphan boy.
'The Orphan Boy's Tale,' by Mrs Amelia Opie.

IN the morning, I awoke early and planned the strategy of my day while I gazed at the photograph of my mother and her two sisters. My mother had been sixty-one when she died, if my father had been truthful when he said that she was forty-five when I was born. The photograph showed that she had been younger than her sisters which meant that these two women must now be at least in their late sixties. My mother, I remembered too, in spite of her flight into romance with my father, had been in many ways a stickler for the petty conventions. All the years in what was called the 'gay Bohemia' of the music-halls, the coy love-making and the little musicales among the red plush and gilt had not stripped her of the trappings of her upbringing, which had hung around her mind like tattered veils or sometimes, suddenly, led to criticism of other people in words as sharp as splinters of whale-bone.

The correct time to serve tea was four o'clock in the afternoon and the guest who called uninvited at that hour was, in my mother's eyes, lacking in gentility. The correct time for such a call was between three and four and, after twenty minutes, the guest should leave unless invited to remain to tea. I decided to arrive at the door of Laurelbank between three o'clock and fifteen minutes past, on the assumption that a convention which had remained with my mother throughout forty changing years might also have remained with her two sisters who had spent forty years without, it seemed, any change at all. Having made this decision, I had breakfast and went out to explore the town of Lochfoot.

Overnight, the weather had changed and the drizzling rain had given way to frost and bright sunshine from a clear far-away sky, the sort of weather when the world looks its best. Lochfoot, however, did not look very well. It was a grey, huddled little invalid of a town, crouching by the side of a cold sparkling lake – or loch, I supposed, this being Scotland. Yes, loch and this was the reason for the name Lochfoot. The first thing I noticed when I came round the corner from the little hotel was a recess in a high wall opposite to the railway station, where the main street of the town turned into a road, along which tramlines ran away towards a smoky haze in the middle distance. The recess contained the town's war memorial which was of a kind new to me in that it was topped by a life-size sculptured bronze figure of a soldier wearing a kilt, the strange dress reminding me that I was now a travelled man.

I turned away from the memorial, crossed the main road and went along a narrower one beside the station yard. The pavement ran along by a high wire fence which enclosed a gravelled rectangle in whose centre lay a grey building with a board above the door which bore the legend: 'O.K. Shirt Factory.' As I passed, the door in the end of the building burst open as if by some explosive pressure from within and a screaming crowd of young women poured out on to the gravel. The youngest of them were about fourteen, the oldest not more than twenty-five but they came screaming forth like prisoners released and gone berserk. Seeing me, the stranger, on the road, they rushed towards the fence, peered through it at me with monkey-like curiosity and as I passed by, hot with embarrassment, I said: 'Good morning.' They fell silent for a second and then one of the older ones, just separated from my shoulder by the steel mesh of the fence, screamed: 'Jesus, it's the Prince o' Wales himsel'! Three cheers for His Highness!' and the others began to yell like furies. To an accompaniment of yells and high giggles, I managed to leave the fence and its enclosed menagerie behind without tripping, falling and giving them further cause for amusement while I swore never to walk this way again.

This little factory building stood by itself and the narrow road led round it in a loop back to the main street, where the usual shops opened on to the narrow pavement, the butcher, the baker, the fishmonger, then the door of a church, then a fish and chip shop, then a junk shop, then two tenements, one of them burned out at the end. It was the squalid little street of any squalid little town and much more ugly than the back streets of Islington or Fulham, the ugliness stressed by the fact that after I had passed the tenements, a public-house and a few more shops, I was practically in open country. There was an old farm-house at a corner with a sign over its gate that declared it to be the Castleside Antique Gallery. It looked expensive, exclusive, prosperous and out of keeping with the rest of the town. A little way beyond this, there was a grey building inside high iron railings, a school, where children were shouting in the playground and I decided not to run that gauntlet. It was probable that the children would have an attitude to strangers similar to that of the women at the shirt factory. I turned round and looked back towards the town. From here, it looked more than ever like an untended invalid because, I think, there was so little of its small grey self in the bright sunshine of this broad countryside. There are so many squalid little streets in Fulham or Islington that they take on the importance of mass and no green countryside is near enough to highlight their ugliness.

On the way back I avoided the main street, took a road to my left under the high stone wall and, having rounded a curve, I found myself in a strangely other world, a little old village, far older than the Victorian town. It consisted of some twenty cottages with neat name-plates on their gates, Ivy

Cottage, Holly Cottage, Lilac Cottage but no Laurelbank. Indeed, the name in this backwater would have been incongruous.

'Good morning. Bonnie day,' said an old man from behind the gate of Rose Cottage.

The greeting cheered me with its friendliness. 'Good morning,' I answered him. 'Can you tell me where to find Lochview Crescent?'

'You are at the wrong end o' the town for that,' he told me and directed me to return to the main street and then take a turning to my left and up a hill.

'Thank you,' I said and he responded with: 'You're welcome, lad.'

I would have liked to talk to him for a little longer but I could think of nothing to say and I turned away with the word 'welcome' sounding in my ears. I chose to regard it as a good omen. Having followed his instructions, it seemed that I was heading for the open countryside again for very soon the pavement ended and the road ran through woodland with, again, that high stone wall on one side but quite suddenly there was a wall on my left as well as on my right, then an opening in this second wall and a large white plate, lettered in black: 'Lochview Crescent'.

The houses were Victorian villas, huge, grey, hideous and rank with the smell of money, great solid lumps of wealth, each lump standing in some two acres or more of garden. 'The Beeches', 'Glendaruel', 'Balmoral', 'Sutherland Villa' said the letters on their solid stone gate pillars, each one more secure and smug than the last, every one withdrawn and hostile even to the one next door, all keeping themselves and their secrets to themselves behind their shaven lawns and heavily curtained windows. Laurelbank, when I came to it, was even bigger and more solid than the others and it seemed also to be more withdrawn and hostile and as I walked slowly past, looking at it, the old man's word of welcome began to fade like an echo in the distance. I went a little way past its walled frontage, the wall topped by tall iron railings, then turned about and came quickly back between the two rows of rectangular blocks on either side of the road, drawn up as if in battle array and hurried out on to the main road and down the hill to the town. My courage had left me. This expedition to Scotland had been a failure. People who had lived for forty years under that heap of grey stone would have no sympathy with me and my ambitions. In houses like Laurelbank, I was sure, live things like sympathy and ambition did not exist. These were houses of the dead where people sat for forty years in their dimly lit solid caves of wealth until, in the end, they died. It was all a dream. My life could not be in any way connected with these houses or the people who lived in them. I would catch the first train back to Glasgow and from there the first train back to London, to Islington, the environment that I knew.

Back in my hotel room, I packed the new suit and shirt in my suitcase but when I picked up the photograph of the two scraggy crows and Kittenpuss, I felt an inner flush of shame. I had not even as much courage as my father when he wrote his last-throw for-auld-lang-syne letter to Lucy. I was a craven coward. I had been a coward all my life but I had always told myself that it was circumstances that made me so, that when I was free and could control my own life I would no longer be a coward because there would no longer be situations, not of my own making, that made a coward of me. If I turned and ran now the shame of it would be with me for ever. It did not matter now if these women refused to lend me the money I wanted. This had become secondary. I had to see them, to let them see me, to come face to face with them, to discover the last thing I was ever likely to discover about the background that had made me what I was.

At last the clock in the hotel hall showed fifteen minutes to three and feeling like an absurd parody of 'Rake' Windermere in my new suit, with head erect I stepped out and up through the town, up the road and along the curve of the Crescent to the gates of Laurelbank.

There was a long sweep of gravel drive between the gates and the front door, firmly shut at the top of its white marble steps and I felt cold and sick as I pulled the brass knob of the bell handle. I should have worn my overcoat but it was too shabby. I could hear the bell ringing faintly, forlornly, far away but there was no other sound. Perhaps the house was empty. Perhaps they were away. No. There was not to be that reprieve. There was a sound of a door opening inside and as the heavy door in front of me began to creak open I drew a deep breath. I have no idea now what horror I expected that opening door to reveal but what it did reveal has remained with me all my life.

A little girl stood there, a girl who seemed to be no more than twelve years old, wearing the afternoon uniform of a parlourmaid of that era, some sort of frilly white cap and a little apron, but it was her face that was so astonishing. When the front door first opened between us, it was the face of any stranger confronting any stranger, a pretty little face, closed, distant, faintly interrogative. Then, as the police sergeant had done the night before, she looked from my face down to my feet, then back up to my face again and as our eyes met, mine looking down, hers looking up, for she was very small, the most extraordinary change came over her. I could hardly have described the change then but in the light of more modern technology I can make an attempt now. Most people have seen those films, taken by slow-motion camera, of some lengthy process such as a butterfly emerging from the chrysalis or the opening of a flower and when the film is shown it is speeded up, so that the butterfly emerges or the flower opens in a few seconds. This is the sort of thing that happened to this child's face. It was exactly like a flower opening, there was a second of full radiance and then it closed again, became distant, very professional, very much the face of the well-trained parlourmaid, but I suddenly seemed to hear again the old man's word of welcome.

'Good afternoon,' I said. 'Are the Misses Simpson at home?'

'What name will I say, sir?' She spoke with the accent of the town in the thin fluting voice of a child.

'Charles Simpson.'

With curious deliberation, she motioned me to step into the hall, whereupon she shut the outer door and then the inner, which was panelled with stained glass. She then looked up at me for a second and it looked as if that strange opening of the flower were to happen once more but, instead, she lowered her eyelids, brushed her small hands over her muslin apron and was dead still for a second before she looked up at me again and said: 'This way, sir.'

I followed her across the large dimly-lit hall past a suit of armour that stood at the bottom of the staircase. It was, like myself, six feet tall, so that, when I passed it, my eyes were level with its closed visor while above its helmet and my own head towered the axe-like blade of the halberd that was held in its mailed fist, the end of the long shaft resting on the floor beside its pointed iron shoe. In my nervous state, my brain jangled with impressions. The thick carpet under my feet felt like a morass, the dim light and the solid richness of everything around me seemed to close in like a jungle in nightmare. I fixed my eyes on the back of the little girl's blue dress with the white bow of the apron at the waist as she led me to a dark mahogany door in the corner of the hall furthest from the entrance. Here, she suddenly seemed to stiffen as if bracing herself before, again with that curious deliberation, she placed her hand on the knob, turned it and pushed the door wide open and said: 'Mr Charles Simpson, madam.'

I understood at once why she had braced herself. The simple announcement of my name was as if she had exploded a bomb in the middle of the heavily-curtained, heavily-furnished room.

Two women sprang out of chairs on either side of the large red fire, snatching steel-rimmed spectacles from their noses as they did so. My mother had been myopic, I remembered, and I believe that she would have preferred to have been surprised stark naked by a stranger to having been surprised wearing her spectacles.

'Jeanie, what does this mean?' thundered the bigger of the two women at the little girl who made no reply but merely bowed her head meekly and turned away as if to leave the room. 'Jeanie, show this – this person out!'

The voice was still commanding but there was a quaver in it and I was suddenly aware of a curious odour in the hot stuffy air that flowed towards me in the doorway, the odour of fear. I felt that I had an advantage of some kind over these two big ugly women with the black shawls round their shoulders, but the whole atmosphere of the house was so inimical and oppressive that I would have ignored the advantage and have gone away if it had not been for the little girl. At the command to show me out, she had turned towards me, her back towards her employers, and now she looked up into my face, her own face utterly expressionless until the lid of her left eye fell shut, the dark lashes forming a fan on her cheek, while the right eye looked at me, vividly blue and brilliant, with what seemed to me to be encouragement. Boldly I stepped past her into the middle of the room and said: 'I am not going quite yet, Aunt Bessie.'

The two women backed away from me and their fear was now almost palpable, seeming to writhe about the room like an invisible serpent.

'Jeanie, you will remain,' the bigger one said. 'Close the door.' She pulled her shawl more tightly round her shoulders and shivered. 'Yes, madam.' The little girl shut the door and sat down on an upright chair which stood just inside it, as if this were a procedure to which she was accustomed. The less big of the two women – she was not small, only less big than her sister – now sat down, almost cowering in her chair, but the bigger older one remained standing, her hands gripping the back of a chair so tightly that the white sharp bones of her knuckles seemed to be about to break through the skin. But on her chair by the door, the little girl sat as if enclosed in a cocoon of calm, her face impassive, waiting, as if she were unaware of any tension.

It was an absurd interview. The sitting woman did not speak at all and the older one spoke only to repeat the one word 'impostor' again and again but, in spite of that, I said everything I had come to say. I offered the standing woman the photograph and the birth certificate, but she would not take them from my hand or look at them. I told her of my knowledge that two hundred pounds a year had come to my mother from this town until the time of her death and asked that a similar amount should be lent to myself each year until I had completed my studies. At every pause, the woman pronounced the word 'impostor' and several times I wondered why I did not turn about and leave the house but, in addition to the fear, there seemed to be also some dynamic force in the room that was driving me on until I had said everything I had come to say. It did not take long. 'Impostor!' said the woman for the last time.

'Very well,' I said. 'Good afternoon, Aunt Bessie, Aunt Jessie,' and I turned away.

The little girl opened the door, we went through and she closed it again and preceded me across the hall where she opened the stained-glass door and closed it behind both of us.

'Turn left outside the gate, sir,' she said quietly and without expression of any kind, her voice like that of the boy at school who used to talk in his sleep. 'Go down to the end of the Crescent, turn left and then left again and come along to the back drive. Wait there till I come out. I'll maybe be a little while. I have to calm the ladies down.'

Before I could speak she had slipped back into the hall and I heard a key turn in the lock of the inner door.

Blinking my eyes in the cold February sunlight, I began to walk down the drive, almost convinced now that the entire time spent inside that house had been a nightmare. I even looked back to assure myself that the great block of grey stone was really there. My feeling was that if the house and the two women were real, the little girl must be a dream or that if the little girl were real, the rest must be a nightmare. Nevertheless, I obeyed her instructions, going left, left and left again, which took me along a sort of mews, bordered on one side by a high wall with trees behind it, on the other by the garden walls of the villas. I waited among tall rhododendrons inside the Laurelbank gates for quite a long time before the little girl came running round a curve of the drive, a coat over her shoulders, a torn scrap of paper in her hand.

'In here, sir,' she said and led me further into the tangle of shrubs inside the gateway, where she handed me the scrap of paper which was the heading torn from a letter.

'This is their men o' business,' she said, pointing to the black copper-plate script, and I read: 'Guthrie, Guthrie, Inglis & Guthrie, Solicitors, Notaries Public' above an address in West Nile Street in Glasgow.

She now laid her hand on my sleeve and looked up at me earnestly from under the frilly white cap. 'Ye want Mr James Guthrie, the old chap. Don't let them palm ye off with anybody else but old Mr Guthrie. He's great, the real mackay. *He'll* make them see sense.'

She spoke hurriedly and her accent and idiom were giving me difficulty. 'Mr James Guthrie,' I repeated obediently.

'That's right. I have to get back. The ladies are up to high doh and like to burst their b'ilers,' she said, ending on a giggle before she became grave again. 'There's just one thing,' she said. 'I'm no' *in* this. I'm no' *in* it, see?'

'In it?'

Small and lithe, she was poised for flight and I now caught her by the arm, arresting her. She made an impatient little movement. 'Tell old Guthrie any yarn ye like about how ye got his address but don't mention *me*.'

'Oh, I see. All right. I won't.'

'Right.' She was about to take flight down the drive but I maintained my grip on her arm. 'Why are you helping me like this?' I asked.

Such a look of scorn came over her little pointed face that I felt she regarded me as an idiot or even suspected me of trying to flirt with her.

'They're ro'en wi' it,' she said. 'Whitry gaun dae wi' it? Leave it ti' the cat an' dug hame?'

She was out of sight down the drive between the dark shrubs before I had made the translation: 'They are rotten with it. What are they going to do with it? Leave it to the cat and dog home?'

'Thank you,' I said quietly to the spot where she had stood.

'Rotten with it.' I liked the phrase. My father had always used the expression 'rolling in it' of people who were very rich, an expression which had always made me visualise a dog rolling in ordure, but the phrase 'rotten with it' carried an even stronger implication of the corrupting power of wealth.

Back in my room at the little hotel, I was full of a new confidence which, when I tried to analyse it, seemed to have been instilled into me by the little girl called Jeanie, hideous name. I was already, in my mind, a member of a medical school, living on an adequate allowance lent to me by the two big ugly women in the dark brown stuffy room and had to make an effort to call myself back to the reality of my situation. But as soon as I began to visualise the reality of Laurelbank, the enmity of my two aunts, the oppressive hall where the coloured splashes of light from the stained-glass fell on the suit of armour at the bottom of the staircase, my mind would be filled with the image of the little girl, so incongruous in that setting and I would hear again her fluting childish voice with its queer turns of expression: 'He's the real mackay. I'm no' *in* it, see?' and once again I would be flushed with confidence, secure in the certainty of my future.

I slept very little that night. I think I was afraid to go to sleep, in case I might awake to find myself back in Islington, and I spent the long hours alternately remembering the red plush, gilt and urine smell of my father's room and the oppressively rich stuffiness of Laurelbank. These were the realities of my world at the moment and the medical school was still a dream but my personal reality was neither in the red plush room in Islington nor among the heavy wealth of Laurelbank. I thought of the former as the Realm of Romance and of the latter as the Temple of Mammon and I belonged in neither place. It was the little girl who seemed to symbolise the true substance of the life I was trying to find. In her ugly accent and defeating dialect she conveyed to me meanings that I completely understood.

CHAPTER FOUR

'Mid pleasures and palaces though we may roam,
Be it ever so humble, there's no place like home;
A charm from the sky seems to hallow us there,
Which, seek through the world, is ne'er met with elsewhere.
Home, Home, sweet, sweet Home!
There's no place like Home! There's no place like Home!

I FELT very nervous the next afternoon when I went up the grey stone steps between the grey stone pillars to the doorway in West Nile Street where a large brass plate announced: 'Guthrie, Guthrie, Inglis & Guthrie', but I paused in the hall of the building and listened for the voice of the little girl inside my head: 'Ye want Mr James Guthrie. He's the real mackay,' whereupon I opened the next door with the frosted glass panels and walked into the office with confidence.

It was a heavy solid place and behind a large wooden counter like that of the police station at Lochfoot the younger of two clerks rose and came forward to meet me.

'Good morning. I should like to see Mr James Guthrie, please.'

'You have an appointment?'

'No, but I should like to see him as soon as possible.'

The clerk opened a large leather-covered book. 'Tuesday next?' That was five days away. I tried to conceal my chagrin, my impatience, my anxiety at five further days of hotel charges biting into my small capital.

'Mr Inglis could see you tomorrow,' the clerk suggested, but the little girl had said Mr James Guthrie and that I was not to be 'palmed off' with anybody else.

'Thank you, but I would prefer to see Mr James Guthrie,' I said. 'Very well, next Tuesday.'

The clerk began to write in the book. 'And the nature of your business?' he asked.

I hesitated and then said: 'It is in connection with the Misses Simpson, of Laurelbank, Lochfoot.'

The words acted like some magic formula. The atmosphere of the mahogany and leather office altered, shifted in perspective, as if it were shrinking and I were growing taller as the senior clerk rose from his desk and came forward to the counter, his manner deferential as that of the police sergeant had been. The effect of the names of these two ugly frightened old women in that stuffy brown room was extraordinary.

'May I have your name, sir?' the senior clerk asked.

'Charles Simpson.'

'Be good enough to wait one moment, sir,' he said and disappeared through a dark heavy door into an inner office.

In less than a moment I was shown into a large room where a thin old man with brilliant shrewd eyes sat behind a large leather-topped table and the clerk shut the door behind me.

'I am James Guthrie,' the old man said, his brilliant eyes sparkling with a curious light as he looked at me. No face could have been more unlike the flower face of the little girl at Laurelbank when she opened the door to me and yet this old man's face brought a fleeting image of that other face flickering across the surface of my mind. 'You have business with the Misses Simpson of Laurelbank?' he continued. 'Well?'

Nervously, I began to tell him my story but I gained confidence as I went along, although I did not know why, for his face did not change and the brilliant eyes still looked at me across the table, keen and shrewd, making me thankful that I was telling the truth. At one point, I handed him the photograph of my mother and her sisters along with my birth certificate but he did not examine them. With his eyes still on my face, he laid the things at the far end of the long table, as if putting them aside as irrelevant.

'And so,' I ended, 'I hoped that, if they were in a position to do so, my aunts – the Misses Simpson, I mean – would lend me the money for my studies.'

There was no more to say and I fell silent but now an extraordinary thing happened. The old man rose from his chair, I too got to my feet expecting to be summarily dismissed from his presence, when he extended his hand across the table, grasped mine and said: 'I am very pleased to see you, young Charles, my lad.'

I felt limp, was afraid that tears might arise to shame me as they used to do at school, as I felt the dry thin old fingers in my hand. I looked at the photograph and the certificate at the end of the table. 'You believe me, sir? You—'

'You are the living image of your Uncle Charlie,' he said.

'My uncle?'

'Dead long ago. Brother of the Misses Simpson.'

'My father always said that I resembled himself,' I said which was irrelevant but was also a release of emotion, an expression of relief that I owed not even my appearance to my father. Perhaps now, when I grew old, I might not turn into a grotesquely swollen yellow idol.

'Never knew your father,' the old man said, 'but I knew you were a Simpson, the real mackay, the minute you came through that door. Well, now, this is very interesting, very.' His use of the little girl's expression 'the real mackay' made me feel warm all over. He sat down in his chair again and a different sparkle, a sparkle of mischief came into his eyes. 'You must have been a proper shock to the ladies at Laurelbank,' he said.

'Yes, I think I was rather, sir.'

'Surprised you got into the house at all.'

'The maid showed me in.'

'Wee Jeanie? Sharp little nipper that,' he said appreciatively, and again I had that feeling that there was something in common between him and the little girl, some bond of similarity. Was it that they were both what they called 'the real mackay'?

'This business can't be settled in a day, you know,' he said next.

'But you think it can be settled, sir – that I am not on a wild-goose chase?'

'Och, if you want to be a doctor, we'll make a doctor of you,' he said confidently, 'but I have to have a little time to get round the ladies, your aunts.'

'Then that's all right,' I said. 'I can get some sort of job here in Glasgow in the meantime.'

'It won't take *that* long, lad, but if I write to the ladies today I'll have to give them a week's notice that I am coming to see them. Always give them a week's notice of seeing them about anything. Gives them time to get used to the notion, you know.' He screwed up his eyes. 'Then they'll need another week to think it over, then – but we should have it settled at the end of a month, say.' He looked at me suddenly. 'How much do you know about the ladies, about the Simpsons in general?' he asked.

'Nothing, sir. I didn't know my aunts existed till I found that photograph. I didn't know my mother had an income from her family until after my father died.'

'It was Mrs Simpson, your grandmother, that arranged that. Your grandfather never knew about it. Was a direct draft from the current account at Lochfoot.' He had been speaking musingly, an old man remembering things long past but suddenly he pounced: 'These transactions never went through this office. How did you get this address? How did you know we acted for the Simpsons?'

'I had heard the name of this firm,' I lied. 'My mother must have mentioned it at some time.'

He continued to look at me for a moment, then got up and turned away, making an um-hum sort of noise that indicated more clearly than any words that he did not believe me but he did not pursue the matter directly. Instead he said: 'The best thing that ever happened to the ladies at Laurelbank is that wee Jeanie Robertson, the maid. Before she took over the house, we were never done engaging and sacking servants for them, but wee Jeanie is a right little jewel.' He took a bowler hat and a black coat from a stand in the corner of the room. 'We'll go down the street and get a bite to eat,' he ended.

Over a very good lunch in the heavily furnished dining-room of a businessmen's club, Mr Guthrie embarked on the history of the distaff side of my family. It was an ordinary enough story for the Scotland of its time, I have since learned, but for myself, at that time, it was full of interest, naturally enough.

'Your grandfather and my father,' he began, 'were both born in Mauchden in Ayrshire, they came up here to the big city to make their fortunes on the same day and they stayed friends all their lives. Your grandfather apprenticed himself in an engineering works. My father took a job as a clerk in a solicitor's office. By the time he was thirty, your grandfather owned the engineering works.'

He paused and I said: 'And your father owned the solicitor's office?'

He smiled. 'Not exactly. They were both lads o' parts but your grandfather was quicker and better at the money-making than my father was.' He paused again, became solemnly thoughtful before he continued. 'But I think my father was better – or maybe just luckier – at everything else and maybe he was a little wiser in some ways than your grandfather. He went back to Mauchden and married a lass he had been at the school with. Your grandfather married an Edinburgh woman – a Miss Minto. She had a little money and a lot o' fancy ideas. In time, my father set up as a solicitor on his own account and it was then that your grandfather began to bring all his business to him. In a way, you could say that he was the making of our business, for by this time he was a wealthy man, with his fingers in a lot of rich pies. From then on, you could say that everything went right for my father. His business went well and so did other things. He had six o' a family – three laddies – I'm the youngest o' them. My two brothers are gone now but my sisters are still alive. But about the same time things began to go wrong for your grandfather. Och, he was still making money. Money reaches a stage when money makes money, like a snowball rolling down a hill. But the one thing your grandfather wanted was sons and he had seven lassies before your Uncle Charlie was born.' He paused again for a few moments, staring at the dark red wall behind my chair. 'Charlie started as a jubilation and ended as a tragedy. Four o' the lassies died young but there were still three left, as well as their mother, to make a ruination o' Charlie. My brothers and I were sent to an academy here in Glasgow and kept under my father's eyes but not Charlie. Charlie was sent to a fancy school down in England and then to Oxford. Your grandfather was a gambler – he had to be to make the money he did – but he was good at it. Charlie was a gambler too but he was no good at it. He gambled and drank his way through a fortune and then drowned himself in the loch down below Laurelbank there.'

'When did that happen?' I asked.

'Eighteen ninety-nine. Before you were born, lad. It was a good few years before that that your mother had run away with your father. I remember fine when that happened too. I was just done with the university and into our office and I remember your grandfather coming in to alter his will. I remember my father saying he was a hard man and that he would rue the day he cut Cathie off but my father couldn't make him change his mind. It made a scandal in Lochfoot, of course, her eloping like that and your grandfather was very proud o' his position and his good name.' Mr Guthrie suddenly chuckled. 'Have you noticed how there's always something comical in things?' he asked and went on: 'The thing that angered your grandfather most about that elopement was – wait a minute. I might as well tell you the whole story so that you can picture it. The Simpsons were all at this party at Lochfoot Castle and your father had been engaged to sing at it. When his singing was over, he was paid and a carriage was brought round to take him to the station for the last train. Cathie, your mother, got into the carriage with him but they didn't go straight to the station. They went round by Laurelbank and she took all her clothes, all her jewellery and most of her mother's and her sisters' as well. Your grandfather never got over that and yet it was just the sort of cool-headed cheeky thing he would have done himself. I have always thought that bit right comical.' He paused again and the smile died from his face before he said: 'But there was nothing comical about poor Charlie, your uncle. Your grandfather never got over his death and your grandmother was no help. She just went off her head and your poor aunties were shut up in that house with the two of them until they died.'

'When did they die?' I asked.

'Your grandfather in 1910, your grandmother a year or two afterwards. By that time, your aunties were too old to come out into the world again. Aye, you must have been a proper shock to them.'

'I am sorry.'

'They'll get over it,' he assured me and then became practical, leaving the past and coming to the present. 'You might as well go back to the hotel at Lochfoot. Are you all right for money?'

'As long as I don't have to stay there too long, sir.'

'Only a week or two. Maybe less. If you run short o' cash, let me know, though.'

'I'll be all right, but thank you very much.'

'No need to thank me, lad. To tell the truth, I'm glad

you've turned up. I like continuity. I think your grandfather would be pleased to see you if he were alive.' He made a sign to a waiter. 'You go back down there and wait till you hear from me. On second thoughts, I don't think I'll write to the ladies. No good giving them time to get into a stew. I'll just get Jim – that's my son – to drive me down there tomorrow afternoon to see them. D'you think wee Jeanie will let me in?' he asked mischievously. 'I'm not as young and handsome as some.'

Until this moment I had liked him but now he had embarrassed me and made me angry. He had distorted what had happened between the little girl and me. I made no comment. We left the dining-room, a porter brought our coats and we parted on the pavement outside the club.

I walked about the streets of Glasgow for a time before I went to the station to catch a train to Lochfoot but I did not notice much as I walked for I had too much to think about. I could hardly believe in my own good fortune in having found such an ally in this kindly and shrewd old man and I would have liked to think about it, to wallow in it and all its prospects for my future but my mind kept returning to the small blue and white figure that guarded the door of Laurelbank. Mr Guthrie was very wise and would be mistaken about few things I felt but I was certain that he was mistaken in his implication that the little girl had helped me – as he shrewdly suspected – because I was 'young and handsome'. I was accustomed to women and girls taking what might be called 'young and handsome' notice of me, but there had been nothing of female-to-male flirtatiousness in the behaviour of that little girl. She had not attempted to make any personal relationship with me but the very reverse with her solemn warning: 'I'm no' *in* this. I'm no' *in* it, see?' And I remembered too her scorn when I asked her why she was taking the trouble to help me. The more I thought about her, the more I heard about her, the more interesting she became, not in any sense as a young woman vis-à-vis a young man but as a human phenomenon and I noted that she was as interesting to Mr Guthrie as she was to myself. His eyes had gleamed with interest every time he mentioned her name and he had mentioned it not out of relevance to our discussion but as if she were a thought on which he liked to dwell.

The next morning I felt restless, which was natural enough, I suppose, with my whole future hanging in the balance, and to occupy myself I set out on a voyage of exploration but I avoided the grey, sickly little town and took the road that led uphill under the high stone wall, past the end of Lochview Crescent and on towards more open country. After I had walked uphill for about a mile, the high wall on my right was pierced by tall iron gates at one side of which was a notice: 'Lochfoot Castle. Private Grounds. Trespassers will be prosecuted.' Inside the gates, there was a lodge and then a long sweep of driveway, flanked by the steel-grey trunks of beeches that gleamed like giant gun-barrels in the frosty sunlight. Involuntarily I smiled at the something comical that Mr Guthrie had mentioned. It was probably through this gateway that the Castle carriage had bowled long ago, carrying Carlo and Kittenpuss on their marauding visit to Laurelbank and then on to the railway station. In that moment, on the quiet roadway, I felt a kinship and even a liking for my parents. They had been young, the whole world lay before them and they had gone towards it, trying to take from it what they wanted, as I myself was now doing.

I followed the road under the wall for a long way, hoping that it would eventually turn back towards the town, but there came a point when the wall swept away to my right, separating the tall trees inside from the open moorland outside while the road went on across the moor into the distance. I turned back and reached the hotel just in time to have lunch. The grounds round the Castle must have been enormous, I thought, for I must have walked five miles out and five back and from no point on the road had there been a glimpse of the Castle itself. The whole of the squalid, huddled little town could have been contained several times in the acreage of woodland I had walked past and this was only a small section of the Castle property. It then occurred to me that our two rooms in Islington could have been contained in that hall in Laurelbank where the suit of armour stood in the coloured light from the stained glass. Money makes money, Mr Guthrie had said. And it was equally true that poverty breeds poverty. The little town was dying of poverty, to all appearances, while the Castle and Laurelbank looked as if they were spawning, by some mysterious self-fertilising process, more and more wealth.

The thought of Laurelbank made me wonder if Mr Guthrie would indeed come down there that afternoon and I was at once taken with the idea of going up there to find out. His son would drive him down there, he had said, which meant that, surely, the car would be visible outside the house. I walked swiftly up to the end of the Crescent and stood there, waiting. I had been there for a long time, it seemed, when a car rolled in at the other end of the curving road, came to a stop outside the gates of Laurelbank and I saw Mr Guthrie and another man go up the drive to the door of the house. Now, feeling as a criminal must feel when the jury goes out to consider its verdict, I sauntered slowly along towards the car but on the other side of the road and paused for a moment opposite the house. There were two big bay windows on either side of the front door and close to the glass of the one to the left, as I looked from the road, there was a small gleam of white under the half-drawn lace-edged blind. Then there was a slight movement as a hand in a white-cuffed blue sleeve was raised and lowered before the gleam disappeared from sight. My heart seemed to pause in its beat for a moment before rushing on into new high hope. Had it been an accident that she was at that window? Or had she, by some mysterious means, known that I was going to come past the house? I hurried away back to the hotel, impatient with myself. The little girl was becoming obsessive, turning into some sort of talisman for me, an uncanny absurdity of the mind not to be tolerated.

I was sitting in my bedroom trying to read a newspaper when a maid came to tell me that Mr Guthrie was downstairs. By the time he had introduced his son to me and had ordered tea I was breathless and wanted to vomit.

'It's all right, lad,' he said then. 'The ladies are sensible enough in their own way if you tackle them right.'

'They are going to do it? I can go to medical school?'

'Aye, aye,' he said soothingly, as if I were a hysterical woman nor could I blame him for thinking so. 'You are a big thing for them to get used to. It was a big decision to make but they made it. We are to pay all your fees from the office and make you a monthly allowance. There's just one thing, though.'

'Not half,' said young Guthrie. 'It's a thing and a half.'

'You are to live at Laurelbank and travel up to Glasgow to the university. I said you should go into rooms in the city but they wouldn't budge,' the old man said.

'Live at Laurelbank? But why? I should have thought that was the last thing they would want. I should have—'

'It's because of your Uncle Charlie,' Mr Guthrie explained. 'A man's sins don't die with him.'

'They are afraid you will drink yourself to death in dens of vice in Glasgow,' young Guthrie told me. 'I'd like to see you do it on a fiver a week.'

'A fiver a week?'

'That's your pocket money. Two hundred and fifty a year, to be exact,' Mr Guthrie explained.

'But I don't want all that, sir,' I told him. 'I want as little as I can manage with. The less I borrow, the less I have to pay back.'

'There is no question of paying back. You are a Simpson. The ladies are reasonable and sensible if—'

'If you ask me, they are a pair of daft old biddies,' young Guthrie broke in.

'Nobody asked you,' his father told him sternly.

'Well, one thing,' the son said in apologetic tones, 'they didn't have that little Orphan Annie of a maid sitting inside the door today the way they did that time you sent me down for their signatures. She gave me the creeps, sitting there like a wooden image.'

'The day you can do your job as well as wee Jeanie Robertson does hers, young fellah-me-lad, I'll maybe be willing to listen to your opinions,' said the old man implacably.

I felt sorry for young Guthrie although he was a good deal older than myself. 'They had her sitting there the other day too when I was there,' I told him. 'Jeanie, you will remain!' I mimicked my aunt's voice.

'Aye, aye, very funny,' the old man said sarcastically, putting me in my place too. 'The ladies are a wee bit eccentric maybe, but folk are the way life makes them.' Turning away from his son, he concentrated on myself. 'Maybe after a month or two I'll get them talked round to letting you have lodgings in Glasgow,' he said.

'Don't worry about it, sir.' The old man had helped me so much that I did not want him to have further trouble on my behalf. 'I don't mind living at Laurelbank. In fact, I shall like it. I have lived all my life in lodgings more or less. Laurelbank will be a change.'

'That's the way to go about it,' he told me approvingly. 'Just take it quietly and disturb the ladies as little as you can and you will be all right. After all, you needn't be in the house except to sleep, if that is how you want it. Well, we must get back to the city. You will come up to the office tomorrow? About eleven in the forenoon?'

'Yes, sir. When do I have to go to Laurelbank?'

'A week today. More important is when you start at the university. From what you told me, your schooling wasn't up to much.'

'You'll have to sit the Prelims,' young Guthrie said, 'if you haven't got a school cert ...'

'A tutor, I think, for the summer,' said Mr Guthrie, 'and try the preliminary exams in September. Jim, what about that crippled doctor that coached Willie Fraser's son? He got young Fraser through, didn't he?'

'I can easily find out about him.'

They made difficulties flow away as if before a strong current and I was lost in admiration for them until I remembered that the force behind the current was money, money piled up by an old man whom I had never seen, money that had taken on a life of its own and had lived on after he was dead.

During the week that followed I spent only the nights at the hotel in Lochfoot for the Guthries were very kind to me, taking me to spend the evenings in their suburban home while, during the days, there were interviews with Doctor Gill who was to coach me, books to buy and in the intervals Glasgow to explore. The week passed quickly and on the appointed day, having been heralded by a letter from Mr Guthrie, I reported at the door of Laurelbank at eleven in the forenoon with my old suitcase and a new larger one that held my books and new possessions. I rang the bell, heard the distant tinkle and waited tensely for the little girl to open the door. When the heavy slab of wood swung back I was once more astounded by her smallness but her little face was radiant with welcome as she said: 'Good morning, Mr Charles. Come in,' and waved her hand towards the dim hall, as if she were presenting me with the freedom of a closely guarded kingdom. Carrying my cases, I went inside and she shut the wooden door and then the door with the stained-glass panels and suddenly it felt as if we were enclosed in a private world.

'This way,' she said, and I followed her towards the staircase where she paused. 'The ladies said I was to show you your room first and explain about meals and things and then you are to go into the morning-room at twelve o'clock.' Her blue eyes under her severe white morning-cap looked at me half-interrogatively, half-apologetically, as if she were saying: 'You are not offended that I am the only one to welcome you?'

'That's fine,' I told her. 'I would like to be on my own for a bit first.'

She smiled, relieved and began to go upstairs, but I stood looking into the iron face of the suit of armour. On the third or fourth step, she stopped to look back at me.

'You don't like him?' she asked.

'Him?'

'The Iron Man?'

'No. I don't.'

'Me neither,' she said. 'Ugly brute,' and turning away, she went on upstairs.

On the big square landing she stopped, pointing to two doors. 'These are the ladies' rooms,' she said, 'and that's their bathroom, but I thought you would like it better at the back, looking out over the trees instead of across the Crescent.' Again there was the implied question in her tone, she waited for my assent that I preferred to look out over the trees and looked pleased when I gave it.

'In here then,' she said, one hand on the knob of the heavy mahogany door while with the other hand she pointed. 'That's your bathroom in there.'

She now showed me into a vast bedroom that would have contained the ground floor of the Islington house. A bright coal fire burned in the marble-surrounded grate, its flames reflected in the polish on the massive pieces of mahogany furniture. In the square bay of the large window there stood a large flat writing table topped with crimson leather and to this the little girl went, laying a small hand on the corner of it.

'I shifted this in here for your writing and studying,' she said, again on that questioning note.

'Thank you very much,' I said. 'It was very thoughtful of you,' while I asked myself how this tiny creature had contrived to 'shift' that massive block of mahogany.

I felt overpowered by the weight of the house and its contents, by the imaginative thought that the little girl had given to her preparations for my arrival and by the strange feeling that was becoming more and more pronounced that this great block of a house and all that it contained were her kingdom and that my aunts, 'the ladies' as she called them, were charges in her care. I also dreaded the moment when she would leave me by myself, as I listened to the silence of the house.

I did not know a great deal about housekeeping and nothing at all about the daily routine of a house of this size but it seemed likely that, between eleven and twelve in the forenoon, one would be aware of movement as people, no matter how well-trained, went about their duties of cooking, sweeping, dusting. In this house, there was no sound of movement and from out-of-doors there came no sound either. It was bright but very cold and no birds sang, no wind blew, no traffic moved along the road between the rows of villas. Even the fire in the grate glowed with a silent life.

I looked around at the rich dark green wallpaper, the thick carpet like a floor of green moss, the long green velvet curtains fringed with gold. I have always been conscious of interior surroundings, an unmasculine trait perhaps, but probably induced by my lifelong dislike of the theatrical red plush and gilt with which my parents chose to surround themselves.

There were several pictures round the walls of this room and above the fireplace, in a heavy gilt frame there was a sombre-coloured painting showing a room that contained a man, a woman, three children, a cradle and a hen on the flagged floor. The people were grouped around a wooden table that held a few utensils and on a small brass plate attached to the bottom edge of the frame was engraved the title of this composition: 'The Frugal Meal'. As a subject, it seemed to me to accord very ill with its costly frame and costlier surroundings and as I drew back, still gazing at it, the little girl confused me further by saying: 'Great, isn't it?' I was startled. If she admired the picture, I would not for the world hurt her feelings by laughing at it, but when I turned to her and saw the mischief in her eyes, I discovered that language or idiom alone was causing the seeming disagreement between us. 'But the one I like the best in the whole house,' she went on, 'is that one over there. Wee Who-did-it, I call him,' and she pointed to the wall above the head of the bed. I went over to examine her favourite. It depicted the head of a child, a child with fat cheeks, cupid-bow lips, big eyes and curly hair, the head floating among billowing clouds and printed in copper-plate script under it were the words which the little girl intoned behind me as I read them:

'Where did you come from, baby dear?
Out of the everywhere, into here.'

and the words were followed by a bawdy little giggle. For a hideous second, I thought that reference was being made to my own bastard birth, my strange arrival in this house, that even, perhaps, this little guttersnipe of a creature had hung the picture above the bed on purpose, but when I turned to face her, that wicked left eyelid dropped over the blue eye for a second before she said: 'Out of the everywhere! Lord help us, it's enough to make ye spew!' and she broke into a gay trill of mischievous laughter. I too began to laugh and loudly, releasing some of the tension of this strange forenoon and went on laughing until the little girl said: 'Sh-sh, Mr Charles! We don't want to disturb the ladies.'

With the words there arose between us a sudden complicity, a bond that was not between us as two people but more of a bond of youth in rebellion against age, of reality against sentimentality, a bond, in the ultimate sense, of the life and the future that animated us opposing itself to the atmosphere of death and the past in this mausoleum of a house. We stood there for a second, smiling at one another while the silence of the block of grey stone lay above, below and on every side of us until the little girl said: 'I have to go down now to see to the lunch, Mr Charles. If there's anything you need, just ring.' She indicated the long gold-tasselled strip of green velvet that hung by the fireplace. 'I'll be in the pantry, the door at the bottom o' the stairs beside the Iron Man.' She went out, the door closed and the silence pressed all around me.

I began to unpack my cases, my few possessions looking very meagre in the large chest of drawers and the larger wardrobe but when I had strewn my few books about, at the bedside, on the table at mid-floor, on the writing table, the room looked better. I had just put my suitcases away in a cupboard in the corner when the little girl tapped at the door. I did not know why I disliked the name Jeanie so much or why I could not bring myself even to think of her by it, except that the unmusical diminutive did not seem to suit her, although I could think of no name that would. A flower name? Rose, Violet, Lily? No. They were too pretty and sentimental, embracing none of her mischievous guttersnipe quality. Marjorie, Alice, Ann? No. 'Mr Charles, it's a minute to twelve,' came her voice through the narrowly opened door.

'Yes. Yes, here I am. I'm ready.'

We went downstairs together, she stopping beside the suit of armour, I going towards the door of the room in the far corner of the hall. Out of the dimness there, I looked back at her. The splashes of coloured light from the stained glass panels flickered over her white apron and over the metal of the Iron Man, as she called it, that towered over her and her left eye closed in that slow wink. I raised my hand and knocked on the panel of the heavy door.

My aunts were sitting one on either side of the fire, tense, fearful and I had the impression that, all forenoon since they had come downstairs, they had been sitting here thus, waiting for this dread moment. I felt sorrier for them than I did for myself, acute as was my own discomfort.

'Good morning, Aunt Bessie, Aunt Jessie,' I said.

'Good morning – Charles,' Aunt Bessie said, hesitating before my name and this hesitation was emphasised by Aunt Jessie repeating ' – Charles' a few seconds behind her sister.

Their nervousness was infectious and asphyxiating. I suppose it was born out of the scandal of my mother's elopement, my illegitimate birth, my unfortunate resemblance to their profligate brother, their spinsterly fear of 'men' in general but whatever its origin, it writhed about the room and seemed to grip my throat and restrict my chest.

'I hope you find your room comfortable,' Aunt Bessie said.

'Yes, comfortable,' echoed Aunt Jessie.

'Yes, thank you. It is very comfortable indeed.'

'If there is anything you require, you must ask Jeanie,' Aunt Bessie said in a rush. 'We are not accustomed to guests – visitors – people staying – ' the confusion rioted ' – we have lived so quietly for so long – ' she made a determined effort to achieve order, her voice quavering ' – that we are out of the way of entertaining peo – entertaining. But Jeanie knows about everything, where everything is. You have only to ask. We want you to be comfortable.'

'Yes, comfortable.'

We had now come full circle. I repeated my thanks and silence fell. I debated whether to take my leave but their faces and the entire room were vibrant with something more, no matter how desperate the effort, that had to be said. I waited, trying not to stare at them too hard. They were probably in their late sixties or perhaps their early seventies but they looked much older, dressed in clothes of the fashion of about 1900 and with black woollen shawls about their shoulders. Their hair, originally dark and now heavily streaked with grey, was drawn up into round coils on top of their heads and their faces were heavy-boned and yellowish-grey, sad and scared. They would have been pathetic except for one thing, a curious implied insistence that this was their house, that they were allotting me a place in it and that I was to stay in that place that they were unwillingly giving me. It was implicit in the fact that they had not invited me to sit down but spoke to me as from the thrones of their black horse-hair armchairs and it became explicit when Aunt Bessie found the courage and the words for what remained to be said.

'We want you to understand that Jeanie is our only servant. We used to keep three—'

'Long ago, we had seven—'

' – three but now we have only Jeanie and the jobbing gardener, of course. Jeanie is a perfect treasure. You may think her a bit rough-spoken but she makes us very comfortable and we do not want her upset. Do you understand?'

'I shall do my best to be as little trouble as possible,' I said, hating them. How dared they make a slave of that little girl in this enormous house? Yet, slave? There was nothing of the slave, the skivvy, in that little – little treasure out there. Aunt Bessie went on speaking into my mental confusion. 'We suggested that when you had to come here we should obtain more help but Jeanie prefers to be on her own and manages splendidly. She is a real treasure, as I said.'

Now that the important business of setting my own redundancy and the value of the treasure before me was accomplished, Aunt Bessie was more at her ease, almost gracious. 'Your – my – your aunt and I have all our meals in this room. We have arranged for you to have all your meals in your own room and as I said you must ask Jeanie for anything you may require. Mr Guthrie will attend to everything pertaining to your studies, of course.'

'You are both very kind and I am very grateful,' I said. I escaped from the brown stuffy room, shut the door and paused, feeling weak, by the Iron Man before I began to climb the stairs.

'Cheer up, Mr Charles, you'll soon be dead,' said the treasure gaily, coming out of her pantry carrying a tray of cutlery, linen and glass and going towards the morning-room. The nervous tension seemed to stream out through the soles of my shoes and I ran, smiling, up the staircase to my own room. I was sitting with my elbows on the writing table, my head between my hands, staring into the trees of the back garden and thinking about my aunts when she arrived with my lunch.

'Well,' she said, putting the tray in front of me, 'the ladies are more like themselves than they have been since you arrived on the doorstep, now that that's over.'

'Why are they so nervous and afraid?' I asked.

'I think it is the money.'

'The money?'

'Money does queer things to folk. Come on, eat your lunch and stop worrying your head. They are all right, the ladies, as long as nothing upsets them or bothers them. They'll get used to ye in time and you'll get used to them. Laurelbank is maybe not everybody's idea o' Home, Sweet Home but it's a sight better than many a place. Eat your lunch, Mr Charles.'

She went away. I lifted the silver covers from the soup cup, the grilled chop and vegetables, the steamed pudding. As she had said, Laurelbank was a sight better than many a place.

CHAPTER FIVE

Oh, no! we never mention her, her name is never heard;
My lips are now forbid to speak that once familiar word.
'Oh, No! We Never Mention Her,'
by Thomas Haynes Bayly.

WHILE I ate my lunch, I concentrated upon my Latin grammar. I was not to begin daily work with Doctor Gill until the following Monday but I knew that I had to attain a certain proficiency in Latin for my university entrance and I also knew that this subject was likely to cause me most trouble, probably because I disliked it, fraught as it was with memories of Mr Cook, my Latin master at school who was always slightly drunk and very bad-tempered. But it was so new and gratifying to be able to do – to be encouraged, indeed – to do what I wanted to do that the shade of Mr Cook evaporated and Latin began to exert a fascination, so that I was startled when the treasure appeared silently at my side to pick up the tray.

'I am sorry,' I said. 'I meant to carry that down to the pantry for you.'

'No need for that, Mr Charles,' she said and as if she had read in my mind my resolve that I would fetch up and carry down my own trays in future, she added: 'but if you do, don't let the ladies catch you. They wouldn't think it right.'

Bending over the tray, she looked at the cover of the *Garland of Gems for Drawing-room Performance* which lay on a corner of the table. 'That book's down in the drawing-room,' she said, 'but it's green instead of red like yours. Great isn't it?' I remembered her use of the word 'great' in reference to the pictures on the walls, nodded my head and waited. She took her hands from the tray, took a step backwards, clasped the hands in front of her apron, took on an expression of coy soulfulness and recited in an accent unnatural to her:

'Now, William, I'll prove if you really are true,
For you say that you love me – I don't think you do;
If really you love me you must give up the wine,
For the lips that touch liquor shall never touch mine.'

She now became herself again as she bent towards the tray. 'I hope poor Willie drank himself into the blues,' she said in her own accent and then: 'Mr Charles, I've been thinking you would like to see over the rest o' the house likely. The best time would be when the ladies are having their lie-down.' She pronounced the last word as 'l'doon' and I was momentarily at a loss. 'They go to their beds every day from after lunch until tea-time at four o'clock,' she explained, 'or at least they do *now*. They used to come down at three o'clock but you and Mr Guthrie put paid to that between you.'

I was at sea and repeated: 'Mr Guthrie and I?'

'First you arriving and then him arriving. The ladies have decided it's not safe so they are staying in their beds till four now. If your wee brother arrives some day at eleven in the forenoon, the ladies'll take to their beds for good, I shouldn't wonder.' This made me laugh and her face suddenly altered. A soft pink flush rose to her cheeks. 'I'm sorry, Mr Charles, honest I am. I shouldn't have said that. I shouldn't be talking like that about the ladies at all but being here on my own I've got into the way of thinking things about them and talking to myself about them and somehow—' she frowned and became suddenly accusing. 'You shouldn't *let* me say things!' she told me angrily. 'The ladies are your connections.'

'I don't feel very connected to them,' I said, 'and I like the things you say and I am sorry if Mr Guthrie and I have made them take to their beds.'

'I don't suppose it matters. They are as well in their beds as sitting in the morning-room,' she decided and added thoughtfully, 'but it's funny how folk do things to folk without meaning to. Sometimes I think it's hardly safe to scratch yourself in case you start an earthquake in Australia.'

She picked up the tray. 'I'd better get down to the pantry and get cleared up.'

'What about seeing the rest of the house?' I asked. I was not over-interested in the house but I did not want to be left alone.

'I've got the dishes to wash first.'

'I'll help you with them.'

'But Mr Charles the ladies won't—'

'If they are in bed, they won't know, will they?' I said and she laughed.

I took the tray from her, she made up the fire, picking up the empty coal scuttle and holding it forward for my notice as she said: 'Rule one in running Laurelbank: never go anywhere empty-handed. Use your head to save your feet. Come on.'

The pantry, as she called the room under the staircase, was unlike the rest of the house in that it was white and light, all new, except for the marble-surrounded fireplace and the big window which looked out towards the shrubs and trees of the back garden. It was really a kitchen, with its gas cooker, its sinks and draining-boards under the window and it was fresh, clean and neat like the treasure herself, very much her own domain.

'This room is new, isn't it?' I asked.

'Doneup, like. We made it into a pantry four years ago when we sacked the rest.'

'The rest?'

'Mrs Tait an' Annie, a couple o' dirty besoms.' She paused for a moment in her stacking of the crockery. 'It was me that got them the sack. Maybe they're in the poor-house by now but I cannae help that. It was them or me for the high road and it wasnae gonnae be me.' She began to stack the crockery again. 'I like being on my own and I told Mr Guthrie that if we could shut up the basement, I could manage. He's great. Well, you know that. The ladies didnae like the idea at first. They don't like things changing. This used to be old Snake-eyes's study and anything connected with *him* is as holy to the ladies as the throne o' God but Mr Guthrie talked them into it.'

'Who was old Snake-eyes?'

'Moses!' She paused in her work and turned large, contrite blue eyes upon my face. 'There I go again! I shouldn't have said that. He was the ladies' father, *your* grandfather, like, Mr Charles. I just can *not* get used to you being connected to the ladies. I keep thinking of you as a proper orphan with nobody, like me. I shouldn't be talking to you or having you in the pantry here at all.'

'You are an orphan?' I asked, because it was the first thing that came to mind, something that might take up her attention and prevent her from dismissing me above stairs.

'Aye, but not legal, like. My father got killed at the war but my mother's still living but she married somebody I don't like and I never go near them. Two years ago when my granny died, I made up my mind I was an orphan, legal or no. It's nothing to do with being legal. If you've got nobody that's in it with you, nobody that wants you or needs you, you're an orphan.'

She began to wash the tumblers and I began to dry them. 'Then I am a proper orphan too. I've got nobody that wants me or needs me. I am not in it with anybody,' I said, using her own phrase, 'especially the aunts'. I thought of the nervous hostility of the morning-room. 'That's old Snake-eyes's portrait above the morning-room fireplace, isn't it?' I asked.

'That's him.'

'Snake-eyes is a good name for him. You have been here for four years?'

'Aye. Ever since I left the school.'

Was the law in Scotland the same as in England? If so, she must have been at least fourteen when she first came here and eighteen now. I looked down at the nape of her neck where the fair wispy hair curled out from under the white cap. It might have been the neck of a ten-year-old child, but she turned her head and looked up at me suddenly and her face was mature, gentle and wise.

'It must be gey queer for you being here like this, Mr Charles. Ye weren't brought up rough like me. Ye were never used to being on your own.'

'I am not so sure about that,' I said and while we continued with our work, I told her something of my childhood and more of the last two years following my mother's death, when my father had degenerated into the drink-sodden hulk in the red plush chair.

'Every time I came in from work, I would wonder if I would find him dead,' I ended. 'I think that the morning I did find him dead I was glad.' It was a relief to say it aloud, to bring the guilty thought out into the light and air.

The little girl stopped working and looked up at me. 'Why should ye have been anything else?' she asked. 'Ach, folk go on about how ye should love your father and your mother as if lovin' was as easy as water runnin' out o' a pipe.' She gushed hot water out of a tap into the sink. 'All that trash about love gives me the boke,' she said disgustedly and then laughed at my non-comprehension. 'That's Lochfoot for makes me want to spew,' she explained and added: 'I wish I could speak proper and sort of Englified like you, Mr Charles.'

I felt embarrassed and also annoyed. I did not want her to mark the differences between us. For the first time in my life I had found someone who thought in a way similar to my own and I wanted the similarities to be stressed and the differences to be ignored.

'The only proper way to speak is to say what you mean,' I said rather pedantically.

She gave her gay mischievous chuckle. 'If I said half the things I mean half the time, I'd end up down in Beery-belly's cells,' she said.

'Beery-belly?'

'The polis sergeant.'

'The big fat one? It was he who told me where this house was the night I arrived in Lochfoot.'

'Och, aye. He'd fairly tell ye where the Miss Simpsons lived or anybody else in the Crescent, come to that. It's a wonder he didnae kiss your arse into the bargain. Excuse me, Mr Charles, but folk like Beery-belly give me the—'

' – the boke,' I supplied when she stopped short.

'Now then,' she said sternly, 'you speak proper. Maybe some day before I'm old and grey I'll speak like you but the loch'll go on fire afore I'll let *you* start speakin' like me. Well, that's that lot cleaned up an' thanks for your help. Come on. We'll go round the house. We'll start with the drawin'-room.'

I stood in the doorway of the room while the treasure made her way through the forest of furniture to raise one of the cream-coloured lace-edged blinds that were drawn down to within a foot of the window-sills. When I looked round the large room I could only conclude that my grandmother had had a liking for the bogus-oriental, or more probably, that this had merely been the fashion of the time when the room was furnished and was no indication of personal taste. There was a profusion of tall Japanese vases, a similar profusion of tables with carved legs and brass tops and over the grand piano was a large shawl of thick black cloth, heavily embroidered and fringed with gold, which might have been of Indian origin. Over it all lay the dead weight of wealth, of no expense spared but ugliest of all were the serpents and dragons. They were everywhere, frozen in their writhing as handles on brass flowerpots, round the legs of tables, engraved on the brass of table-tops, in the gold embroidery of the shawl and finally on four long painted scrolls that hung from ceiling to floor, one on either side of the fireplace, one on either side of the large bay window. The golden dragons, spitting red flames against a dark blue background writhed two from ceiling to floor and two from floor to ceiling, like petrified moments of long-ago evil. Between the snarling teeth and upon the tongues of flame in the mouth of a gold dragon on the piano shawl, sat a silver-framed colour-tinted enlargement of the photograph of 'Bessie, Jessie and me in our dresses for the soirée at the Castle'.

My eyes on the piano, I said to the treasure: 'Would you go up to the upstairs landing for a moment?'

'What for?'

'Go on,' I said coaxingly. 'I am not going to do any damage.'

'All right.' She was doubtful but she indulged me. 'Just watch your eye, though, that's all.'

She went away. As I remembered the upper floor, my aunts' rooms were above the other large room, probably the dining-room, on the other side of the hall. I shut the door, put two pink satin cushions from the sofa along the bottom of it, put down the soft pedal of the piano and played a verse of 'Home, Sweet Home'. I then went upstairs and fetched the treasure down again.

'Did you hear anything?' I asked.

She shook her head. I shut the door, replaced the cushions and went back to the piano. 'Oh, Mr Charles!' she protested. Disregarding her, I began to strum out a tune and speak softly to it, in mimicry of my father, the words to which he used to ogle my mother:

'Queen rose of the rosebud garden of girls,
Come hither, the dances are done
In gloss of satin and glimmer of pearls,
Queen lily and rose in one.'

I did not ogle the treasure but the bronze figure of a Greek warrior that stood on the piano top and when I finished the verse, she wriggled out of her spasm of laughter and said: 'Help, Mr Charles, ye'll be the death o' me! Where did ye learn to play the piano?'

'I can't really play,' I said, closing the lid over the keyboard. 'This thing is in tune, though.'

'Aye, the man comes from Glasgow to tune it three times a year. It's only half-past two. The ladies are dead to the world. And ye can *so* play the piano. Play another tune, go on.'

'I *cannot* play the piano,' I insisted, despite my feeling that I was giving the subject an excessive importance. For some reason that I could not clarify, I did not want this little girl to endow me in her estimation and through her ignorance with gifts that I did not possess. 'I can only strum out cheap rubbish in a cheap way,' I said.

'Keep your hair on, Mr Charles,' she told me. 'I know you're not Paderoosky as they call him.' She frowned, searching for words. 'When I was at the school, they were awful partic'lar about writing. Your pen had to go up light and down heavy and if your writing sloped back, you got the strap. You had to do what they called *good* writing. It was only after I started to read books by Jane Austen and folk like that that I saw that how you make letters on paper is nothing to do with good writing. What you mean is that your piano-playing slopes back like, but it's better to play the piano like that than not play it at all, like me. Go on. Play another tune. It's great to hear it playing, honest!' She turned her eyes up towards the ceiling, began to sing: ''Mid pleas-ewers and pal-a-ce-ez tho' we may roam,' in obvious mimicry of some amateur concert singer she must have heard and I began to accompany her on the piano. It was in this way that our 'little musicales', as we came to call them, began and they became almost a daily feature of our lives thereafter. On this afternoon, however, while we 'gave' 'Home, Sweet Home' to the hushed house, I was much more interested in the treasure's remark about reading Jane Austen.

'You read Jane Austen?' I asked when we had finished our rendering of the ballad.

'Aye,' she replied, but her suddenly closed face indicated that she did not want to discuss the matter further. 'Well, come on and we'll take a look at the dinin'room.'

The dining-room, the smoke-room or library, the billiard-room, like the rest of the house, were heavy with wealth and sullen with disuse but the treasure pointed out to me the features which she considered 'great', which were for the most part paintings of kittens in beribboned baskets or of stricken-looking men and women above brass plates with titles like 'The Last Farewell' and 'Never Again'. She also drew my attention to the several bronze figures that adorned every room. 'Rotten, aren't they?' she asked, applying the adjective which was her antithesis of 'great' and which she pronounced as 'ro''en' with a glottal stop in the middle. As we passed through the hall on the way to the billiard-room, however, she jerked her thumb towards the suit of armour and said: 'But He's the worst of the lot. *He's* a real bugger, excuse me, Mr Charles.' I stopped and stared at the closed visor. I felt that the little girl really hated this thing, she could not look at it, even seemed to be a little afraid of it. 'At your service, Lord Mammon,' I said, making a deep bow to it, making fun of it, as we had made fun of 'Home, Sweet Home' in the drawing-room. The little girl uttered a nervous little laugh and I knocked on its breastplate as if on the panel of a door: 'Anyone at home?'

As if she were afraid that I was going too far now, she said: 'Don't, Mr Charles. And don't let the ladies see you doing anything like that. He is very valuable, they say.'

'Valuable? It wouldn't raise five bob from a scrap-dealer!'

'Oh, Mr Charles!' She was fearful, yet relieved and became

her practical self. 'They'd have to give more than five bob for him. There's twenty quid inside the ugly brute.'

'Twenty quid? Inside him?'

She moved away and opened the door to the billiard-room. 'The ladies hide the housekeeping money from the burglars,' she explained. 'I bring it from the bank once a month and they put it under rugs and in vases and all over the place. Three years back Miss Jessie put her share into the Iron Man's face and it went right down to his feet and we've never got it out. This is the billiard-room. Dash, I forgot the key to the Killection. It's in the pantry. Just a tick an' I'll get it.'

Before she went away, she raised one of the drawn blinds a little that I might look round the room but I was bored with the crushing weight of it all, as well as half-scared by the deadness that seemed to close round me when the presence of the little girl was withdrawn, as if I had been left alone in a tomb.

When she came back, she inserted a large key in the lock of a door in a corner, disappeared into a dark cavern and raised a blind, dark green in this instance, to reveal a window with iron bars on the inside as well as the outside of the glass. Even with the blind raised, the room was dim for, beyond the window but close to it, were high green laurels.

'This is the Killection,' she said.

'Killection?'

'Old Sn – your grandfather's killection o' silver,' she explained, waving a hand at the trays, bowls, candlesticks, boxes that littered every surface and pulling open a drawer of one of the many chests that lined the walls to expose several dozen silver spoons.

'He collected silver?' I asked weakly.

'Aye. It was his hobby, like.'

'All these drawers are full of silver?'

'Aye. Thank God I'm not supposed to clean it. It would

take a year. It takes long enough to clean the big stuff that's out—' she indicated the litter of bowls and trays. 'That brute there is a real bugger,' she told me, pointing to an inkstand that squatted on a writing-table in the middle of the floor. 'Still, shut up like this all the time, the stuff doesn't get dirty. I only give it a rub every six months or so.'

My eyes were fixed with horror on the 'real bugger'. It was a massive inkstand in the form of a bird of prey with outspread wings, around which two snakes coiled in writhing confusion, the creatures locked together in combat that would never end until someone had the good sense to drop the hideous monster of vulgar ostentation into a melting pot. The outspread wings of the bird supported a tray that held a silver penholder and among the coils of the serpents were two crystal ink-bottles, topped with silver. I looked from it to the little girl and saw her repress a shudder.

'Don't laugh at me, Mr Charles,' she said, 'but I am just about *frightened* o' that damn' thing.'

At her words, my own horror of the hideous thing abated. I went to the table and picked it up, using the curved neck of the bird as a handle. It weighed three pounds if it weighed an ounce and my two years in the Islington grocery had endowed me with the ability to estimate accurately small weights.

'It is nothing to be afraid of,' I told her, 'but it is just about the ugliest bloody thing I've seen in my whole life.'

'Put it down, Mr Charles. I hate to touch it.'

I set the thing back in its place. 'Do my aunts ever come in here?' I asked.

'No. They never go in any of the rooms except maybe the drawin'room or the dinin'room to hide the burglar money. That's why I have the key o' the Killection in the pantry, so as not to bother them for it when I need to clean the stuff.'

I felt that my aunts' need 'not to be bothered' could hardly go further when they must not be bothered at intervals of six months to hand over the key to this miser's hoard. I looked round the room, saw the large mahogany log-chest beside the fireplace and raised the lid upon emptiness. As the little girl watched fearfully, I put the inkstand in the box, closed down the lid and sat on it.

'I wouldn't clean it any more when you dislike it so much,' I said.

Her eyes became round. 'Aren't you the bright one?' she said. 'Just imagine me never thinkin' o' that.' She looked round at the trays and bowls. 'We'll let the rest alone, though, just in case. I quite like cleaning the rest. I like cleaning things.' She drew the blind down again, locked the door and we returned to her pantry where the clock indicated fifteen minutes past three. She put the key of the 'Killection' in the corner of a drawer as she said: 'We'll not bother with the bedrooms up the stairs. Ye can take a look at them any time. They're all alike, 'cept for the pictures. There's a great one in old Sn— – in the big front bedroom. "A Father's Love" it's called. It'll fairly make your hair curl. Come on down below. There's just time before I make the tea.'

We now descended a straight flight of stairs that lay beyond a green baize door in the corner of the hall next to her pantry. On the wall above our heads as we went down, there was a long row of bells on coiled springs, with a row of labels underneath: 'Morning-room. Drawing-room. Front Door' and many more. From the bottom of this stairway, a stone-floored passage ran straight ahead to a door at the end and to this the treasure went, withdrawing two large bolts and turning a key in a heavy lock before she could open it. I went to join her in the aperture which gave on to a narrow area with stone steps leading up to ground level.

'I only brought ye down here to show ye this door, Mr Charles,' she said, taking up a corner of her apron and pleating the white cloth between her small fingers, looking down as if she were concentrating on this activity. 'Sometimes I feel real angry at the ladies,' she told me now in a low voice. 'Miss Bessie said she forgot to tell you that we lock up at half-past nine at night and that you will have to be in by then. She said I was to tell you. I think she should have told you herself but she said I was to tell you—' She broke off in confusion.

'So you are telling me,' I said.

She looked up at me gratefully and her eyes became gay before the left one closed in that dramatic wink of hers. 'I aye do what the ladies tell me,' she said demurely. 'And now and again I do a wee bit more than they tell me. That's the way I'm such a perfect treasure.' I do not know if she heard my rapidly snatched breath at this, but she probably did. I had become aware that very little escaped her observation.

'The ladies are frightened o' the dark,' she continued. 'It's dark down here by half-past nine, even in the height o' the summer. It's a handy door this. Ye just come down the back drive and down the back steps an' lock it behind ye an' Bob's yer uncle.'

'Very handy,' I said.

'Never going out, the way they do, the ladies don't know how handy it is,' she said and dropped the subject. 'You go back to the light o' the pantry stairs, Mr Charles, afore I shut it again,' she instructed me.

'Just a minute. What are all these rooms down here? Where does that staircase go?' I asked, pointing to a wooden-stepped cavern that disappeared upwards.

'The old kitchen, scullery, larder, pantry, laundry. The stair goes up to the attics. My room is up there and five more forbye. This is the old laundry.' She opened a door. 'That new bit o' wall in the corner is my bathroom. Mr Guthrie got the men to make it when they did the pantry. Mr Guthrie's great. He thinks about folk. There was no place to wash your face before except the scullery sink. Here, I'll have to go up an' change into my afternoon uniform. Ye'll find your own way up the stairs, Mr Charles?'

'I think so,' I assured her.

She went away up the back staircase and I opened one or two doors and peered into the dank rooms with their heavily barred windows, their ceilings on the level of the ground up above. The weight of the three upper storeys towered over me and I suddenly thought that this was not so much a house or a home as a miser's treasure chest, partially sunk in a great hole in the ground. I ran up the staircase and into the hall, releasing the green baize door which the treasure had hooked back and as it swished shut behind me, I was face to face with the Iron Man, Lord Mammon, who stood on guard at the foot of the stairs. The big clock in the hall announced that it was twenty minutes to four but except for its slow tick, there was no other sound in the house. 'The ladies are dead to the world,' the little girl had said in her own idiom. It seemed that her words were more true than she knew. With the exception of herself, this house, along with all it contained, was dead to the world. I let myself out of the front door and went for a long walk across the moor above the town, although it was growing dark even as I set out.

When, about two hours later, I returned to the Crescent, I paused under the street lamp near the front gate and looked at the house, a rectangular black lump against the dark grey of the sky. No light showed anywhere. There were no streaks of light at the edges of curtains as at the windows of the other houses, nothing to indicate that people lived and breathed inside that block of stone. I turned away from the gate and, for some reason that I did not examine at the time, I turned left at the end of the Crescent, then left again along the lane, then left again into the back drive between the overgrown rhododendrons and laurels and down the steps to the back door. I hoped that the treasure had not locked and barred it again and she had not. When I came through the doorway at the top of the stairs, her head in its frilly afternoon cap popped out of her pantry.

'Ye don't have to come in that way as early as this, Mr Charles.'

'It was the most convenient way,' I excused myself. 'I was up on the moors.'

'It's great up there, isn't it?' she said and returned to the sink where she was preparing vegetables. 'Ye'll be ready for your dinner after a walk like that.'

'Dinner? I thought we had that at the middle of the day. What do we have now?'

'The usual – three courses an' cheese an' fruit.'

'Listen, I can't eat another big meal like that,' I protested.

'Ach, well, we're not going to force it down your throat. What would ye like, Mr Charles?'

'A sandwich or some bread and cheese and some milk or cocoa or something.'

'Well, well. The same as me. I cannae go two dinners in a day either.'

'How do my aunts manage to eat so much when they only sit about and lie in bed all day?'

'Ye'd better ask them. I suppose it's a case o' what folk's used to. The ladies are fond o' their grub. I'll bring your tray up about half-past seven,' she added dismissively.

'Can't I get what I want for myself?'

'The ladies won't like that.'

'They won't know, will they?'

She sighed, then smiled. 'Right. Ye're on. Help yourself. There's cold chicken and cheese and stuff in the larder over there and the bread's in the bin here.'

While I found what I wanted, she put cutlery, glass and linen on the tray and set out to lay the table in the morning-room but, having gone into the hall, she came back.

'Mr Charles, was it you that left that stick leaning on

the Iron Man?' she asked, putting her tray down on the table.

'Yes. I picked it up on the moor. I was using it as a walking-stick. Why?'

She fetched the stick, stood it in a corner of the pantry. 'Don't leave anything about the hall or the upstairs landing,' she said in a gentle pleading voice. 'The ladies are that blind and they won't wear their specs. They might trip over anything they are not used to. Ye didn't know that likely,' she excused me, 'but they can only see things that are close to, ye see.'

'I'm sorry. I'll remember. But if they turned up the gas in the hall they might see better.'

She sighed. 'The ladies are very economical,' she told me.

'Economical?' I looked at the battery of pans on the gas cooker, the slab of butter and the black grapes on their crystal dishes on the tray.

'Waste not, want not, as our dear papa used to say,' said the treasure in exact mimicry of Aunt Bessie's voice and then with exasperation: 'Ach, Mr Charles, I wish ye wouldn't stand there an' make me make fun o' the ladies! It's not right. But I've got that used to making fun o' them inside my head all this time – ' she paused ' – it just came out without me meaning it, like,' she apologised.

'If we don't make fun of them, I'll go off my rocker,' I told her.

She nodded. 'I know what ye mean but ye'll not turn up the gas, will ye? They like it turned down to a peep in the hall an' on the stairs. That was how it aye was in old – your grandfather's time and it's what they're used to an' it's no good upsetting them.'

'I won't turn the gas up ever, ever, ever,' I promised her ham-dramatically with my hand upon my heart which brought back her gaiety.

'Ye're a proper caution, Mr Charles, so ye are,' she said, picking up her tray.

'And you must keep telling me all the things I must and must not do. After all, I am new here.'

'Aye. It must be gey funny for ye at first but ye'll get used to it come time, Mr Charles.'

When she returned from the morning-room, I was sitting at the pantry table, eating my supper of cold roast chicken and bread and butter while I read a page of *Pride and Prejudice* which lay beside her knitting.

'In the name o' the Kingdom o' Heaven, Mr Charles,' she protested from the doorway, 'if the ladies see—'

'But they are *not* going to see me, are they?'

But she stood firm. 'All the same, this is not the thing at all. Ye are the gentleman o' the house, Mr Charles and—'

'You know that isn't true,' I interrupted her, making her look strangely discomfitted but I went on: 'You know that my aunts regard me as a cross they have to bear, a charity child that they don't want. Maybe if I have any sort of pride, I should clear out of here, give up my fancy ideas of studying medicine and earn my living some other way.'

I did not know that the humiliation I had felt in the morning-room in the forenoon had gone so deep, that I had been filling in my day in the company of this little girl so that I might forget about it. Now, however, it was exposed, red and raw and I thought of my few pounds in the bank and of Glasgow, that seething city which must be able to employ, feed and house one more body.

'Don't you talk like a bliddy goat!' said the little girl sharply, jerking me out of my shame and self-pity. 'If you act the cod after a' the bother that Mr Guthrie an' me went to, so help me I'll throttle ye, so I will. Sit back down there an' get on wi' your supper. I've got to get the dinner in.'

I sat in silence while she carried course after course to the morning-room and when she returned after delivering the coffee, she put her small fists on her hips and looked at me gravely. 'Mr Charles, I shouldn't have spoken to ye like that but ye made me real angry, so ye did.'

'I am sorry,' I said. 'You have been very kind to me and I don't want to make you angry.'

She turned away from me awkwardly, poured herself a glass of milk and began to spread butter on a piece of bread. It was a few seconds before I understood that she was unaccustomed to gratitude and did not know how to respond to it.

'Why did you bother with me that first day? Bother to tell me about Mr Guthrie, I mean?'

With her back still towards me, she said: 'It's a kind o' a long story an' maybe a bit silly as well.'

'It doesn't seem silly to me. Tell me.'

She sat down at the table opposite to me. 'It goes right back to when I first came here to Laurelbank.'

'Four years ago,' I encouraged her.

'Aye. This Mrs Tait an' Annie that was the cook and the housemaid here, they were a pair o' dirty besoms like I said an' when they left I had a proper turn-out o' the house from top to bottom. In them days, Miss Jessie was a lot more spry than she is now. She got the 'flu a couple o' years back an' she's never been so good since. In them days, she liked a wee bit o' a chat, behind Miss Bessie's back, like. She came up the back stairs one day when I was thoroughing out the attics. I'll have to take ye up there one day, Mr Charles. It's like a high-class secondhand shop, so it is. Anyway, I had just come on this picture – a paintin' o' this lassie with blue eyes an' curly fair hair an' Miss Jessie said: Oh, poor dear Cathie and began to greet – to cry, ye know. And then she told me about how long ago they all went to this party at the Castle an' Miss Cathie ran away with this drunken Irish singer. Sorry, Mr Charles, it's your father an' mother I'm speakin' about but that was what Miss Jessie said.'

'It is quite true. He was Irish and he was drunken too. Go on.'

'Then she said I was to forget everything she had said because dear papa had said that Miss Cathie's name was never to be mentioned in this house again and that she'd die in the gutter an' she was no daughter of his.'

'Old Snake-eyes,' I said.

'Aye. But it's stupid to say things an' then tell folk to forget them. I didnae forget about Miss Cathie. I asked my granny about her my next time-off. My granny was great. She could mind on everything that happened in Lochfoot for years an' years back. She could mind on when the town wasnae here at all, just green fields where the buildin's are, but she couldnae tell me any more about Miss Cathie. But she said something.' The little girl paused, her eyes soft and wide as she remembered her grandmother. 'She said she hoped old Snake-eyes was wrong, for it would be a pity if a bonnie young lassie died in the gutter. An' maybe this is kinda silly, Mr Charles but I believed that my granny had a better chance o' being right than old Snake-eyes had, in spite o' all his money an' his Killection an' everything. From that time on, I aye hoped an' believed that Miss Cathie would come back. Only she didn't but *you* did. That's why, that day you came and I opened the door I must have – must have looked kind o' funny. It was like as if you'd proved that my granny was right.' She got up and stood with her back to me while she rinsed her glass at the sink. 'Imagine that old bu—that old Snake-eyes sayin' that she was no daughter o' his. It's like that thing in the *Garland o' Gems*:

Oh, no we never mention her, her name is never heard,
My lips are now forbid to speak that once familiar word.

It's enough to give ye the boke,' she ended, coming back to the table. 'It just goes back to what we were sayin' after dinner-time about fathers lovin' their bairns an' all that rubbish. Old Snake-eyes didnae strain himself lovin' Miss Cathie an' I am right pleased he was wrong an' her Irishman never left her an' she never ended up in the gutter. I am right pleased my granny was right.'

'Yes, your granny was right,' I confirmed. 'My mother and father had eyes for nobody but one another.' In this light, at this point in time, I was glad that all the coy love-making on the red plush sofa had taken place, that I could say with conviction that my parents had behaved like lovers until death separated them. At this moment, the quality of that love, its reality, did not matter for, after what I had seen of this house, after what I had heard from Mr Guthrie, after hearing the treasure's version of Miss Cathie and her drunken Irish singer, I questioned the reality in my own terms of all these antecedents of mine.

Between my mother and myself there had always been an intangible insulating screen that prevented mental contact, as a row of footlights between actors and audience creates a barrier of distorted truth or actual illusion. Between old Snake-eyes and myself there was the barrier of time, of an outmoded way of life and thought, of death itself and between my aunts and me there was a physical barrier of the heavy door of the morning-room, behind which they led their cloistered lives and the mental barrier was almost as palpable as the door, so conscious was I of being an intruder coming late into their lives and probably the last fell trick that life could play upon them before they died.

'And there was something else in it besides my granny that day you came to the door, Mr Charles,' the treasure said as she laid a hand on the open pages of *Pride and Prejudice* that lay on the table. 'I pinched a book once, the first book of my own I ever had. It wasn't *bad* pinching though. The folk I pinched it from had no use for books. It was an old second-hand book and they would only have burned it anyway, likely.

It's called *Cranford*. I've still got it up in my room. It was it that started me reading real books like this.' She patted the book on the table. 'But after I pinched it, I found out it had been a present that a brother had given to his sister long ago. Their names are inside it.' She paused, looked at me, looked away. 'The names are Charles and Jean.' There was another little silence. 'So that was inside my head too when you came to the door that day. It's funny how many things are in a wee ordinary thing like you ringing a doorbell and me opening the door. Ye see, I've got strict orders from the ladies not to let anybody in and I mostly obey their orders but that day there was my granny and old Snake-eyes and Miss Cathie and *Cranford* – they were all *in* it so I showed ye into the morning-room.'

The pantry seemed to stir with life, to glow with warmth. It is one of the saddest conditions of human kind that it can recognise happiness only by hindsight. Few people have said: 'I am happy now', but the commonest phrase in the language is: 'I was happy then', although the words used may be 'Those were the days' or 'Où sont les neiges d'antan?'.

When I went to bed at nine-thirty on that first night at Laurelbank, I did not know that I was embarking on the happiest period of my life. I did not recognise the happiness until it was in the past.

'Are you going out again the-night, Mr Charles?' the treasure came to my room to ask about nine o'clock.

'No.'

'Then I'll go and lock that back door before I forget it.'

'I'll do it,' I said. 'I'll do it every night and then there will be no muddle.'

'Righto. I'd better bring up some more coal for your fire.'

'There is no need. I don't need any more fire tonight and when I do need coal, I'll carry it up myself.'

'But Mr Charles, the ladies—'

'Oh, no, we never mention them, their names are never heard,' I sang to the tune of 'Home, Sweet Home'.

'Mr Charles, you are a real comic, so ye are,' she told me. 'You should be on the stage, like your father.'

CHAPTER SIX

How doth the little busy bee
Improve each shining hour,
And gather honey all the day
From every opening flower!
'Against Idleness and Mischief,' by Dr Isaac Watts.

BY the end of the following week my life had settled into the surface security that is born of routine. Every day from Monday till Friday, now, I was travelling by train from Lochfoot to Glasgow to work with Doctor Gill, the tutor that Mr Guthrie had found for me. I left the house at a little before nine in the morning and did not return until about six in the evening but I spent only the forenoons with Doctor Gill. After a light lunch, I read in one of the many libraries or loitered around bookshops or explored the great grey sprawl of a city from the top deck of a tramcar, from which I descended if I saw anything that particularly interested me. It was possible to travel a long distance by tramway for a halfpenny, I remember.

Doctor Gill was a man of about thirty-five but he had become a victim of what in those days was known as infantile paralysis. His legs were paralysed, confining him to a wheelchair but the disease had in no way impaired his mind. He had one interest which was medicine and one hobby-horse, which was money and he took two pupils for coaching, myself in the forenoons and another youth in the afternoons.

In the atmosphere of friendly welcome which he generated, in the presence of his quick interested intelligence, study was easy and pleasant and even the terrifying mathematics, in which I had to reach a fairly high standard, began to come under the subjection of my brain. But what was of much more value than the formal tuition in the specific subjects for my examinations was his conversation after it was over and he had set me my reading for the following day. I reached his house shortly after ten in the morning and at twelve-thirty Mrs Gill would bring him the glass of beer that he took before lunch. This was a signal for my tutor to finish with business and mount his hobby-horse which he galloped with much vigour.

'There is only one disease in the world today,' he would begin, 'and that is the love of money. It is the root of all the evil and the basic cause of every disease that attacks the human organism. I was a doctor. You want to be a doctor. Very well. But who is going to operate on humanity and extract the malignant tumour of greed? Rickets – bad food because no money. Heart disease – wrong food because too much money. *You'll* be a doctor, young fellow. You'll get through these Prelims on your ear. Nothing to them. But when you are a doctor, you won't be able to do much good. You'll only be healing temporarily a few of the scabs on the surface that are generated by the malignance at the core.'

Perhaps he galloped his hobby-horse too hard and too straight, generalised too much and made too few allowances but when I left his house and spent a few hours exploring Glasgow by tramcar before I went home, I could see plenty of evidence for his argument in the squalid slums, the tall smoking chimneys, the infernal rattle of chains and riveters' hammers around the dirty grey river. Many great and elegant ships were built and sailed away down this famous waterway but the men who built them were small, dispirited and ugly so that my own six feet of healthy height towered over them, making me self-conscious and ashamed, making me crouch my shoulders to look smaller when I mingled with them on the greasy pavements, as they hurried into the bleak pubs or towards their bleaker homes. Then, when I made my way to the station, came the contrast. In these more central streets of the city, about five in the evening, the big cars would be starting out for the large suburban villas, for the hillside residences that overlooked the Clyde estuary, for the Laurelbanks. The distinction between the Them of the rich and the Us of the poor was never more pronounced than it was in Glasgow in 1924.

It seemed that I lived in two worlds. There was the world of the city, where so much happened every second, seconds when fortunes were lost or won, seconds when happiness turned into misery, seconds when high aspiration turned to failure, seconds when the life of a back street turned to tragedy, as a slum building collapsed, killing the teeming women and children it contained. And then, Up-the-line, at the other end of a short railway journey, there was Laurelbank, where nothing ever happened at all, where, for over forty years, two women had been sitting inside a cocoon of wealth, behind half-drawn blinds. And inside Laurelbank, although I was unaware of it at this time, a new life-cell was forming. This was the world of the pantry behind the staircase which was inhabited by the treasure and myself. It would be more correct to say that this world had existed ever since she had come to the house and that it was now extending its boundaries to include myself and I think it would be true to say that I made some contribution to it. For me, the comfort of this world was its honesty and simplicity. In it, there were no problems of rich and poor, no deviousness of motives, no petty selfishness, no hidden currents, no social barriers. The treasure insisted upon calling me 'Mr Charles' and pointed out, occasionally, improprieties in my behaviour in relation to my position but these were things of the surface only. The moment we were confronted by some of the small realities of our lives, such as my recurring fear that I would fail the mathematics examination and never reach medical school, truth would rise from the depths and the treasure would address me not as 'Mr Charles' but as 'ye witless thowless big sapsie'. Social distinctions were secondary in the pantry world, not primary and dominating as they were in the world outside.

I had expected to have to pay such expenses as railway fares out of my monthly allowance but on the Friday before my first visit to Doctor Gill I received a letter from Mr Guthrie's office which contained a season ticket on the railway for three months. In those days, in railway terms, social cleavages were even more pronounced than now and there was no second-class travel, but only first and third, and I found that Messrs. Guthrie, Guthrie, Inglis & Guthrie regarded me as a first-class traveller.

On my first Monday morning at the station, there were three other youths and two girls of about my own age, all carrying large black stiff-covered notebooks bearing a gold crest which, I soon discovered, was the crest of Glasgow University. I longed to talk to them, to be one of the chattering group, but they gave me no encouragement. I remembered that, as I had emerged from the road that led to Lochview Crescent, this group had approached the station from the town and the treasure had already indicated that town and Crescent did not mix. Still hopeful, however, I followed them into a third-class compartment, but my presence merely brought a constraint upon them until one by one they opened their notebooks and began to read, casting furtive glances at me as they turned the pages. At the first stop, two further students joined us, filling the compartment, and a ticket inspector also joined the train, an occurrence which, I was to discover later, took place at irregular intervals of anything from five weeks to three months. My ticket was the first to be requested and I produced the rectangle of thin white cardboard, noticing with something akin to dismay that the other seven hands held pale green rectangles.

'You should be forward in the firsts, sir,' the inspector told me, although kindly. 'Will you move forward at the next stop? The train will be filling up, ye see.' And while I stammered an apology he turned to the others: 'And what are the learned professors going to teach you the-day? Spellin' or 'rithmetic?' he asked them jovially and did not trouble to examine their tickets. At the next station I left the compartment, walked towards the engine and travelled the rest of the way alone, in a first-class carriage that was sealed off from the rest of the train.

I have described this incident, not of my own making, which separated me on that first day from those who should have been my fellows because it was typical of my life in relation to the rest of Lochfoot. At the end of three months I insisted at Mr Guthrie's office that a third-class ticket was a desirable factor.

It was known by now that I lived in Lochview Crescent and although the other students gradually began to greet me in the mornings and even include me in their conversations in the train, I was never completely accepted. My own nature was partly responsible for this. Except when I had been at school, I had never been with people of my own age and at the school I attended, enmity was more common than friendship and the friendships that were formed had a basis of social class as a rule and I, with my raffish background, had not been acceptable to any class. I was shy and diffident and most telling of all I was different from the other students on the train in that I went to a private tutor and spoke with an English accent. That both my parents were dead they also seemed to regard as peculiar. They distrusted my differences and most of all they distrusted my Crescent background. I could feel this every morning as I came round the corner from one direction and they came down the street from the other. We met on the neutral territory of the station yard but the cleavage was accentuated by the girls of the shirt factory.

These girls seemed to burst forth from their prison at times of their own choosing, under the leadership of the one who had referred to me as the Prince of Wales on that first day.

She was their ringleader and I came to know that her name was Maisie. Having burst forth, they would run screaming about the gravelled yard or dance about behind the fence until hounded back into the building by a fat red-faced man, presumably their employer. He treated them in a good-natured bawdy way and after they had worked off their high spirits for a few minutes they would quieten down and allow him to shoo them in through the door like a flock of unruly chickens.

When I began to catch the train regularly the girls took to bursting out each morning to greet my arrival in the station yard. This seemed to me very strange at first, for I did not understand the reasons behind it until I summoned the courage to discuss it with the treasure.

'Och, you're far too soft an' sensitive, Mr Charles,' she told me with some disgust. 'You're new, that's all. They know all the other folk that go to the station and you make a change for them.'

'They call me Princie now. It's awful. It's because of that skinny one calling me the Prince of Wales that first day.'

The treasure giggled very much as the shirt factory girls giggled, a lewd sort of cackle. 'Then you're all right,' she assured me. 'If they called you Rudy or Valentino, it'd be different. If it's the Prince o' Wales, it means that they like ye.'

But despite her assurances, I still regarded the mesh fence as an embarrassing gauntlet I had to run on my way to the train, but the treasure had imbued me with some confidence and I began to feel that the girls were more high-spirited than hostile. One morning, Maisie the ringleader was waving her shawl enthusiastically behind the fence when the wind caught it and carried it over into the road. I picked it up and carried it back to her and they were all quiet as I handed it over the fence. 'Many thanks, Bonnie Prince Charlie,' she then screeched with a high-pitched giggle. I had a non-plussed second of hesitation before I remembered the confidence with which the treasure had assured me that they liked me. 'Don't mention it, Miss Flora Macdonald,' I replied to Maisie in her own coin and the other fifty or so girls rounded on their leader, making a mocking ring around her while they danced and screamed: 'Miss Flora Macdonald, for Jesus's sake! Serves ye right, Maisie!' and I walked unmolested into the station.

Thereafter, we exchanged friendly greetings through the fence, although the other students seemed to disapprove of this. The name of Prince Charlie persisted but when I asked the treasure how they could have discovered my name, she said: 'Likely they don't know it's your real name. If I know anything about Maisie Anderson, all the history she minds on from the school is Bonnie Prince Charlie. From Princie to Prince Charlie – it's just an accident.'

It proved more difficult, however, to achieve acceptance among my fellow students than among the shirt factory girls and this was an area where I felt the treasure could not help me. To the factory girls I was a 'student', a representative of another genus of which they knew nothing but whom they would accept on terms of live and let live. To my fellow students, I was a variation from the norm of the student genus, a sport of the kind that all species distrust.

It was a pity that they could not know how I envied them and what I had learned of their backgrounds. They were all products of two large schools called 'academies' in two suburbs on the railway line between Lochfoot and Glasgow. They had sound education in preparation for university behind them and around them they had the backing of parents interested in them and ambitious for them. They were the sons of doctors, policemen, factory workers, clergymen and railwaymen, a truly democratic mingling of the academically fit, bonded together by a desire to enjoy a better world, as they saw it, as expressed by the doctor's son in: 'The old man wants me to specialise. A G.P. has a dog's life, he says' and by the railwayman's son in: 'My father always says that he wants my sister and me to have things easier than he and my mother had.'

There were plenty of girls on the train too, pretty girls with university-crested notebooks in bundles on their forearms, gay and full of chatter like girls anywhere but with a vein of seriousness and ambition lying under it all. They were the girls of the new world of after-the-war, girls with a new freedom which they cherished and because of this I felt more akin to them than I did to the boys, but I did not dare to talk to them at any length. The snake-like head of prurient sex was very close to the surface and I was already suspect enough without declaring myself to be 'a greasy Valentino' as those who showed too much interest in girls were called.

When the train left Lochfoot in the mornings, it carried only about a dozen passengers as a rule, one or two women embarking on a day's shopping in Glasgow, a few railwaymen going to work at the next town, one or two workers of other kinds and us students. But quite often, two or three times a week, perhaps, the Pauper, as I thought of him, would be waiting on the platform in his greasy too-big bowler hat which came low over his ears and his long black overcoat that flapped about his shins. He was always alone, spoke to nobody and nobody spoke to him, which was not surprising for he looked down at the ground all the time, seemed to be huddled inside himself and content to be alone and apart. He made me think of the verses in the *Garland of Gems* that had the refrain:

Rattle his bones over the stones!
He's only a pauper, whom nobody owns!

Feeling that I myself was something of an unowned pauper I felt that there ought to be some kinship between this old man and me, outsiders as we both were on the platform and in the train, but I could not bring myself even to bid him good morning. There seemed to be an impenetrable barrier around him. One dull wet morning, while we waited for the train, I happened to look round and see him standing in a darkish corner, beside some bundles of iron rods that stood upright against the wall. I had a curious sensation that I had seen him before, but in another place, in another life, even. There came the sudden shriek of the whistle of the approaching train, in its echo I seemed to hear the voice of the treasure: 'I'm just about *frightened* o' that damn' thing,' and I realised with relief that the old man, with his stooped shoulders and forward-bent head, was reminding me of the curved neck of the vulture on the silver inkstand that had belonged to my grandfather.

One evening, over supper in the pantry, I said to the treasure: 'That queer old man was on the train this evening. I call him the Pauper. He wears an old bowler hat that's too big for him and—'

She sat quietly while I described the old man and then rose from the table and went to the sink, to speak with her back towards me. 'You don't want to have anything to do with *him*, Mr Charles.'

'*He* doesn't seem to want to have anything to do with me or anybody else,' I told her.

'No. He doesn't like folk.'

'Who is he? What does he do?'

'He owns the Secondhand. It's a shop down the town that sells old furniture and carpets and stuff.' She turned round, pressed her elbows close to her sides as she did when she looked at Lord Mammon. 'He is nothing to do with *you*, Mr Charles,' she said.

I dismissed the Pauper as just one more puzzling feature of this eccentric little town, one which the treasure did not like to discuss and let the matter drop. There were other more interesting things to think about and talk about.

In spite of the shadowy barrier that Laurelbank and its wealth raised between me and the other young people, in spite of the irritating deference shown to me in the local shops and by the staff of Mr Guthrie's office, I found my new way of life much preferable to the old. From long habit, I was still careful with money but I could not resist the bookshops and there came, once, a thrilling moment when I realised that I could afford to buy the watch I had always wanted.

And I made the strange little discovery that, during the two years between my leaving school and the death of my father, I had never had enough sleep, that I had been constantly tired, although unaware of it. The regimen of Laurelbank, whereby we were all in bed by ten in the evening, brought me the extraordinary pleasure of waking early in the morning, truly refreshed and with the desire to be up and doing. At first, I did not get out of bed when I awoke, for the early spring mornings were frosty and cold, but a morning came when I bethought me that the pantry was always warmed by the boiler that heated the water, and with my book under my arm I crept downstairs. When I opened the door the gaslight was burning cheerfully, the fire glowed in the grate and the treasure was sitting at the table, knitting, a cup of tea beside her while she read *Emma*, which was propped against the teapot. I ought to have known, I thought as I stood in the doorway, that I could not go anywhere in this house, at any time, without the knowledge of its presiding genius.

'Good morning, Mr Charles,' she greeted me. 'Cup o' tea? Help yourself.'

The clock indicated that it was not yet six. 'Are you always up as early as this?' I asked.

'Earlier in the summer. I like the early morning time.'

When she had drunk her tea she put away her book and her knitting and went away to clean the morning-room. I followed her, picked up the coal scuttle, took it to the cellar in the basement, filled it and brought it back.

It was in this way that we began to spend the early mornings together, doing the work of the house between us, my main duties being the carrying up of coal and down of cinders, the stoking of the pantry boiler, the shoe-cleaning and the dusting of Lord Mammon. The treasure could not touch him without betraying that little shudder of repulsion and all my attempts to turn him into a figure of fun were unsuccessful.

'Say what you like,' she said, 'he is the worst circumstance in this whole house. I'd rather scrub every floor in the place than lay a finger on him.'

'Circumstance?'

'Is that bad grammar? I've aye thought that circumstances were the things round about you that you had to put up with.'

'Yes, I suppose that is quite a good description of circumstances. It is simply that I had not thought of old Lord Mammon being important enough to be a circumstance all by himself.'

'He is a circumstance all right, the ugly b – sorry, Mr Charles.'

The treasure was a natural mimic and her speech and accent began to grow into more and more of an imitation of my own, but I was glad that she lost none of her graphic quality, none of her acute observation and none of her ability for hitting ideological nails accurately on the head. And when she was amused, angry or deeply interested, out would come some phrase straight from the backyards and gutters where, I learned, she had spent most of her childhood. Her formal education had seemed to consist mainly of the learning of hymns and sentimental verse by heart and as she went about her early morning work, she would sing to the tune of 'There is a happy land' or some other hymn words that had no relation to the hymnary or the classroom. Her bawdiness was totally inoffensive because it had the clean cutting edge of a scalpel and her early morning singing seemed to me to be, like birdsong, a hymn of praise to some secret joy that she carried and cherished within herself.

Having lived my life among the second-rate, having attended a second-rate school and having grown up among second-rate music-hall artists, I had an appreciation of the first-rate in no matter what form and I admired greatly and wondered at the treasure's absolute mastery of her post as custodian of Laurelbank. Her standards for all the varied work of the house were very high but she never appeared flustered, always had time to stop to chat, to laugh, to take an interest in my books and studies. As far as the studies were concerned, her attitude to me was that of an adult to a retarded child who had to be coaxed and encouraged to learn his alphabet.

'There's no good being fed-up with it, Mr Charles,' she rebuked me during a struggle with a problem in trigonometry. 'You'll never do it if you're fed-up with it.'

'I don't see why I need trig to find out if somebody's got a sore throat or a broken ankle,' I protested pettishly.

'Likely the teachers think that if you can do that sum you won't be stupid enough to give somebody a bottle o' cough mixture for a broken ankle. Come on, now. Have another go. You say I can cook. When I came here an' got rid o' Mrs Tait, I couldn't boil an egg. In our house there were never any eggs to boil. But I found a big book down in the old kitchen. *Mrs Beeton's Household Management* it's called and I read it and got interested in cooking and cleaning silver and laying tables and all that. If you're interested, you can do anything. If you don't watch yourself I might get interested in that trigathingummy and turn into a doctor myself. Come on, now, have another crack at it, Mr Charles.'

Her frequent phrase 'If you don't watch yourself' always made me think of the tale of Little Orphant Annie in the *Garland of Gems*, every verse of which ended: 'An' the gobbleuns'll get ye if ye don't watch out'. I could understand why Jim Guthrie had referred to her as 'that little Orphant Annie of a maid' for she had a guttersnipe courage and an inexplicable dominating power like the character in the ballad.

'Another crack or the gobbleuns'll get me?' I would say on these occasions.

'Ye never can tell,' she would reply gravely.

She had tremendous decisiveness, seemed to suffer from none of my own morbid uncertainties and fears and yet, deep in her mind, there seemed to lurk some knowledge and fear of 'goblins', which showed itself physically in her shrinking from Lord Mammon, the other numerous bronze figures about the house, the silver inkstand and the embroidered snakes and dragons that rioted around the drawing-room. But this hidden knowledge and fear showed itself very seldom and for most of the time she was gay, forthright, mischievous and for all of the time she was busy. When she was not active about the house, cooking or cleaning, she sat knitting, with a book, usually by Jane Austen, propped up in front of her. She purloined the books from the smoke-room, explaining to me with her wink that she had no business to be reading the books that belonged to the house, that the ladies would not like it. The knitting was always some small white garment for an infant and on my weekly forenoon visits to the morning-room, the only times I ever saw my aunts, I noticed that they occupied themselves with similar knitting.

'You and the aunts must know a tremendous number of babies,' I said one Saturday forenoon, after I had left the aunts and had discovered the treasure knitting and reading in the pantry while the lunch cooked on the stove.

'I knit for a shop down-the-line,' she said, by which she meant a shop in one of the towns on the railway line to Glasgow. 'They give me the wool and pay sixpence the half-cut for knitting it.'

'Surely the aunts aren't knitting for money!' I protested.

Money! Hadn't they enough already? Or could they never have enough?

'No,' said the treasure. 'The ladies knit to amuse themselves and to be kind to the heathen.'

'The things they knit are for heathen babies?'

'Or slum ones.' There was something of mischief in her voice.

'How do the things go to the heathen or slum babies?'

'The ladies give them to me to take to the Missionary Society.'

'Where is that?'

'Down the line.'

She stopped knitting for a moment, looked out of the window and then straight into my face before her left eye closed in that disconcerting wink. On a gasping breath, I realised that, unknown to themselves, she had my aunts in her employ, knitting half-cuts of wool for which she was pocketing the sixpences.

'Treasure,' I exploded in her own phrase, 'you'll be the death of me!'

She looked suddenly innocent, even wan, her big eyes wide and lost so that I began to wonder if I had dreamed that wink, the mischievous implication in the phrase 'down the line'.

'Why, Mr Charles?' she asked, her fine eyebrows raised under the white cap. 'I wouldn't want any harm to come to you any more than to the ladies.' Now her tone and expression changed. 'By the way, what was that you called me just now?'

Logically, she should have been at a disadvantage, having tacitly admitted to swindling the aunts but, illogically enough, she had myself at a disadvantage.

'I am sorry,' I said. 'I didn't mean to say that.'

'You mean you didn't mean to say it out loud,' she told me with accuracy. 'But you've been thinking it inside your head for a while.'

'I don't like the name Jeanie,' I said, half-apologetically, half-belligerently.

'Me either,' she disarmed me. 'I never heard of anybody called Treasure before,' she continued. She put her head on one side and seemed to consider her knitting and the name at the same time. 'I suppose it's because the ladies have told you that I'm a perfect treasure?'

'How do you know that they told me that?' I asked, for I was sure that it would be against my aunts' principles to tell the girl herself of her treasurely qualities. Did she listen at key-holes? It seemed more than likely.

'I don't know.' She took thought for a moment. 'It's the kind of thing they *would* say. The ladies never say anything that's real.'

'Real?'

'Never anything that is their own. They say things they've heard other folk say, mostly dear papa, things they've picked up, like honesty is the best policy. Honesty isn't a policy. A policy is something you do because it suits you.'

'Like you taking the aunts' knitting down-the-line?' I enquired.

'That's right,' she agreed calmly.

'And what about honesty?'

'If you are honest it is something you have to be whether it suits you or not,' she informed me. She went to the cooker and tested the potatoes with a fork. 'If the ladies knew I was getting money for their knitting they would say I was dishonest, but I see it different. They think the things go to heathen babies and that makes them feel real pleased with themselves and they think they are being good. I got them started on this knitting ploy away back when we got rid of Mrs Tait and Annie and they were paying me a pound a month. It was more honest, I thought, for them to pay me a bit more than knit for heathen babies that are not even real to them and that they'd run a mile from if ever they saw them. I suppose you think I am terrible to swindle the ladies when they trust me and everything but, so far, they don't know they're being swindled and they are quite happy. But they would be very, very upset if I asked them for more wages instead of swindling them. I found that out the time I asked for another five bob a month after we got rid of Mrs Tait and Annie.'

'A pound a month?' I said, clinging to the only thing she had said that was concrete and familiar to me for I was not yet accustomed to her unconventional views on honesty and I was also a little stunned by her keen estimate of the aunts' characters. There was no doubt that she was correct when she implied that they would rather be swindled, although they would never admit it, than have to revise their idea that servants should be paid as little as possible. 'A pound a month?' I repeated. 'Is that all they pay you?'

'No. I get two-ten now. Mr Guthrie has got them to raise me bit by bit.' She looked straight into my face. 'Do you think I am really dishonest about the knitting, Mr Charles?'

'If you will teach me to knit I'll give it to you to take down-the-line to the Missionary Society,' I said and she laughed. I then said: 'I don't know why you told me about this.'

'You asked,' she told me, 'and like I said being honest is something you have to do whether it suits you or not. I am a good liar but I never tell dishonest lies.' I found this statement of a private morality too complicated and made no comment, whereupon she continued: 'You know, I don't sell the knitting so much for the money now as for the fun. I just think it's comic, the ladies being so economical and clever with their own way of it and being so easy to cheat. It gives me the same feeling as going Up-the-Burn when I was at the school.'

'Up-the-Burn? What was that?'

'It was great. You know the Castle? Nobody's supposed to go into the grounds and there are lodges at all the gates and that, but there's a way in all the same. You go up the Burn, through a tunnel and through a big iron grating. I used to go up there and wander about all over the place. In the name o' the Kingdom o' Heaven,' she lapsed into her dialect in her delight, 'I went into the very glass-houses once an' pinched a load o' flowers!' She became what she called 'proper' again. 'I pinched the flowers for the funeral of a poor baby that died, a slum baby, if you like, like the ones the ladies think they are knitting for. It just didn't seem real or right or honest to me that there should be all these flowers at that Castle and no flowers for the baby's coffin.'

It struck me, as she began to make the final preparations for lunch, that her views were similar to those of Doctor Gill but less wordy and more practical. Treasure did not merely fulminate against the maldistribution of the goods of the world. She did not fulminate about anything. In her small way, she tried to set small corners to rights, in particular Treasure's own small corner.

'Ever since I came here,' I said, 'I have wondered if the aunts have paid you more because of me. They told me that they offered to get extra help but that you didn't want that. Did they raise your wages instead?'

'No, Mr Charles,' she said. 'I don't think you understand the ladies right. I am higher paid than any other servant in the Crescent already and the ladies don't like that. It gets on their consciences, paying me so much. They only do it because Mr Guthrie told them to and because he is a gentleman who knows what's what, like dear papa. It's not just that the ladies are mean, although, mind you, they *are* mean. They think it's *wrong*, a sin, to pay servants any more than they can help. It's not their fault either. It's the way they were brought up to do and say things that other folk like dear papa did and said like honesty is the best policy and waste not, want not.'

She spoke kindly and gently, as if she were anxious that I should understand her ladies, be less critical of them and then she went on in energetic tones: 'Don't you worry your head about *me*, Mr Charles. I do all right for myself in ways that don't upset the ladies.'

'But, Treasure, I have quite a good allowance and I would like to pay you something for all you do for me.'

'Lord a'mighty, but that name is real comic! No, Mr Charles. You are not to think of giving me anything. It wouldn't be honest, me taking money from you.'

'Not honest? But why?'

'You and me's in the same boat, orphans with nothing except what we get from the ladies, and then we're *real* to one another. It's right hard to talk about real things, but listen, the ladies don't see you and me as folk. They see me as a servant, a perfect treasure, a – a *thing*.'

'And how do they see me?'

'As Miss Cathie's disgrace, I wouldn't be surprised or *something* like that,' she told me, not mincing matters, and I felt that again she had hit a nail accurately on the head. 'But you are not to blame the ladies for the way they think, Mr Charles. It's the way they were brought up and the money and everything.'

'The money?'

'Ach,' she became impatient with my stupidity, 'ye ken damn' fine that folk that make a god o' money are bound to get frightened o' it. Folk are aye frightened o' gods like folk were frightened o' auld Whiskers in the Bible. Here, I'm goin' to be late. Get the silver for the ladies' lunch out for me, will ye?'

Early on a morning shortly after this, Treasure was cleaning the front hall, a form of cleaning which she called 'thorough-ing' which happened about once a month to the few parts of the house that were in use. I had finished my coal-carrying and other jobs and offered my help, whereupon she said: 'Lift that mat in the porch, Mr Charles, and take it down the back stair and give it a good bang or two against the wall.' The porch was an area some fifteen feet square between the heavy outer door and the inner one with the glass panels. Like the hall, it was lit by stained-glass windows but where the hall was parquet-floored, the porch was tiled with a shallow oblong well just inside the outer door, in which lay a thick, heavy coconut-fibre mat. I lifted this thing out as instructed and uncovered four one-pound bank-notes.

'Treasure,' I said, 'come here.'

She stood looking down at the money. 'Burglar money,' she said. 'Don't touch it, Mr Charles. Take the wee brush and sweep round about it and say your prayers while you're at it. If that's still there two months from now, we'll both be two quid better off. I aye give burglar money two thoroughings, to make sure the ladies have forgotten about it.'

'I see,' I said.

'I don't suppose ye do,' she informed me candidly. 'The way I look at it is that if folk have to hide money because they're frightened that somebody will pinch it, they deserve to get it pinched if they forget where they've hidden it.'

My training and the tradition in which I had been reared indicated that Treasure was a dishonest member of what my mother called 'that class', a petty thief whom I, in my position, should report to my aunts but her candour about her petty peculations delighted and flattered me, for not only did it indicate her trust in me, it also showed her acceptance of me as what she called a 'real' person, someone of her own kind who looked hard facts firmly in the face. And in addition to this there was my gratitude to her for the intervention that had opened this house to me. None the less, I was shocked and troubled at first as I learned more and more of her activities, but when I looked beyond the face of her 'dishonesty' I found it impossible to regard her as dishonest. She gave to my aunts full value and a good deal more for all the money she acquired. She made it possible for them to have the way of life they wanted on their own terms of personal sloth and self-indulgence while congratulating themselves on running their house economically. They gave no thought to their treasure, accepting without thanks and as of right all that she did for them while she had constantly in mind their comfort, their eccentricities and stood always between them and any form of 'upset'. I came to regard her as the busy bee improving each shining hour precisely in the manner advocated in high moral tones in the verses in the *Garland of Gems*.

After some weeks, Saturday forenoons, when I paid my visits to the morning-room, took on in my mind the character of the ceremonial day of the week and on the last Saturday forenoon of each month, ceremonial rose to a high peak. Punctually at eleven o'clock, Treasure went into the morning-room dressed in a neat navy coat and a navy felt hat and emerged a few moments later bearing two cheques. With these, she set off to the bank and when in the town she might have instructions to buy some small haberdashery items such as buttons or elastic. She also brought home the week's supply of fruit. All the other food came in horse-drawn vans to the back door where Treasure bought the meat, bread, fish and vegetables day by day.

Her departure to the bank was the signal for me to enter the morning-room to pay my weekly visit to the aunts which was a penance to all of us. As time went on, they became less obviously nervous of me but they remained awkward because they were ashamed of me and the air in the dim room was always filled with frantic searchings and writhings as we tried to think of things to say to one another. Like or dislike did not enter into the relationship for I think this faculty in the aunts had become dessicated by their long sequestration from human company. They had grown together and away from the rest of the world to the degree where I felt I was dealing with one distant shut-away mind which inhabited two very similar big-boned bodies, dressed in long dark skirts and shawls and wearing the spectacles which they hastily hid away when I came into the room. In spite of this, or perhaps because of it, I always saw them as and always remember them as wearing steel-rimmed spectacles.

The same remarks were made Saturday after Saturday. They hoped that I was making progress with my tutor, they hoped that I was attending to my studies, they hoped that Jeanie was attending to me properly. We would then make an excursion into the wider field of the daily news, perhaps. Those terrible Clydeside men were making a fuss in Parliament again, always wanting more money. People thought about nothing but money and we did not know what the world was coming to. Tea was going up in price again. Prices were rising every day. We would all end up in the workhouse. And there was the weather. It was still very cold for the time of year and we were sure that Jeanie had had windows open again this morning. Really, servants had no consideration for our weak chests.

The return of Treasure from the town at about noon gave me my release and I would emerge from the morning-room despising myself for listening to them, for not 'standing up' to them, for fawning on them like a whipped dog until Treasure would join me in the pantry, put the housekeeping money for the week into its box and say: 'We are grand pleased with ourselves this morning. The ladies think ye'll be a credit to them yet, Mr Charles,' or some such nonsense which invariably had the effect of sweeping away my humiliation and self-disgust.

Now the final monthly ceremonial would begin. I would leave the pantry, Treasure would shut the door, I would retire upstairs and soon there would come the furtive movements around the ground floor while the aunts hid their money from the burglars. It was a little uncanny, this monthly furtive disturbance of the silence and stillness that normally prevailed, as if this were a witching hour when the spirits of this stone temple came out of their sleep and prowled at large. Sitting in my room, visualising the hall down below with the light filtering through the stained glass, one black-clad votary kneeling to put money under a carpet, another reaching up to put money in a tall Japanese vase, it was only too easy to imagine Lord Mammon at the foot of the stairs coming to life and raising his tall axe in grotesque sacrilegious blessing. Then the door of the morning-room would shut and the aunts would not be seen for another week. It embarrassed them to meet me on the landing, the stairs or in the hall because, I thought, servants and dependants should not be seen in the 'front' of the house except in the course of their duties and I had no duties except my weekly visit to the morning-room. When the door had been shut for five minutes I would come quietly downstairs and rejoin Treasure in the pantry where we would take up life again.

'I'll bet ye there's some under the stair-carpet this time,' she would say. 'I heard a bit of a creak.'

It seemed to me, at first, ludicrous that the aunts should think, firstly, that they could hide money unknown to Treasure and, secondly, that they should think that she would not find it in the course of her cleaning, but Treasure explained to me.

'Annie,' she said, 'that was supposed to do the morning-room, the dining-room and the drawing-room when I first came here never lifted a rug or dusted the inside of a vase. Annie never thorough-ed anything. After her and Mrs Tait left, I found money all over the place. And then, they were down in the basement while the ladies were hiding the money. The ladies went to the bank themselves in those days. The whole place was filthy, Mr Charles, to tell ye the truth but the ladies didn't know that. They can't *see*, ye see, and they won't wear their specs if they can help it. Besides, they don't know about housework. They don't know that you lift rugs an' shake them an' so on. It was right dishonest of Mrs Tait an' Annie to take advantage the way they did of the ladies being blind and the basement was like a dung-midden because they knew the ladies wouldn't bother going down there. If folk are taking money to do a job they should *do* it, but Mrs Tait an' Annie were just two lazy, dirty dishonest bitches.'

I am sure that I did not discover all of Treasure's methods of 'looking after' herself as she called her peculations. If I had asked her for details, I feel sure that she would have told me but I did not ask. I discovered that in the time of Mrs Tait and Annie there had been 'books' for the grocer, the baker and other tradesmen which had been paid at the end of each month, but after their departure the aunts had decided to trade on a cash basis because they felt that 'the books were always too high'. I do not know to what extent Treasure influenced this decision but I have always suspected that the weekly allowance of cash was not all spent on food bought at the back door or the change returned to the morning-room at the end of each week all that it should have been.

But I came to feel more and more surely that Treasure was entitled to every penny that she guided into her own pocket. The money from under carpets and inside vases was, after all, a reward for her 'thoroughness' and it seemed to me that the aunts, too slothful to interest themselves even in the choice and purchase of their food, deserved to pay a little extra to have it delivered to them, perfectly cooked and served by the efforts of their treasure.

The most amusing to me and the most revealing of the aunts' characters among Treasure's lookings-after of herself was the laundry. Lochfoot was less prosperous now than it had been in the nineteenth century when my grandfather had built Laurelbank, and Lochview Crescent was no longer the exclusive residential area that it had been in former times. There were no longer the staffs of servants, the dinner parties or the At Home days and many of the large villas were occupied by aged couples or widows who seemed to live almost as quietly as my aunts, although in less morbid seclusion and on more slender means. Some of the villas were divided and occupied by several households, the men of which drove in cars to work in banks and insurance offices in the towns down-the-line or in Glasgow. Two of the villas had been turned into nursing-homes and a third was a boarding-house for elderly ladies. As the nature of Lochview Crescent changed, there had come changes in the ancillary services which it had demanded. The livery stable which had supplied the cabs for the dinner parties and afternoon visits had gone out of business and another enterprise which had more recently closed its doors had been the Lochfoot Steam Laundry. This, Treasure told me, had upset the ladies very much, disliking change as they did and, in addition, the laundry from down-the-line which now came knocking at the doors of the Crescent tore the sheets and lost the table napkins to a degree that made the aunts' departure to the work-house immediately imminent.

'It was the only time I ever invented a *person*,' said Treasure. 'I was always one o' the best liars when I was at the school, like I told you, but when the laundry got so bad and the ladies were in such a state, I invented Mrs Grey and I had to invent Mr Grey as well, because they live down in the Village and Mr Grey has to come on his bicycle to collect the washing and bring it back.'

I came to know of the imaginary Mr and Mrs Grey one day when I found Treasure sitting at the pantry table, writing laboriously in a grey notebook with a pencil held in her left hand. I had seen her write before, producing a clear fluent script, rapidly, with her right hand. 'What in the world are you doing?' I asked.

'It's Mrs Grey. She's not a very good writer.'

I stood behind her and read: '6 table napkins 1/-, 4 hand towels 8d., 8 sheets 4/-.'

'Who is Mrs Grey, Treasure?'

'Me,' she said and went on to tell me how Mrs Grey had come to be 'invented'.

'But why?' I asked. 'Couldn't you just have told the aunts that you would do the washing and they could pay you instead of the laundry?'

She sighed. 'Mr Charles, sometimes I think you will *never* understand about the ladies, honest I do. They wouldn't pay *me* to do the washing. I'm doing it in *their* time and they're paying me for that already.'

'But it's dotty!' I protested. 'If they were willing to pay the laundry, why can't they pay you for doing the same job?'

'Because I'm getting paid already and ever since they couldn't get a laundry-maid any more, the washing has gone out to be done. The ladies are used to that now and there's no use upsetting them with new ideas. Mr Charles, start getting the dinner tray ready, will you, so that I can get Mrs Grey's book finished.'

During the cold months of February and March, I had not penetrated to the overgrown wilderness that was the back garden, but when the milder weather came and it was still daylight when I came home from Glasgow, I went through the dense screen of rhododendrons and laurels facing the back door by a little path made by Treasure. Beyond the rank shrubs, the area opened out into grass dotted with tall trees and clumps of bushes, with pieces of stone statuary and iron seats here and there and in the part furthest from the house there was a decayed summer-house with, behind it, what had once been a kitchen garden and an area of grass with poles and a clothes-line on which flapped some of 'Mrs Grey's' laundry.

I sat down on the low wall that divided the trees and bushes from the erstwhile kitchen garden and looked towards the house but, from here, no part of that large block of stone was visible. The wilderness had obviously been laid out and planted at some considerable expense as a woodland garden but nobody, with the exception of Treasure, had set foot in it for so long that it had a curious nostalgic charm, as if ghosts walked between the trees with a faint rustle of silk.

It was on a little thrill of pleasure that the thought came to me that some of the trees in this place were older than the house, that the site of Laurelbank had originally been woodland. The brooding solidity of the older trees seemed to nullify some of the menace that the house had for me, as if the trees in their watching silence were aware that even this great block of stone was subject to decay. And it now came to me too that the aunts were mortal. Until this moment, I think, they had appeared to me as two of the fixtures of the house, more mobile than Lord Mammon who was screwed to the floor of the hall, but not much so as they pursued day after day their confined orbit from bedroom to morning-room and back to bedroom. What would happen to the house when they had gone? I did not care, but I hoped that they would live until I had qualified in medicine.

'Don't the aunts ever go out?' I asked Treasure as the spears of the daffodils thrust through the grass in the wilderness. 'Even into the garden in the fine weather?'

'No,' she said. 'The ladies are too busy to go out. Busy as bees they are, what with eating and sleeping and looking after their weak chests and their knitting for the Missionary Society and their library books. They are reading a book called *The Sheik* just now, all about passion in the desert. Saw you going up the back garden. It's great out there, isn't it?'

CHAPTER SEVEN

I don't go much on religion,
I never ain't had no show;
But I've got a middlin' tight grip, sir,
On the handful o' things I know.
'Little Breeches,' by Colonel John Hay.

IN September of that year, 1924, I sat the preliminary examinations at the university during a period of dull grey weather with low cloud that hung like a pall over the big grey building on top of the hill. As the days went by and I answered paper after paper, I became more and more depressed. The other examinees were all a year or some two years younger than myself and I seemed to be the only one who was sitting a full curriculum of entrance examinations. The others were sitting only one or, at the most, two subjects in which they had failed at their final examinations at school. Also, these others were examination-hardened in a way that I was not. They had been accustomed to rigorous yearly examination in their strict Scottish academies while, at my school, examinations had been a joke, as if we were all subconsciously aware that we would be given reasonable reports as long as our parents continued to pay our fees.

When the ordeal for each day was over, I would moon around the park on the hillside below the university, catch a train that would bring me to Lochfoot after dark, moon along the road by the lochside and come down the back drive to the back door of the house. I regretted all the time I had spent in carrying coal, stoking the boiler and indulging in musicales in the drawing-room with Treasure, precious time when I should have been studying anent these examinations.

It was the custom at that time – it may be so still – for the authorities to post a list of names of candidates who had passed on a notice-board at the university and to publish a similar list in the *Glasgow Herald*. The night before these notices were to appear, I could not sleep, then fell asleep towards morning to writhe, feeling giddy and sick, in a nightmare in which the aunts stood in the hall beside Lord Mammon, pointing bony forefingers at the front door as they ordered me, the failure, the waster, the bastard son of that drunken Irish singer to leave their house for ever.

'Mr Charles,' came the faint voice across the cloudy stained-glass hall of the nightmare. 'Mr Charles.'

I struggled up to a sitting position, struggled out of the serpent coils of the nightmare, hastily wiping the tears from my face while the sweat made my skin itch as it broke through the pores on the back of my neck.

Treasure threw the open pages of the *Glasgow Herald* on to the bed and went dancing round the room while she chanted one of our musical monologues:

> *I sprang to the stirrup, and Joris, and he,*
> *I galloped, Dirck galloped, we galloped all three—*

By my writing table in the window she came to rest. 'Jings, the ladies'll hear me! Read it, Mr Charles! In the name o' the Kingdom o' Heaven, I'll be callin' ye *Doctor* Charles yet! Ye've got them *all*!'

I could not believe her. I looked down at the tightly printed column of the newspaper but the print blurred and my stomach came heaving, humiliatingly, up into my throat. I had to get to the bathroom to be sick. What would Treasure think? I ventured to look up but Treasure was gone. Only the newspaper remained to prove that she had ever been there. My stomach subsided, my sight cleared and I began to look for my name in the various pass-lists. It was not difficult to find. In each list it had been ringed in pencil by Treasure.

By the time I had washed and dressed, I was feeling acutely

ashamed of myself because I had allowed Treasure, who would have been almost as disappointed as I myself would have been had I failed, to take the first shock of the pass-lists. I also wondered with humiliation how much she had seen of my struggling nightmare, of the tears on my face, how long she had been standing by my bed trying to wake me.

As I went down to the pantry to breakfast, I was nervous of facing her and paused at the foot of the stairs, trying to collect myself. Treasure must despise me, a grown man having nightmares about the results of examinations. What was that word she used for weaklings such as the milkman who was afraid of his horse? Sapsie. She must be thinking of me as a sapsie. Beside me, Lord Mammon stared blindly across the hall and I had a sudden idea of a way to reinstate myself, of demonstrating to myself and to Treasure that I was not a sapsie like the milkman, but someone quite fearless, more fearless, even, than Treasure herself. She was afraid of Lord Mammon to the degree of fearing to touch him, but I was not afraid of him. I would get that twenty pounds of burglar money out of him if I had to take him to pieces to do it. I would get it out and present it to Treasure. Squaring my shoulders, I strode into the pantry.

'Treasure, have we a screwdriver in the house?'

'In that drawer over there. What do you want it for? Better watch your hands. Doctors' hands are important, especially if they turn into surgeons.'

'Shut up. It will be five years and more before I am a doctor, if ever, that is.'

'Don't talk like a sapsie!' she said. 'If folk want to do a thing as much as you want to be a doctor, they can do it. Look at all the times you told me you would never pass in maths. You think too little o' yourself, Mr Charles. I suppose it was your father being so conceited about himself that made you go the opposite way.' She surveyed me critically while she revealed to me this truth about myself. 'And you might have put on a clean shirt the-day. Your cuffs are as black as Lewie Leadpipe's Sunday hat.'

'They are not!'

'That shirt's been on your back for three days, ye mean brute, when poor Mrs Grey gets sixpence a shirt! Sit down and eat your breakfast.'

'I'll change my shirt when I go upstairs,' I promised her.

The next morning I got out of bed as dawn began to break and opened both front doors to let the maximum of light into the hall. At first glance I had taken the figure at the bottom of the stairs to be a suit of armour but it was to be precise an effigy of a suit of armour, the only moving part being the visor which swung on two screws at either side of the helmet. The whole was one large bronze casting, whose mailed feet grew out of a bronze plate which was screwed at its four corners to the parquet of the floor. The holes in which the screw-heads were sunk were full of the accumulated floor polish of the years, the screws themselves at first seemed to be immovable but at last, as the clock ticked away the precious minutes, the first one began to respond to the screwdriver. Round the four corners I went, slackening each screw a turn at a time until the figure began to wobble slightly, but terrifyingly enough to make me fetch some rope from the basement and lash it to the newel-post of the stairs. If Lord Mammon fell over he would not only wake the household, I thought, but probably cause considerable damage as well and all the time that I worked there was the fear that the base-plate was solid, sealing off the soles of the feet, sealing in the twenty pounds and rendering my entire effort useless. I was removing the last of the long screws when the whisper came from behind me: 'Oh, Mr *Charles*!'

Kneeling on the floor, holding the thing by its thighs, I looked over my shoulder. 'You are just in time. If I tilt him a little, will you put your hand in underneath and feel if there is a hole in his feet?'

Treasure came close to me. 'Mr Charles, I don't—'

'Don't be so silly, Treasure!' I said impatiently. 'If the money is there, it won't bite you!'

'No, but—'

'Hurry or I won't have him screwed back before the aunts come down.'

'But, Mr Charles—'

'Oh, don't be such a sapsie!'

Kneeling on the floor, she looked up at me while I braced myself, took the thing by the waist and tilted it over. A small bundle of notes held by an elastic band dropped out on to the parquet.

'Pick that up,' I said. 'I can't hold this bloody thing all day.'

'Oh, Mr Charles,' she said again and lifted the money from the floor while I raised the effigy upright again.

'Go and make us some tea,' I said, and began to replace the screws. It was almost as difficult to re-drive them as it had been to take them out for they were rusty, no doubt from water that had seeped down when the floor had been washed, but all went well if slowly until I came to the last which suddenly broke when it was half-driven. Fortunately, it was one of the two screws which were covered by the rug that lay at the foot of the stairs and equally fortunately, even without the rug, the short-sighted aunts would never see it. And the effigy was steady enough, firmly back in his place, rigid, solid, standing guard over his temple. Treasure came out of her pantry, looked at him and then at me.

'Gyad,' she said, 'you haven't half got a nerve! If the ladies knew we'd been interfering with that bugger they'd murder us.'

'I'd like to see them try,' I said grandly. 'And anyway, *you* didn't interfere with him but you've got the money and that's what matters.'

'Mr Charles, it's *your* money. I did nothing to get it out of him.'

'And I couldn't have got it out of him if you hadn't told me it was *in* him.'

'It's not right, Mr Charles. You never take any of the burglar money and I can't take all this money especially out of *him*.'

'Are you trying to tell me he has made the money no good? That he has poisoned it?' I asked.

'Gyad, no. Money can't get poisoned but it can poison *folk* if they don't watch themselves. But all right, Mr Charles. I knew it was in him and you got it out of him so we'll go halvers,' and she counted out two little heaps of crumpled notes on to the pantry table.

'All right. I'll use mine for books,' I said. 'What will you do with yours, Treasure?'

'Put it in the bank.'

I was feeling very pleased with myself, very confident and different from the morning before. 'Saving up for your bottom drawer, are you?' I asked.

'No. I don't go much on the marriage business,' she told me ' 'though I might consider it if someone came along with an estate of six thousand a year like in Jane Austen. Here, it's time we got stuck into that morning-room.'

I now had time to spare, with my examinations behind me and my classes at the university not scheduled to begin until October and Treasure and I embarked on a round of gaiety. We had a musicale in the drawing-room each morning before the aunts came downstairs and another each afternoon when they went up for their 'lie-down'. Treasure took me on a tour of the attics at the top of the back stairs which consisted of six rooms in all, one occupied by Treasure, one other furnished as a servant's bedroom and four which were full of the less valuable acquisitions of the years. This was a house where nothing had ever been thrown away, where everything was stored against that rainy day of which the aunts lived in constant fear.

The room that Treasure had chosen for her own had been furnished with items chosen from the storerooms by herself. It was directly above my own and looked out over the trees of the back garden. It had a sloping ceiling and dormer window and everything in it was white – white-painted wooden furniture, white curtains, a white counterpane on the bed, all in complete contrast to the weighty over-furnishing of the rest of the house. It suddenly came to me that, during the silent locked and barred nights when the house slept, Treasure was above all the weight and wealth, floating clear of it in her white bed, near the tree-tops and the sky.

'Do you want to be rich, ever, Treasure?' I asked her as we stood among the marble-topped wash-stands and brass hot water jugs in one of the lumber-rooms.

'No. I just want to have enough.'

'Enough for what, though?'

'To live the way my granny did in Lilac Cottage in the Village.'

'Lilac Cottage?'

'My granny's house. She left it to me when she died. It's got folk living in it, a business gentleman from Glasgow and his wife and invalid son. Mr Guthrie found them for me and looks after the rent and all that side of it.'

'So you are a woman of property, Treasure?'

'You could put the whole of Lilac Cottage into these attics and have a bit left over,' she told me. 'But I like it. I like it because of my granny, I think and because it's been there so long, longer than the town and the Crescent here. You've been down to the Village, Mr Charles?'

'Yes. It's charming. It was one of the first parts of Lochfoot that I happened to see. I walked down there by chance that first day, before I came up here even.'

The first day, now, seemed infinitely far away as did all the time before I had known Treasure, for it seemed that she had shed a different light on the world for me, making me see it, I thought, more clearly and truly.

There were about a dozen pictures in black wooden frames that crossed at the corners stacked against the wall and idly I began to tilt them backwards against my legs to look at them. They were dreary sepia prints of Old Testament subjects, Jacob climbing a ladder, the top of which was hidden in cumulous cloud, Moses on top of a mountain with his long forefinger pointing upwards into more cloud.

'They give me the creeps, that bunch,' said Treasure. 'They were in the bedroom that was your granny's but I brought them up here. It seems she got religion right bad in the years before she died. Used to preach sermons to herself and everything, poor soul. But then, I don't go much on religion, like that man in the American poetry in the Gyarland.'

Treasure had a trick of inserting a superfluous y after the g of garland, which was very expressive of her scorn of the book and all it contained and in a similar way she said 'Gyad' as an expletive of disgust.

'But that man said he believed in God and the angels,' I argued.

'I believe in goodness, so maybe that's kind of believing in God.'

'In goodness? Why?'

'Because I know there's badness and if there's badness there must be goodness, although I ain't had much show of it, like the man in the American poetry.'

'What sort of badness do you mean?'

'Just pure badness.'

'Greed? Cruelty? Murder? What?' I persisted.

'All these things are bad but there might be reasons for people being them or doing them but there is pure badness that's worse than any o' these things. It's just *pure* badness.'

'I don't understand, Treasure.'

'I can't explain any better. I think it's to do with just hating folk and wanting to hurt them and make them suffer and and grabbing everything for yourself and not caring about other folk at all.'

'Like the aunts eating and sleeping all day and not bothering about anybody or anything?'

'Mr Charles,' she was stern with indignation, 'the ladies are not *bad*. The ladies just don't want to be upset but they don't upset anybody else either.'

'So bad people are the kind who upset other people?'

'You try and laugh at me and I'll give you one in the eye,' she threatened. 'Bad folk don't just upset other folk. They don't care what they do to anybody else as long as it's something bad. And they *like* doing the badness.'

'Very unpleasant.'

Her little face sneered at me. 'It's well seen *you've* never come up against real badness,' she told me. 'If you had, you wouldn't be asking silly questions about it and making me give silly answers. Well, you've seen the attics. I'm off down to take in Mrs Grey's washing, poor soul.'

When my beginning work at the university became imminent, Mr Guthrie, who invited me to lunch with him at his club every fortnight or so, told me that he believed that he could now persuade the aunts to let me have rooms in Glasgow. At this point, the last thing I wanted to do was to leave Laurelbank and I could not explain to Mr Guthrie my true reasons for wishing to remain there, for he would at once, I was sure, put a wrong construction on my relationship with Treasure. In the end, I must have appeared to him as a very smug, holier-than-thou young man with all my protestations of not being interested in games, dancing, the cinema, of liking the quiet of Laurelbank and its proximity to the moors where I could walk. The falseness of this portrait of myself that I had been forced to construct irritated me. It seemed that only with Treasure could I be the person that I actually was. The aunts saw me as a potential reincarnation of my Uncle Charlie, the other students on the train saw me as a rich 'toff' to be distrusted and Mr Guthrie, if he knew about Treasure and me and our relationship would become watchful and slightly lewd, as he was about his youngest son, Hugh, who was in his final year in law at the university and 'a bit of a lad among the girls'. I did not want to be leered at as a bit of a lad among the girls and I knew very well that if I tried to be a bit of a lad with Treasure, I would suffer the same fate as the dashing fishmonger's man who had recently received a ringing slap in the face at the back door and the injunction to keep his 'stinkin' paws among the herrin' guts where they belong'.

Reluctantly, I had to bear with Mr Guthrie's view of me as a studious young man whom he would privately describe as 'a bit of a cissie' and he began to invite me to lunch less frequently, but this ensured my remaining at Laurelbank where Treasure and I continued to live in our private world, which was like a glass bubble out of which we could see but into which the rest of the world could not see. It was a world with its own laws and its own views on every subject under the sun and it even had its own language, for we communicated largely in the phrases of the Gyarland, in the words of the sentimental ballads of the sheet music in the stand under the piano and in the titles of the sickly pictures that hung upon every wall in the house.

This world was peopled, too, with fantasy figures like Mrs Grey the washerwoman, old Snake-eyes, Lord Mammon and even the aunts, shut away in the morning-room, were part of the fantasy world under the title of 'the ladies'.

By hindsight, it is easy to observe that Treasure and I were ill-developed adolescents. When we were children, I can see now, we were in a sense both old without ever having been young and now in adolescence we brought out in one another the childhood we had never had, but we were still lop-sided in development. Academically, I turned into the most advanced student of my year while knowing nothing of and being rather afraid of the world at large in which I had no integral place, while Treasure, academically totally ignorant, seemed to have a clear inborn wisdom that the chaotic tumult of the world could never cloud, although she had chosen to leave the outer world that she had known for the small enclosed area of Laurelbank.

The private world which we inhabited had been originally the creation of Treasure. On an accidental impulse, she had admitted me to it on that first day when she showed me to my room and introduced me to the picture that she called 'Wee Who-did-it' and the caustic turn of her mind, its complete freedom from sentimentality had appealed to me, the unwanted physical by-product of Cloud Cuckooland.

My main contribution to the private world was my ability to strum upon the piano, for this led us to set all the verses in the Gyarland to music, to play and sing all the sentimental ballads stored in the music stand and as we both had keen aural memories, the phrases of the verses and songs remained with us and became the verbal coin of our conversations. We both used the sentimental and sanctimonious verses and phrases obliquely and cruelly, as when we caught the two mice in the traps I had set in the basement and Treasure stood over them and intoned:

Billy's dead and gone to glory – so is Billy's sister Nell;
There's a tale I know about them were I a poet I would tell;
Soft it comes with perfume laden, like a breath of country air—

at this point she left the text of the Gyarland and improvised:

Gyad the stink down here would kill you get on an' catch another pair.

Thus, in the private world, we trampled underfoot all the

sentiments that the solid Laurelbank had been built to house and we scorned Lord Mammon, the effigy of its god, whose chief commandment was: 'Thou shalt love, cherish and protect thy money to a life beyond life.'

With time, my Saturday forenoon visits to the aunts became less of an ordeal for, through Treasure, I gradually came to some sort of understanding of them and it became my chief goal, when in the morning-room, to lead them into talk about Treasure herself. On this subject, as on many others, it seemed to me that the minds of the aunts looked in two opposite directions, as if each mind were a pair of grotesquely squint eyes. With one mental eye, for instance, they would talk pitifully of 'the poor', of their duty to help them by knitting industriously for the Missionary Society while with the other mental eye they would deplore those dreadful Clydeside members of Parliament who were agitating for more wages for the workers. There was a similar built-in contradiction in their view of Treasure. They would begin by telling me that she was a perfect treasure – this cliché recurred and recurred – and by enjoining me distrustfully to do nothing to upset her but, this said, they could go on to tell me in the same breath that I must not leave money lying about in my room. 'It is only a temptation to her,' they would say, 'and you cannot trust any of them.'

Gradually I came to accept that what Treasure had said of the aunts was absolutely accurate. They saw her, myself and the rest of the world as things rather than as people. It took me much longer to come to understand that they saw the world like this because they themselves had turned into 'things', vegetables, living passively inside their cocoon of comfort. They could not imagine how Treasure or Mr Guthrie or I or anyone felt or thought because they themselves had long ago ceased to feel or think. Their minds were governed by second hand shibboleths – 'dear papa always said', and their feelings were reduced to the minimum of physical comfort or discomfort – 'Charles, shut that door properly. There is a draught.' For a long time, before I came to this understanding of them, I resented their attitude to Treasure, their miserly return for all the thought, care and effort she expended upon them and their comfort but, after I understood, the aunts dropped into their place in the private world as a composite fantastic entity, under the name that Treasure had always used for them: 'the ladies'.

Treasure's orbit in the world of actuality was very limited but the little section of the world she knew, she knew in depth. I learned that, when she entered the service of the aunts, she had broken her connection with the world of the pavements and backyards of Lochfoot where she had grown up and the death of her grandmother had broken her slight connection with the old Village. She had no friends and seldom went out, except for her weekly trips to the bank and shops and for occasional trips down-the-line to the 'Missionary Society' and to the public library to exchange the romantic novels in large print which the aunts read. It was one of the topsy-turvy features of the house that the aunts read novels which I had been brought up to regard as the reading matter of 'skivvies' while Treasure read, illicitly, the leather-bound classics from the house library which, I believe, she was the first ever to open. The library and its books were part of the furnishings of the house, to be cherished and carefully dusted like Lord Mammon and the ladies would have been very angry had they known that their servant was presuming to make use of the books for the purpose for which they had been created.

Gradually, in the way that other aspects of Laurelbank became clear to me, I came to understand that Treasure's passion for reading had driven the first wedge between her and the way of life in which she had been reared.

'I aye had to read in secret,' she said. 'My mother said that reading was just idleness and if the rest had known about it they would have called me a sapsie.'

By 'the rest' she meant her school-fellows and companions of the backyards. It seemed that the solitary reading had turned her into a solitary in other ways, so that she broke away from the troupe of children that roamed the streets and began to pursue on her own the illicit pastimes that she had formerly pursued as a member of a child gang.

'I stopped running with the rest,' she said. 'They did things I didn't like very much, like watching the drunks getting thrown out of the pub at night. I just stopped thinking that the drunks were funny, that's all.'

Her coming to Laurelbank had separated her physically from the world she had known and she at once, it seemed, determined to take over the stagnant hulk of a house and remould it to her desire.

'The worst thing about it,' she told me, 'was Mrs Tait and Annie. As I told you before, it was them or me for the high road. Apart from liking to be on my own, they were so dirty I couldn't abide them. Mrs Tait used to sell the dripping to the baker's man and she and Annie used to take to their beds after lunch, like the ladies. In those days, I used to go down to my granny's every Wednesday afternoon after I'd taken the tea in and one Wednesday the baker's man came back with the shilling for the dripping and asked me to give it to Mrs Tait. He had forgotten to bring it that morning. When I took the tea in, I gave the shilling to Miss Bessie. It's for Mrs Tait, please madam, from the baker's man for the dripping, I said and then I got changed and went down to my granny's.' Her left eye slowly closed and reopened. 'When I came back at nine o'clock, the ladies were very upset but Mrs Tait and Annie – Annie was her daughter and half-witted – were away.'

'And then *you* began to sell the dripping to the baker's man?'

'Aye, but I charge him one-and-six. He can well afford it, a bachelor like he is and putting half-a-crown in the kirk plate every Sunday. And I bet he's selling it over again to somebody else for two bob.'

From this day forward, Treasure had become the presiding genius of Laurelbank, establishing her dominion over the ladies by playing on their weaknesses, their love of good food, their love of comfort and the sloth that increased daily with every little household care and duty that Treasure took out of their hands. Gradually but inevitably, the young energetic hands with the keen intelligence behind them had caused the old lazy hands and the stagnant minds to relinquish the reins of the household but Treasure did not neglect the cumbrous machine or allow it to run to seed. She governed it carefully, kept it clean and polished and any tradesmen who tried to cheat it of a penny of its due received very short shrift from her. Treasure might 'look after herself' at the expense of the ladies but no other person could look after himself at the expense of the ladies, Laurelbank or Treasure.

In my early days in the house, Treasure had once or twice said apologetically that she could not 'get used' to my being connected to the aunts and I see that this non-connection of the aunts with anyone was the chief factor in drawing Treasure and myself together, causing us to establish our world within a world, to create some coherence of relationship in this place that was fundamentally hostile to both of us but the relationship developed as gradually and naturally as the turn of the seasons so that our private world came into being and surrounded us without our being aware that it was developing at all.

One afternoon in late September, during a few golden days of Indian summer, I had been reading in my room and went out to take a walk in the wilderness of the back garden. At one place near its centre, there was a weeping elm tree and under it a small stone statue of the god Pan. The leaves of the elm were yellow now, the branches drooping to form a tent about the little figure but the tent held a second occupant today. Treasure, sitting on a piece of old carpet spread on the grass, was knitting and reading as usual.

'Come in,' she said in a welcoming voice. The secluded place had the air of every place that Treasure liked, an air of belonging, of being completely her own, as the pantry and the attics of the house belonged to her and were her own.

'This is a lovely little place,' I said.

'I'll never forget the first time I found it. Gosh, it was great that day! It was my third day here and Mrs Tait spat in the frying-pan to see if the fat was hot enough to fry the chops and Annie wet her knickers all over the kitchen floor. Annie was simple-minded, a sort of idiot like I told you and she couldn't help it but I thought I can't put up with this and I'll have to do a bunk but where can I go and then I came running out here and there he was.' She waved her hand at the little statue of Pan. 'That's wee Sammy,' she said.

I looked at the little stone figure. It was only about two feet high, undoubtedly a statue of Pan, the god seated on a rock, the left leg bent upwards at the knee, the hoof resting in a crevice in the rock, the right hoof on the ground.

'I don't suppose that's his right name, if he's got a name,' Treasure was saying in an uncertain little voice, 'but that's what I call him.'

I went on looking at the figure. Treasure was never uncertain unless she felt deeply involved, unless she was emotionally concerned. This was a facet of her strange individuality that I had newly discovered.

'Why?' I ventured to ask, still looking at the archaic figure, part goat, part man, its bunch of grapes in one hand and its pipes in the other. One of the little horns above the forehead was broken.

'I had a friend called wee Sammy, long ago, when I was at the school,' Treasure said.

I had learned to listen to her words very carefully. This had begun when I first came to the house, because her dialect was strange to me but, later, I had to come to know that much could be learned about her by observing the words she chose and the tones in which she spoke them. This was the first time that I had heard her say 'I had a friend'. Her usual custom when speaking of people she had known was to say 'A girl I knew at the school' or 'a boy that lived in Tramway Buildings'. I also noted again, as I had noted many times in the past, the phrase: 'when I was at the school'. Treasure never said 'when I was young' or 'was wee' or 'was a wean' as she might have said, using the words of her dialect for 'little' or 'child'. Treasure, it seemed, had never been young, little or a child or had never felt herself to be so.

She rose from the carpet and went to stand beside the statue with her back against the tree trunk. 'Wee Sammy got run over when he was wee,' she said. 'He was a cripple. He had iron things on one of his legs and it was shorter than the other one. He used to stand against walls like this—' She took up a pose, her legs exactly like those of the statue but where the statue was an archaic god, Treasure was a crippled child. Her shoulders and arms drooped, her head hung forward, her small body slumped and she had a pathetic air of hopelessness, of being left behind by the world so that, compared with her, the little stone god seemed to be filled with pulsing life.

'Where is your friend Sammy now?' I asked.

She came to sit down on the carpet again. 'Dead. He got drowned. It was an accident, sort of—'

The uncertainty was there again. She frowned, tracing the faded pattern of the carpet with her forefinger. 'There was this – this old – this man that stole things from folk. Not honest stealing, though. He took things like jewellery from folk that couldn't pay him their rent. He stole a watch from a lady I knew but I found out where he kept some of the stuff he stole and one day I pinched the bloody lot out of his house and threw it all in the burn, all except the watch. I sent that back to the lady but I didn't know who the rest belonged to. But wee Sammy saw one of the brooches I had pinched in the burn and he tried to get it out. He fell in and got drowned.' She fell silent, her forefinger following the loops and whorls of the pattern for a long moment before she said: 'When it happened, I thought at first that it was my fault that wee Sammy was dead. If it hadn't been for the brooch I put in the burn – see? But it wasn't *all* my fault.'

'I don't see that it was your fault at all.'

'Oh, yes, it was a bit,' she said. 'I was in it all right but so were a lot of other folk. But since then I've been very canny about trying to do folk good turns, like I did when I tried to get the lady's watch back. You never know how they might turn out.'

'They must turn out better in the end than doing bad turns all the time like the man that stole the jewellery,' I said, although I was very uncertain of my ground, for Treasure's sad little story and the thought she had drawn from it had opened up moral territory that was new to me. Until then, I had thought of good actions and evil actions as being in two distinct unrelated categories, had never thought of the good turn that could turn out badly. 'After all,' I added, 'you did me a good turn the day you gave me Mr Guthrie's address and it seems to be turning out all right.'

She sat silent for a little time before she looked up at me and said quietly: 'It's funny how things get clearer when you speak to folk about them. I've never spoken to anybody about wee Sammy before – never had anybody to speak to, like. I think I see where I went wrong that day I pinched that jewellery, Mr Charles. I should just have taken the lady's watch and left the rest. But I took the rest and threw it into the burn just for pure spite. That was a bit of real badness that I did because I hated old – the man. And it was no use anyway. Old Beery-belly got it all out of the burn after wee Sammy was drowned and gave it all back to him.'

'The police?' I said. 'The police got the jewellery back but you were never caught for stealing it?'

She turned her head towards me. The blue eyes under the fair hair and the frilly white afternoon cap held the innocence of flowers. 'Me?' she asked. 'Why should old Beery-belly think that a stupid wee thing like me would pinch all that jewellery? No. They never found out how it got into the burn,' she ended.

From the manner in which she spoke the words 'a stupid wee thing like me', I felt that she was quoting a phrase that had frequently been applied to her, probably at the harsh school she had described to me, the grey stone school at the other end of the town. Next, I remembered that, on one or two occasions, Aunt Bessie, when talking about Treasure, had described her as 'simple-minded'. 'She is not like others of that class,' Aunt Bessie had said in justification of this. 'She never asks for extra time off to go to the picture house and she gives no trouble by having followers in the basement or anything.' Aunt Bessie had a simple mind which knew that all members of Treasure's class, if they gave no trouble in the way of extra time off or followers in the basement, were simple-minded.

I became suddenly aware that Treasure did not cheat people as to her nature. True to her dictum of: 'You mind your business and I'll mind mine', she merely stood passively by and allowed them, in the simplicity of their minds, to cheat themselves. And they cheated themselves about her because they did not interest themselves in her sufficiently to look upon her as a person. They judged her by preconception, as Aunt Bessie judged her, as a member of 'that class'. Treasure herself made the opposite approach to people. She studied them as individuals, in detail and in depth so that she came to know them, as she knew the aunts, better than they knew themselves. I looked down at her as she sat on the old piece of carpet. She had taken up her knitting again, the fine white wool moving rapidly between her fingers. There was about her a young innocence and at the same time an age-old wisdom, as if she were a little more than human, as if she had come down from that innocent yet instinctively-knowing time when men believed in gods like Pan. She looked up at me suddenly.

'It's all past long ago,' she said, startling me, as if she were aware of my thoughts of that long-past time, 'but anyway, that's why I call the statue wee Sammy. Do you know who he really is, Mr Charles, the statue, I mean?'

'I think it is meant to be the Greek god Pan.'

'Pan? You mean the one in that daft song o' yours: Come, follow, follow, follow the merry merry pipes o' Pan?'

At some of our musicales, I gave an imitation of an off-key soprano coyly singing this song, a performance which never failed to 'roll Treasure in the aisles', as my father would have put it. 'That's the one,' I agreed.

She gazed at the statue. 'In the name o' the Kingdom o' Heaven, when you sang that song it always reminded me o' Sandy the Tinker playin' the bagpipes an' us all dancing the hooligan! A Greek *god*, you said?'

I was not well versed in Greek mythology and knew better than to pretend, in the presence of Treasure, to a knowledge that I did not have. 'The Greeks had a lot of gods and Pan was one of them. I don't know much about them. There are a lot of stories about them, called myths.'

'Here, listen,' said Treasure, 'there's a book in the library called *The Myths o' Ancient Greece*. I looked up myth in the dictionary and it said it was a fictitious narrative about supernatural creatures an' by the time I'd looked all *that* up, I decided I didn't go much on myths. Would Pan be in it?'

'Perhaps.'

'I'm going in to get that book.'

When she came back with the large volume, we found that it contained two pages about Pan, and lying side by side and prone on the old carpet, we read about the god. The first paragraph described him as the god of shepherds and lonely places and went on to give his ancestry and position in the hierarchy but the second paragraph began: 'Pan was a great lover of the nymphs.' The book was the work of some Victorian Scottish divine and the exploits of Pan as a lover of the nymphs were recorded in decently veiled language but the veil was not proof against the penetration of Treasure. 'Aye,' she said as we came to the end of the paragraph and turned the page, 'he was a bit different from Sandy the Tinker, the wee rascal, but likely Sandy was a bit of a lad as well, in his young days.'

We now read of Pan's love for the nymph Syrinx who was turned into a reed as she fled from him and how Pan cut the reed into different lengths and made his Pan pipes from it, at which point the divine slipped thankfully from Ancient Greece to Victorian Scotland with the pretty comment: 'And even today, when the wind blows, the reeds by the water's edge may be heard whispering Pan's love for Syrinx.'

'Maybe aye an' maybe hooch aye,' came the comment of Treasure.

Then came the conclusion of the section: 'Plutarch relates that in the reign of Tiberius a mysterious voice was heard by some travellers in the Ionian Sea proclaiming: Great Pan is dead.'

Treasure raised her eyes from the book to look first at me and then at the statue. 'Who was Tiberius?' she asked.

'A Roman emperor.' A shaft of light seemed to strike a corner of my mind as I recalled the reading I had done for my examination in Latin. 'He was the emperor who was in power when Christ was crucified. It was after the Crucifixion that Christianity took a real hold on the world. I suppose Pan and the old gods died when Christianity was accepted and established.'

Treasure looked up at the statue again. 'God of Shepherds

and of wild and lonely places,' she quoted. 'I like shepherds and lonely places. I would rather have Pan than what Christianity has turned into nowadays.'

'What is that?' I asked. 'What has it turned into?'

'Something like the Iron Man in the hall, mostly,' she told me. 'Lord Mammon, as you call him.'

CHAPTER EIGHT

It is Christmas Day in the Workhouse,
And the cold bare walls are bright
With garlands of green and holly,
And the place is a pleasant sight;
For with clean-washed hands and faces,
In a long and hungry line
The paupers sit at the tables
For this is the hour they dine.
'In the Workhouse: Christmas Day,' by George R. Sims.

WHEN the university term opened, I began to travel by a train that left Lochfoot a little later than the one I had used when I was going to Doctor Gill, which meant that the pattern of passengers was different. There were no railway or factory workers on this train, only a few women shoppers and sometimes the Pauper while the only other student besides myself was a girl who disappeared each morning through the doorway of a secretarial college near the station in Glasgow.

I found the university very large and overpowering. It was probably my own diffidence and uncertainty that lay at the root of the matter but it seemed to me that everyone except myself knew his way by instinct around this complex of buildings, that everybody except myself had his place in some noisy group of young men. In my own mind my difference from my carefree fellows became more and more marked until I almost believed that I must be wearing a mark on my forehead to show that, unlike them, I was not a schoolboy undertaking a new phase of study but a man who had buried his father and had come to a new country to seek his fortune. In relation to the others, I felt sometimes like a child who had wandered into an adult world whose laws I did not know and at other times I felt like an old man, caught in a web of youth in which I had no place.

As the winter term ran its course through the lecture rooms and laboratories, I came to know a number of men of my own age or a little younger by name but that was all; but I made a friend in an unexpected place, not in the lecture rooms or the laboratories but at the tram terminus behind the main building of the university. Our friendship began one day when I was running after a departing tramcar. He was running ahead of me, sprang on to the back platform where, holding the rail, he held out his other hand and hauled me on board. He was the first of my fellows to hold out a hand to me either literally or metaphorically and this induced in me a gratitude so deep that I began to stalk him round the complex of buildings so that I might discover his timetable and meet him ostensibly by accident. I was delighted to discover that he was, like myself, studying medicine but his first year was already behind him while I was only at the start of mine. He was a quiet sort of man with none of the rugby football enthusiasms or clumsy banter so common in the Union and around the laboratories. For much of our time together, we did not talk at all and when we did we talked in the main about our work and even then I was the more voluble of the two. His name was Adair and his home was in the heart of the city. We would part at the tramway-stop and he would walk up a dingy side street while I went downhill the short distance to the station and my train. When we were together, we formed a small entity, separate from the rest of the world, as if we had no connection with the other students who shared our lectures, as if we had no homes or relations. When it rained, we travelled by tram and sometimes we would have a cup of coffee in a little teashop near the station until it was time for my train but when it was fine we would walk to the station and often we would loiter in the park on the hillside below the university and I would catch a later train. Adair had a liking for the park. He did not say so but his liking for it was something that could be felt, almost seen. He seemed to grow taller, to move differently, to become more confident when he was in the park.

One bright frosty afternoon in early December, we were sitting side by side on a park bench, our overcoat collars turned up round our ears, our black and gold university scarves wound round our necks when a ridiculous thing happened. A fat old lady in a fur coat, with a little Pomeranian dog on a red lead, came toddling along the path, stopped in front of us and said: 'And you two boys are twins and both at the university! How very nice!'

We shambled to our feet, our embarrassment acute and painful, Adair feeling I think, as I felt, that his deepest privacy had been invaded. From the corner of my eye, I could see red blood travelling up under the skin of his jaw and on to his cheek and my own face felt as if it were on fire, while my tongue clove, speechless, to the roof of my mouth.

'What a beautiful day,' the old lady maundered on. 'Flossie and I are having a lovely walkies. We always come to the park for walkies on nice days, don't we Flossie? Well, it has been so nice to talk to you two dear boys. Good day,' she ended and toddled off, muttering: 'Twins. How nice!'

Adair and I sank back on to the bench and as the old lady disappeared round some bushes, Adair gave a sort of hiccup and in the next second we were rolling about in an agony of laughter, clinging to one another and the wood of the bench as we tried to control ourselves. At last, with my tongue and throat parched and cold from the frosty air, my jawbones aching from laughter, I managed to say: 'I hadn't realised that you looked like me!'

'Neither had I – you like me, I mean.'

We stared solemnly at one another, really observing one another for the first time and discovered that the old lady was right. We resembled one another very closely for two men completely unrelated. We were of similar height and build, with blue eyes and fair curling hair. Adair's hair was darker than mine, what my father would have called a more manly colour but otherwise there was more similarity between us than difference. I was about to begin laughing again at the absurdity of it when Adair suddenly burst forth: 'I wish to God we *were* alike!'

'What do you mean?'

'Inside, I mean, as well as out.' He frowned at the black cranes of the shipyards by the Clyde which showed above the roofs of the intervening buildings like the gaunt black skeletons of long-legged wading birds, herons or – or *cranes*, I thought. 'You are really keen on this medical stuff, aren't you?' Adair asked.

'Yes. I am. Why? Aren't you?'

'I hate it,' he said, shrinking inside his coat and shivering. 'I hate it all – the labs, the cut-up dogfish, the – I hate the whole bloody thing!'

'Then why are you doing it?'

He frowned at the ground between his feet now. 'I sort of got into it by accident,' he muttered. 'I didn't think. It just sort of happened.' He raised his head to look at me. 'I suppose you think I am off my rocker?' He rose from the bench. 'We'd better get on the road down town,' he said.

'If you want to talk— Well, why don't we hang on a bit and I'll catch the five-forty-five?'

He sat down again. 'Listen,' he asked abruptly, 'who are your people?'

'People?'

'Father, mother, sisters, brothers?' He was irritable at my slowness of wit.

'Dead,' I said, 'my father and mother, I mean. I haven't any sisters or brothers, only the aunts.'

'Aunts?'

'Yes. I live with my two aunts.'

'Oh.' He was silent, as if he were trying to visualise my life with my aunts and I had a sudden impulse to laugh for, on this seat beside Adair in the wintry park, even I could barely visualise the aunts at Laurelbank, although Treasure's left eye seemed to wink at me over a vast misty distance. Adair sighed and moved his shoulders under his coat as if trying to shrug off something too difficult and remote.

'What about *your* people?' I asked now because his people seemed to be connected with his difficulty.

'Have you ever felt you were the odd man out?' he asked me instead of replying to my question and I was startled into silence because the truthful reply would have been: 'I have *always* felt I was the odd man out' and yet it was a reply that I found impossible to make.

'Odd man out?' I repeated while I thought that this must have been the bond that had drawn Adair and me together.

'I don't suppose you would understand,' he said surlily, 'not knowing what it's like to be surrounded by family.'

'Is yours a big family then?' I asked awkwardly.

'A sister and four brothers. And my father and mother, of course. The thing is they are all doctors or want to be doctors.'

'Your father is a doctor?'

'No.' He sounded angry at my stupidity, as if he felt that I ought to know without being told about his family situation so familiar to him. 'My father's a shepherd,' he snapped at me, as if cutting off sharply the final words 'you bloody fool'.

'A shepherd?' I repeated, also growing angry. Who was Adair to take me for a fool? 'But your home is in the middle of Glasgow!'

'What are you talking about? My home is in Perthshire. That hole in Dunn Square is only our digs.'

'Digs?'

'Digs are very uncommon,' he said with heavy sarcasm. 'Only about half the students up here live in digs.'

'Listen, Adair,' I said, trying to be conciliatory, 'I am

sorry. I simply took it that your home was in Dunn Square. It was natural enough.'

'I suppose it was.' He looked shame-faced. 'But it's not my home. It's digs and it's full of medical books and Isabel who is a doctor at the Western down there – ' he jerked his head at the hospital at the corner of the park ' – and my brother David who is in his fourth year in medicine up here and my brother Ian who is in his first year in medicine up here and me in my second year in medicine up here and back at home at school is my brother Peter who can't wait to get into medicine up here.'

'Why—' I began but Adair, the non-talker, having begun to talk, was like a runaway horse.

'It all started with Isabel. She is the oldest of us and she was brilliant at school and came into medicine, then David followed her and somehow it became a family habit. It got to be taken for granted that we would all do medicine. It was an idea that we all grew up with. I never thought of being anything other than a doctor but I never really thought about being a doctor either. It wasn't until after I had passed my first-year exams that I found out that I hated medicine. That sounds daft but it's true. I suddenly found out that I was committed to spending my whole life looking after sick people and that I hated it.' He rose to his feet suddenly. 'There's no point sitting here blethering,' he said and strode away down the path, his hands in his coat pockets, his shoulders hunched.

I followed him and we did not speak again until we were out on the pavement where the street lights glimmered in the misty greyness of the falling dark. I drew abreast of him as he walked along and we had gone some way before he muttered. 'I'll just have to go on with it. Maybe I'll get used to it – even get to like it in time.' I felt that he was retreading familiar mental ground that he had trodden often before and I halted under a street lamp and stood in front of him.

'Look here, Adair,' I said, 'you will never be a doctor if you don't like it. And if you don't like it now you will never get to like it. You don't need me to tell you that. Oh, yes, you will pass the exams and qualify but what then?'

'Do you think I haven't thought about that?' he asked, growing angry again.

'Nobody can force you to study medicine!' I protested.

His anger died away. 'No – o?' he asked quietly and suddenly he seemed to be very old and far away from me and my young certainty. As we began to walk again, he said: 'You and I come of different kinds of folk.' His sudden use of the Scottish idiom marked more distinctly the distance between us. 'My mother and father saved hard all their lives – they are still saving – to send the five of us to university. It all started with Isabel, as I said and she is helping now too, giving up part of her salary to feed the rest of us. She will be a great doctor some day. She is as keen as mustard and so are all the others but I just didn't think – —' His voice trailed away, to be lost in the noise of the traffic.

'But now that you have thought about it, surely you can change your mind?'

'It's not so easy. I would like to do what my people want and then – well, there's the money.'

'The money?'

He became irritable again. 'I've used up a year's time and a year's fees and everything,' he snapped at me impatiently and then, as if he regretted his irritability, he added: 'It's hard for you to see it like I do. We come of different folk, as I said. But my mother and father have worked so hard and saved so hard that it can't be right for me to waste their money and disappoint them.'

We went on walking in silence now for, try as I might, I could not imagine Adair's position and feelings as the son of parents who were ambitious for him, who had made sacrifices for him. We parted at the street corner above the station as usual, he going uphill, I going down and as the train rattled me along towards Lochfoot, I thought that perhaps it was easier to be alone as I was, rather than one of a closely knit family like Adair. Looking out into the smoky dark, I heard his voice again: 'And there's the money. I have used up a year's fees and a year's time and everything.' The money lay at the root of the matter for 'a year's time and everything' meant the money spent on food, tram fares, clothing, a year of time lost to money-earning if Adair left the faculty of medicine and changed course.

Until now, I had not thought of money in connection with Adair, for he did not belong to the group of students who were obviously poor. This group had no money to buy lunch but ate a few sandwiches, carried in their pockets, in some quiet corner between classes. The Scottish drive towards academic education in the face of grinding poverty was typified indeed by the university holiday in November, which was known as 'Meal Monday'. This was a survival, I had been told, from the times when young men from all over Scotland set out on a Friday evening to walk from the university to their homes to bring back the oatmeal which would be their staple food for the rest of the winter term. Brought up, as I had been, among the shabby genteel at a cheap boarding-school to think of university in terms of Oxford and Cambridge and the degrees of fashion between their various colleges, the Scottish attitude was very strange to me but it had a harsh pleasing reality. It also brought me the comfort that there were other eccentrics like myself who were prepared to go to some lengths to obtain the education that they wanted and that I had not been called upon to go to lengths as stringent as some.

When I reached Lochfoot, I walked slowly uphill by the lochside, past the end of the Crescent road and on to the lane that would lead me to the back drive and back door to the house. Before I turned into the lane, I went close to the fence on the other side of the road and looked down at the black water of the loch beyond the rocks. Further down the hill towards the station, the rocks on the lochside gave way to swampland where tall reeds grew and although the air was frosty and motionless, the reeds still made a susurration, like a sobbing over past sadness. I remembered reading with Treasure under the elm tree about the god Pan and like a cry of mourning I heard again the words: 'Great Pan is dead'. Depressed, I turned away from the black water and hurried towards the house.

Over supper in the pantry, Treasure suddenly said: 'What's up, Mr Charles? You are so down in the mouth that your chin is like to trip you.'

'I'm all right,' I said and tried to think of some small incident in my day that might amuse her. I remembered the old lady in the park. 'A funny thing happened in the park today, Treasure,' I said. 'I was sitting with a second-year man I know, a chap called Adair and—' I told her about the old lady and before I realised what I was about, I was also telling her about Adair and his difficulty.

Treasure, as always, listened with interest and sympathy, making few comments until I came to the end of my tale. 'He is a nice chap,' I ended, 'and I feel sorry for him. It must be rotten to have a family like that.'

'Like what?' Treasure asked suddenly and angrily. 'Colin Adair must have gone daft!'

'*Colin* Adair?'

'That's his name. If he's not David or Ian or Peter, he's Colin.'

'How do you know?'

'I've known the Adairs since I first went to the school.'

'But his home is in Perthshire. I *told* you!'

'It's in Perthshire now,' she said, 'but it used to be down in the Village, next-door to my granny. Mr Adair was in the service o' the Duke, like his father an' gran'father before him and when the Duke sold the Castle and went to Perthshire, the Adairs went as well.' She was as impatient as Adair had been with me in the park, as if these were all facts of which I should be aware. 'Colin Adair must be off his bloody head!' she said.

'Why do you say that?'

'If he thinks Mr an' Mrs Adair would want him to be a doctor when he doesn't want to be one, he must be daft and just you tell him that next time you see him.' She was indignant, taking items from the table and slamming them down by the sink and into cupboards as she spoke.

'Treasure,' I said, 'calm down. I can't tell Adair that he is daft and wrong about his parents, if he *is* wrong, that is.'

'He is *so* wrong!' Far from growing calm, she seemed to swell to twice her size as she stood over me. 'Mr Adair is *great*, I tell ye, just great and he wouldn't want *any*body – much less his own son – to be doing a job they didn't like.'

'But how can you be so sure about Mr Adair? How do you know—'

'Ach, away an' don't gimme the boke!' she interrupted me. 'How can you be so sure? How do you know?' she mimicked me and then: 'How do I know if it's winter or summer or night or day? I know *folk* an' I know the Adairs.'

This seemed to be unanswerable. When I thought about it, there was no doubt that Treasure 'knew folk'. She knew them deeply and acutely, as she knew the aunts, so that she knew how they thought and how they would re-act. For the first time, it came to me that, from the first time we met, she had had an uncanny intimate knowledge of myself and that through this she had smoothed my way into this new strange way of life in this eccentric household.

Her certainty of her knowledge of Adair's parents was very convincing and although she led me to believe, when I was with her, that Adair was mistaken about his own father and mother, the belief did not stand firm in the face of Adair's hopelessness. I found myself in a silly quandary. Days passed without my telling Adair that I lived in Lochfoot, in Lochview Crescent or that my aunts' maidservant was a former schoolfellow of his. I was afraid that this would put distance between Adair and me as it had done between me and the other students on the train when I was travelling to Doctor Gill's. As it was, Adair could become edgy very easily, as he had done when I had carelessly mentioned being tutored, because my English boarding-school had failed to bring me to university standard.

At the end of about a week, over supper in the pantry, Treasure enquired: 'Have you knocked any sense into that Colin Adair yet or is he still wasting his time?'

I was now tired of Treasure's tirades in the evenings after Adair's sighs of despondency in the park and said: 'Since you are so sure about everything, you ought to knock some sense into him yourself.'

'I help my Jimmie Johnson,' she said, 'an' so I will. If I come down the line on the four o'clock on Wednesday, will you bring him to meet me?'

'But, Treasure, are you sure that—'

'If you ask me again if I'm sure, I'll clout you one. There's a wee tearoom – the Sutherland, they call it – just round the corner from the station. D'ye know it?'

'Yes.'

'Get him there by quarter-to-five. I've got to catch the five-thirty to attend to the ladies' dinner.'

'But—'

'Ach, give it a bye,' she told me impatiently and then added: 'There's one thing though. Don't you go calling me Treasure in front of him. If he's gone as daft as you make out, he might think things that aren't good for him. I am the ladies' servant and on Wednesday you'll meet me accidental near the station an' take me in for a cup o' tea like the decent gentleman ye are.'

'But—'

'Give it a bye, d'ye hear me?'

'Treasure,' I capitulated, 'I agree to everything. I'll get him to the Sutherland and do everything you say but—'

'But what then?'

'Why are you so interested in Adair? Why are you going to all this trouble?'

'I'm not interested, as ye call it, in Colin Adair. Not for himself, like.' She frowned. 'It's hard to explain but his mother an' father – well, they did me a good turn once an' I cannae abide Colin being so – so damn' *wrong* about them.'

With a little judicious lying on my part, the meeting was arranged and in the little teashop I introduced Adair to Miss Robertson. She was wearing a deep blue felt hat, I remember and I discovered once more how small she was as she looked up from under the hat-brim at Adair who immediately said: 'Wee Jeanie Robertson! Jeanie, you haven't grown an inch. You are still the same wee smout you always were. Are you still as cheeky?'

'Aye, when it comes up my back,' she told him calmly.

The first words over, Adair began to look uncertainly from one of us to the other, as if he could not understand how we had come together and Treasure, with her knowledge of 'folk', read his mind and said: 'I'm the maid to Mr Charles's aunties in Lochview Crescent. I met him on the way to the train an' he asked me in for a cup o' tea. This is my afternoon off. I've been up for a look at the shops.' She went on to enquire about Adair's parents, his sisters and brothers, recalled a few exploits of their school days and then: 'So you are learnin' the doctorin' like Mr Charles?' Her dialect was very pronounced. She was very much the cheeky little guttersnipe, emphasising the distance between herself and us two university men. 'I never thought you would take to the doctorin'. I always thought you would be a shepherd like your father or maybe a farmer. My granny used to say you made a better job o' her garden than any o' the other Village laddies. She used to say you had green thumbs.' She then moved away into more talk of their schooldays but subtly returned to her insidious attack. 'It's funny the whole five o' you Adairs takin' to the doctorin'. In a way, your mother an' father must be kinda disappointed. Your folk have been Castle folk for so long, aye workin' on the land, it must be kinda hard for your father an' mother to see ye all takin' to a new kinda job. I mind once I had a notion to work in the shirt factory up-the-line an' my granny was terrible against it. She said I should go into service an' as it turned out, she was right. Of course, you Adairs aye bein' top-o'-the-class folk at the school, it was natural you should go to the university. It's a shame they don't make farmers at universities, instead o' only doctors an' ministers an' that.'

'But they *do* make farmers at universities,' I said when she paused and immediately felt that the words had been put into my mouth, as if I were a ventriloquist's dummy, speaking a part. Treasure's eyes, deeply blue under the blue hat, looked at me, wide and innocent, across the table-top. 'Ach, don't try to cod me, Mr Charles,' she said.

'They *do*,' Adair assured her gravely. 'You can take a B.Sc. in agriculture – ' he then looked at me and repeated slowly and wonderingly ' – a B.Sc. in agriculture.'

'What's a B.Sc.?' the innocent one enquired and Adair explained that it was a scientific degree.

'Just fancy!' she said. 'They'll have degrees for domestic servants next. Imagine me wi' letters after my name!'

She prattled on as I had never heard her prattle before until it was time for our train but when we parted from Adair, he seemed to be lost in a dream, hardly aware of our going.

When we were in the train, I looked sternly at Treasure and said: 'You are more than a good liar. You are a real actress.'

'Aye,' she agreed calmly, 'it's what ye might call a real gift. I wonder if it'll work though?'

'It seemed to be working before we left him. How did you hit on the farming notion?'

She looked out of the window. 'Since you told me about him, I've been thinking about him a lot, going back over all the wee things I could mind about him. He was the quietest o' all the Adairs. Och, he could fight like the rest o' them when it was needed but he never fought just for a fight like Isabel an' David. Isabel was a heller at the school. Colin was more like his father than the rest. He is still like him an' his father was a shepherd an' a farming man. I don't think he could ever have been anything else.' She looked down at her hands, her face hidden by her hat. 'He was a good shepherd,' she said, 'just a good shepherd.' She turned her head to look out of the window again, her face still hidden from me. 'If Colin turns out half as well, he'll be better than most,' she ended.

When I met Adair the next day, I felt a little guilty, felt that I had played a trick on him and he was inclined to be bristly and very different from his former despondent self.

'Funny,' he said in aggressive tones, 'that you never mentioned that you lived at Lochfoot.'

'You never mentioned that you once lived there either,' I countered, 'and what does it matter anyway?'

Some of his aggression died away but an awkwardness remained as he said: 'I thought I had forgotten Lochfoot but it all came back last night. When we were at the school, Lochview Crescent where you live was another world.' He made an effort. 'Your people must be rich.'

'My people are dead, as I told you,' I said. 'There are only my aunts.'

'I meant your aunts.'

'My aunts are just two spinsters living very economically in a house they inherited that is far too big for them and paying for my education.'

Had Treasure imparted to me something of her 'real gift' for the distortion of the truth or was I generating it on my own? I did not care. Adair was looking relieved and less aggressive still.

'Funny the ideas you get when you are young and how they stick with you,' he said. 'At school, we all believed that all the people in the Crescent were millionaires. Our place was down in the old Village. Do you know it?'

'I walk down that way sometimes. It is the best part of the town.'

'It is the oldest part. But I am sure Lochfoot is different now. It was changing before we left, even.'

Once more on his former footing with me, as if he had put Village and Crescent behind him, he chatted on more freely than he had ever done in the past but he did not mention the renewal of his acquaintance with wee Jeanie Robertson. I had gathered from the prattle in the teashop that, in former days, he had been Treasure's champion and defender in the rough and tumble of the school playground and I thought it probable that he wished this to be forgotten, especially by me, seeing me as he did as the 'young gentleman of the house' in which Treasure was a servant. I was glad that he did not talk about her because I was afraid of betraying an intimacy with her that he would misconstrue, apart from which I did not wish to discuss her with anyone. As we came near to the station and to the corner where we would part, he said very casually: 'If I make up my mind to give up medicine, I have been thinking I needn't waste the year I've done. I never thought of it till last night but if I went for the B.Sc. Agri., say, the subjects I've taken already would count.'

'That's true,' I said. 'You would go in for the B.Sc. with three of your subjects already under your belt. Are you thinking seriously of it?'

'Thought I'd put it to my people when I go home at Christmas,' he said in an offhand way, like a man who had a variety of choice before him, a very different man from the trapped rather desperate creature who had made the outburst in the park after the old lady had mistaken us for twins.

With the coming of the Christmas vacation, I and my life retreated within the boundaries of Laurelbank like a tortoise retreating into its carapace. I reported to Treasure that Adair intended to discuss his transfer to the science faculty with his parents during the holidays and then I forgot about him. Without him, the university had seemed very large, over-powering and friendless but in the private world of Laurelbank, both Adair and the university slipped away into the background.

The weather had turned grey, drizzly and dreary but the pantry was warm and cheerful and the drawing-room gay with song each early morning and each afternoon. There was no heating in the big over-furnished room but Treasure and I were kept warm by our own gaiety and the energy we brought to our performances. She never tired of my rendering of 'The Green Eye of the Yellow God' and when, on Christmas Eve, I came to the end of it, I was suddenly struck by the difference between this Christmas and the last. My mind went back to my father in the red plush chair, anticipating the celebratory 'little bird and little bottle' and then further back to another Christmas I had spent at home, at the Fulham house when, as soon as lunch was over, I was told to go to my room and play 'because Mumsie and Daddy want to have a little rest'. They were entwined on the red plush sofa before I was out of the room, I remembered.

'What are you thinking about?' Treasure enquired. 'You look like the Lost Chord.'

'I was thinking that my mother must have played this piano long ago,' I lied. 'If anything, she played worse than I do. Will you do "A Lost Chord" for me?'

'All right. And stop going on about your playing. It's great. You never think enough of yourself or what you can do. It's funny when you think about things. My mother worked here at Laurelbank once, away back. She knew *your* mother likely. Sometimes when I'm dusting, I think: my mother must have dusted this thing once. It's funny both of our mothers being here long ago and us being here now. Right. "A Lost Chord". A song with actions by Jeaneta Roberta, Carlo Simpsona presiding at the pianoforte,' and took on a soulful expression while I began to play.

As Treasure regarded 'The Green Eye of the Yellow God' as my masterpiece, I regarded 'A Lost Chord' as hers. As she sang, she looked, physically, for the chord under rugs and behind cushions, producing first a parody of the aunts hiding burglar money and then a parody of their failing to find it because they had forgotten where they had hidden it. On the final couplet –

It may be that only in Heaven
I shall hear that grand Amen

– she was a miniature of Aunt Bessie, staring searchingly at the ceiling, while she wondered where she had put the money for which the coalman was waiting at the back door.

In the course of one of our many conversations, Treasure had told me that she had never received a Christmas present in her life until she came to Laurelbank, when the aunts had presented her with a set of morning and afternoon dresses, aprons and caps.

'But that wasn't a present!' I protested. 'They would have to have given you your uniform anyway.'

'It felt like a present to *me*,' she said. 'Up till then, I had been wearing the stuff that the parlourmaid before me had had. She must have been a six-footer and I looked a proper little Orphant Annie with my skirts trailing around my feet.'

Since that time, the aunts had given her replacements to her uniform each year and I determined that, this Christmas, she was to have a genuine present, to which end I had bought all Jane Austen's novels, bound in red leather with gilt lettering and also a large box of chocolates tied with blue ribbon.

When I came down to the pantry on Christmas morning, I gave her the packages and was rewarded by a tremulous joy and gratitude such as I had never seen. She sat at the table, her small hands caressing the books, fingering the blue bow on the chocolate box, unable to speak and at last I had to turn away, leave the room to escape the intensity of feeling that vibrated about her. When I came up from the basement with my first two buckets of coal, she had disappeared but her books and sweets had been placed carefully at the end of the dresser, the papers in which they had been wrapped folded beside them, along with the string in neat bundles. This care for even the wrappings was a further mute appreciation of what I had given her.

It was then that I noticed the little oblong package on the otherwise bare table-top. It was wrapped in heavy dark green paper, sealed at the ends with red wax, an expensive-looking little object with 'Mr Charles' written in blue ink on the green paper. With care, I opened it, uncovering a slim black leather case, inside which was a slimmer silver propelling pencil. On the barrel of this, beside the hallmark, on a little panel that was not engine-turned like the rest of the pencil, were the initials 'CS/TR'. It was by far the most tasteful thing I had ever owned, ever held in my hand even and I laid it back in its blue velvet groove and admired it for a long time before I went to the morning-room to find her. She was kneeling on her square of grey linen on the hearthrug, her hands encased in her too-big fireplace-cleaning gloves.

'Thank you, Treasure,' I said. 'You shouldn't have but it is beautiful, really beautiful.'

She looked up at me. 'You like it, Mr Charles?' She closed her left eye. 'Folk will think more of your cough mixture if you write it with a good pencil, I thought.'

'Treasure, it must have been very expensive and you shouldn't—'

'I love buying pencils and books. Pens too and paper for

writing on. Listen, let's get this fire going and get across the hall and have a bit of a musicale.' She sprang to her feet, stretched out her arms with the big black gloves on the ends and carolled: 'It is Christmas Day in the Workhouse—'

To the aunts, Christmas Day was as any other day and they made no gesture towards it except in instructing Treasure to buy herself some new items of uniform at their expense. Christmas was to them, it seemed, a reminder date for this small chore that life imposed on them and that was all.

Their year, I was discovering, had its own strange calendar. The monthly ceremonial of hiding the burglar money was the only festival which they seemed to enjoy, for all the other different days that marked their year were invasions from the outside world which they both feared and hated. During the last week of every third month, Mr Guthrie paid them an afternoon visit and Treasure made a special cake for tea and during the last week of every fourth month, the piano-tuner came, had tea in the pantry and there was no special cake. These were the only visitors and towards the days of their arrival, of which warning had been given by letter, tension seemed to mount in the house until the air vibrated. This tautness in the atmosphere was at its most marked in the hall where Lord Mammon seemed to grow taller and to swell with resentment, while the filtered coloured light became more purple than usual and the big clock ticked away more loudly the watchful minutes.

Treasure and I had often talked of that first day when I had arrived at the front door and she had shown me into the morning-room and she had often described to me the aftermath. She had had strict instructions not to admit anyone to the house other than Mr Guthrie and the piano-tuner but it was only now, after nearly a year in the house, that I began to appreciate what an explosion in the lives of the aunts my sudden appearance in the morning-room must have been.

During an interval in our musicale that Christmas afternoon, we talked again of that first day and Treasure said: 'I had to make up my mind in a hurry that afternoon. If I'd told the ladies you were there, you wouldn't have got into the morning-room at all. If I had told *you* about the ladies, you wouldn't have believed me and you'd have thought I was up to something funny. And then I'd been hoping for you for so long that I couldn't *not* let you in although I knew it would be a proper Battle o' the Boyne.' She paused. 'Not that I'd been hoping for *you* exactly,' she amended, 'but I'd been hoping for proof that my granny was right, like I told you before.' She now gave her gay mischievous laugh. 'When I saw you standing there, saying you were Charles Simpson – that was old Snake-eyes' name, for gyad's sake – you could have knocked me down with a feather. I think now that all the time I was hoping, I was hoping I would open the door to Miss Cathie – your mother – and she would be standing there all dressed up like Doris.'

'Who was Doris?' I asked.

'We-ell,' Treasure hesitated momentarily, 'we might as well call a spade a spade. She was a whore that came here to Lochfoot at the time o' the war but she was great. She was one o' the kindest folk I have ever known.' Her eyes grew large as they always did when she looked back into her memory. 'I didn't know her for very long. When the war stopped, she went away.' She was momentarily sad but became gay and mischievous again as she said: 'Doris used to wear pink frilly blouses and white frilly petticoats and flowery hats and feather boas and a fur coat in the winter with a big hairy skunk collar. I think that I hoped that Miss Cathie would come in the summertime, in a flowery hat and a frilly blouse and I would show her into the morning-room and she would say: In the name o' the Kingdom o' Heaven, Bessie, what the hell are ye doin' in that auld black shawl? That's what Doris would have said.'

'But my mother wouldn't have said that,' I told her. 'She was very genteel. Maybe it's as well she didn't come.'

'Maybe. Things hardly ever turn out as ye hope or expect they will, but I'm not complaining. Genteel. I think my mother was genteel too or she tried to be. When I was at the school, I didn't know the word genteel. I said un-vulgar instead because my mother was always talking about other folk being vulgar.'

'My mother talked a lot about vulgarity too.'

'I think I like your father better even if he was conceited and everything like you said. Come on. Do "The Green Eye o' the Yellow God" for me, Mr Charles.'

I now learned that my aunts were not so unusual in that they did not celebrate Christmas and that the main time of celebration in Scotland was the New Year, a celebration that took the form of an orgy of drunkenness, a primitive bacchanalia in honour of the new-born year, but it was a far cry from the Dionysian feasts of archaic vine-wreathed Athens, as described in our copy of the *Myths of Ancient Greece*, to the drunks lying on the greasy pavements of Lochfoot under the grey drizzling rain. The aunts, of course, did not indulge in an orgy of drunkenness, for their only beverage was a concoction called 'Dr Abernethy's Tonic Wine' which they drank 'to keep up their strength'. It was delivered by the case to the back door every fortnight and it was kept in a cupboard in the morning-room in case, presumably, it might tempt Treasure or myself into intemperance.

During the week between Christmas and the New Year, however, other things besides tonic wine began to arrive at the back door, large parcels of all shapes which I helped Treasure to carry upstairs and place on the large table that stood between the doors of the aunts' bedrooms.

'The Discounts,' said Treasure, when the first of these packages arrived. 'There will be about a dozen of them before we're done. They're sort of presents from the grocer and the butcher and the tonic wine shop in Glasgow and all the folk we deal with – hams and tangerines and all the like o' that. It aye makes me think o' that bit in the Bible about to him who hath shall be given.'

'What happens to all this stuff?' I asked when I had carried up a large heavy package that looked like a side of bacon and had placed it like one more offering on the mahogany altar. 'And why do we carry it all up here anyway?'

'This was how it was done in dear papa's time,' Treasure explained in the voice of Aunt Bessie and added in her own voice. 'The ladies will open all the parcels on New Year's Day after tea and say that the ham from the butcher gets smaller every year.'

'And then?'

'We'll all have baked ham one day – ' her left eye fell shut ' – and I'm not saying that the wee Murphys down in Railway Terrace won't get a New Year's dinner after all, although maybe a day or two late.'

The ritual of the discounts took place exactly as Treasure had predicted. On New Year's afternoon, by pre-arrangement, Treasure brought my tea up to my room while the aunts had theirs in the morning-room as always. As soon as they had finished, I heard the bell ring for Treasure to take away the tray and then their footsteps on the stairs. With my ear to the crack of my door, I listened to their appraisal of the various tributes and when Treasure tapped on the panel, I darted back to the table in the middle of the room.

'May I take your tray away, Mr Charles?'

'Yes, thank you,' I replied formally to the formal question.

Treasure bent over the table to pick up the tray.

'Jessie,' said the voice of Aunt Bessie from the landing, 'this ham from the butcher gets smaller every year.'

Treasure's left eyelid dropped down, I clapped my hand over my mouth and she went out with the tray, shutting the door behind her.

The discounts was the final ceremonial of the aunts' year from my point of view although, from theirs, it was probably the first ceremonial of the New Year, but I counted the year from February when I had first arrived at Laurelbank. During January, the aunts hibernated even more energetically than before, to use a contradiction in terms, as if to recuperate from the effort of opening the votive offerings and soon Treasure and I were celebrating the anniversary of my arrival with a special musicale, 'giving' each other all the Gems from the Gyarland of which we never grew tired.

CHAPTER NINE

Love, sweet love is the poet's theme;
Love, sweet love is the poet's dream.
What is the love of which they sing?
Only a phantom unreal thing.
'Love, Sweet Love,' by Felix McGlennon.

WHEN the spring term opened at the university, I did not see anything of Adair for the first week and I began to think that the cleavage between Lochview Crescent and the rest of the world had, after all, come into operation, that Adair had decided that I was 'not his sort', that once more I was on my own but on a cold wet January evening, I found him at the ticket barrier when I arrived at my Glasgow Station.

'Where have you been?' I asked, trying for some unknown reason to conceal my delight. 'I thought you must be ill or something.'

'Far from it. Never felt better in my life but I have transferred to the B.Sc. course, different time-table altogether. One of my classes is down at the Tech. even. Listen, do you have to catch this train?'

'No. Why?'

'Come round to the Sutherland. My brothers are round there. I'd like you to meet them.' He had a brave new ebullience and a different much warmer attitude to myself.

In a corner of the little tea-shop, I began to understand that he was giving me all the credit for showing him the way out of his difficulty and that to introduce me to his brothers, to admit me into his family was the best thanks he could offer. I recognised Ian, the younger brother, as a leading member of one of the most boisterous groups in the laboratories for he was in his first year, like myself, but I was completely overawed by David, the elder son, a fourth year medical and a forward in the first Rugby fifteen. I ventured only one remark to him. 'You play for the Fifteen, don't you?' and he replied: 'Aye, I'm one o' the stupid eight.'

Colin, I saw, was the odd man out physically as well as mentally. Although he and I were six feet tall, we were small compared with the others, especially David. Ian was only eighteen and still lanky and gangling but David, at twenty-two years old, was massive, his huge shoulders straining the seams of his shabby tweed coat. And both brothers were darker than Colin, more colourful and less elusive as personalities.

'Either of you two got enough money for another cup of coffee?' David asked when we had drunk the first.

'I'm skinned. It's Friday,' said Colin.

'I've only got the money for the sausages,' said Ian.

'I—' I began but David interrupted me, rising to his feet. 'Then that's it. We'd better get back to the digs. Come on, Simpson.'

As if in a trance, I went with them up the street, Ian and Colin in front, David and myself behind, David talking easily of the professors and lecturers in the faculty. We stopped at a butcher's shop, David and I waiting in the doorway among the smell of sawdust and raw meat while Ian and Colin bought the sausages before we went on to Dunn Square.

Until now, Dunn Square had been only a name to me and if I had imagined anything, I think I had imagined it to be like one of the London squares, with some trees in the centre and steps leading up to the doors of the houses. I suffered something of a shock for Dunn Square was made up of four four-storey tenements built round a square with openings at the corners and the area thus enclosed was laid with concrete which sprouted a forest of iron clothes poles instead of trees. In the grey rain, in the pale shafts of gas-light that came from the surrounding windows, dingy garments hung limp from the clothes-lines and among the iron poles, boys played football with a bundle of rags for a ball while girls played a singing game, their voices thin and shrill in the wet smoky air. I had a sudden mind picture of Treasure and felt that if I went over to where the little girls were, she might be there, singing among them.

I followed the Adairs into a passage with a concrete floor and walls and up some stone stairs with iron banisters, where a blue fan-shaped gas jet flared, turning the ruddy faces of David and Ian to a sickly yellow. On a stone landing, they opened a door and Ian called: 'Eeba, we're here!'

'And about time too,' came a female voice. 'Did you bring the sausages?'

Suddenly a door opened and framed in a rectangle of gaslight stood the goddess. She was tall for a woman and she was the all-male David subtly transmuted into female form. In her presence, a change came over the three brothers, as if they became younger, smaller, quieter, less colourful.

'Eeba, this is Simpson,' David said. 'We brought him to supper. Our sister Isabel, Simpson.'

She held out her hand to me, looked straight into my eyes, smiled and turned to her brother. 'Did you bring some extra sausages as well?' she asked.

'No oof,' said Ian.

'Honestly, you three are the limit.' She turned to a coat that hung on a hook in the little passage, took a purse from the pocket and handed a coin to Ian. I wanted to run to the butcher's shop, buy the great heap of sausages in the enamel tray in the window, bring them back and lay them at her feet but I was frozen, speechless and motionless.

'Better get another pound,' she said. 'Come in, Mr Simpson.' She led me into a room with a sink under the window and a black iron range where a coal fire burned. 'I'll take your coat. What's your name?'

She was holding out her hand for the coat. 'Name?' I stuttered. 'Oh, Ch-Charles.'

'Sit down, Charles.' She moved a heap of books from a chair to the top of a wooden coal bunker. 'Col, peel some more potatoes.'

'Isabel was a heller,' Treasure had said. 'Heller' was as good a description as any for this extraordinary creature, I thought. Extremes were the only words my mind could apply to her – angel, goddess, heller, words for creatures not of this world but of some remote region shrouded in clouds of mystery. Over the fried sausages, onions and mashed potatoes, there was plenty of noisy conversation but I do not think I spoke at all. The talk was mostly of medicine and Adair family affairs but it was dominated by Isabel, who seemed to wield over her brothers a long-established dominion. 'Eeba' they called her, this being, I gathered, David's first childish attempt at the word 'Isabel', which had been perpetuated in the family. The little name had an archaic ring, reminiscent to me of names like Io and Ida that Treasure and I had come across in the *Myths of Ancient Greece*.

The feeling of family unity was extremely strong, making of that sordid tenement flat a home, a hearth, almost a temple although it contained only the barest necessities for day to day living and well-thumbed heaps of medical textbooks. As a member of the semi-circle round the black range, I understood fully for the first time the nature of Colin's dilemma when he made his outburst in the park. I had never known before that family unity could be such a compelling force and I felt myself to be the most privileged of people, admitted as I was into this sacred circle.

Thereafter, I went to the Sutherland Tea Room every Friday evening in the hope that I might meet some of the Adairs and be invited to Dunn Square. Sometimes they were there, sometimes they were not. Sometimes I was invited but sometimes I was not, but I came to understand that money was the controlling factor in this. More often than not, they could not afford the extra sausages for my supper. I once tried to contribute to the meal but this was a mistake on my part that I did not repeat. In a subtle way, it was borne in on me that my contribution was an invasion of their family privacy, an infringement of their dignity, and that although a small box of chocolates as a tribute to Isabel was acceptable, a contribution to the basic hospitality of the house was not.

The circle dominated by the Adairs, however, extended far beyond the tenement flat in Dunn Square. David was a member of the leading set in the Union and sporting life of the university and Ian was at the centre of the first year in the medical faculty while Colin, having found the work he wanted to do, became less of a solitary and blossomed into importance in the debating society and in the columns of the university magazine. Towing me along in their wake, the Adairs opened all doors to me and I found myself accepted and integrated as I had never imagined I could be and only very occasionally, amidst the interest and enjoyment of it all, would I remember that the real key which had opened all the doors was Treasure, determined to repay what she called 'a good turn' to the Adair parents.

The only regulars on the trains I was now using to and from Lochfoot were myself and the girl I mentioned earlier and I discovered that this girl was also a regular at the Sutherland Tea Room. She was there not only on Fridays but every evening between four and five o'clock.

The journeys through the smoky suburbs between Lochfoot and Glasgow were very dreary and boring in the winter drizzle and I began to chat to this girl. Her name was Mary Lawrie and she was a large, plain lumpy creature with a broad pale face, a clumsy body and an air that was half sullen, half pathetic. She conversed mainly in monosyllables and in the intervals of replying yes or no to some remark, she would sit looking vacant, vegetating, as if the mind behind her eyes had been extinguished like a light. I think that, boredom apart, the main reason why I spoke to her at all was that she was in such complete contrast to Treasure or Isabel. It was amusing to make a remark to Mary Lawrie, watch her come slowly out of her apathy to say yes or no before slumping back again and then imagine making the same remark to Treasure and imagine her lively response. Isabel was constantly in the depth of my mind but I did not imagine making remarks to her. Instead, I would look at the lumpish fleshy Mary, then close my eyes and see against their lids an ethereal vision of a creature compounded of light and fire.

Mary and I had been sharing a compartment morning and most evenings in unrelieved gloom on her part for about three weeks when, one evening, as the homeward train made its first stop in the Glasgow area, she sprang from her seat, looking more alive than I had ever seen her look and said: 'I'm getting out here tonight. Cheerybye!'

Feeling that my eyes were glazed with stunned astonishment, I watched her cross the platform and join a young man. A few evenings after this, I spent some extra time in the biology laboratory and caught a train that left at six-ten instead of five minutes past five and at the first stop on the line Mary, who had probably been on the earlier train, joined this one, bidding an affectionate farewell to the young man. He was a sleek, flashy young man with dark hair and side-burns, a young man of the kind that my fellow students described as 'a proper greasy Valentino', but in his presence Mary Lawrie was different, placid rather than lumpish for she could never be vivacious, solemn rather than sullen for she could never be gay. In an unmoved clinical fashion, I was interested in this change that could come over Mary Lawrie and which fell away from her as soon as she turned away from the man and got into the train. She would step into the nearest compartment in an unseeing way and drop sadly down on the seat, seeming not to see me if I happened to be in the compartment that she joined.

'Treasure,' I said one evening over supper, 'there's a girl called Lawrie who travels on the train.'

'Big feet and a face like a scone?' Treasure enquired.

'Yes,' I had to agree.

'Old Boney Lawrie, the butcher's daughter. Her name is Mary. What about her?'

I told of the evening assignations between trains. 'It seems so pathetic. They must just walk about the streets for an hour or so in the rain five evenings a week. She is always so damp and dreary-looking when she gets into the train.'

'She was always pretty damp an' dreary anyway,' was Treasure's comment. 'What's the chap like? Long an' weedy an' dark an' conceited-lookin'?'

'Yes,' I had to agree again.

'Gyad, old Boney would bust his boiler if he knew. That's Pat McPhee. He was born a tinker but I don't know what he works at now, if he works at all, that is. The McPhees were never famous for working. They never even played the bag-pipes for pennies.'

'He must be doing something,' I said. 'He is well enough dressed in a flashy sort of way. Anyway, he seems to make Mary happy.'

'Aye. He always did that. Mary's been daft about him since she was about ten years old. If she doesnae keep her eyes open an' something else shut, Pat'll maybe make her happier than she bargains for. What's she travellin' up and down to Glas-gow for anyway?'

'She goes to the secretarial college in Sauchiehall Street.'

'Mary Lawrie a secretary? Ach away for pity's sake, Mr Charles! Mary Lawrie never got the upper hand o' the two-times table.'

'Well, she goes to the secretarial college.'

'Old Boney must have got her shoved into it somehow. They are an uppish pair, the Lawries. He is an elder in the kirk an' high up in the Freemasons with a fancy wee apron. But imagine Mary switching trains like that to meet Pat McPhee! I never thought she had it in her. Well, well, amor vincit omnia!'

The last phrase startled me. 'Treasure, since when have you been learning Latin?'

'There's a picture called that up in the attic. Amor vincit omnia – love conquers all, it says underneath it an' the band played: believe it if ye like,' she ended in scathing comment.

'It certainly works for Mary Lawrie,' I said.

My life now became very full. In addition to my new friends the Adairs and my new acquaintanceship among my fellows, I still kept in touch with Doctor Gill to whose coaching I owed my university entrance and at his house, one afternoon, I was introduced to a friend of his, a Doctor Mason. After a little time, this man rose to take his leave with the words: 'I have to be off. This is one of my nights for the Settlement.'

'You'll have to take Charles down there with you some night, Mason,' Doctor Gill said. 'If that doesn't put him off medicine, nothing will.'

'The Settlement?' I asked.

'The Dockland Settlement. It's financed by the church – a soup-kitchen, lodging-house and so on. We have a clinic down there, six to ten – ten if you're lucky – Monday to Saturday.'

'Will you really take me some evening, Doctor Mason?' I asked, and Doctor Gill and his wife laughed at my enthusiasm. 'I don't suppose I'd be any use,' I added, deflated, 'I'm only in my first year.'

Doctor Mason looked at me, smiling. 'All you have to do to be useful down there is to do what you are told,' he said.

'I can do that, sir,' I assured him and so began my attendance, at some periods six evenings a week, at the Dockland Settlement.

The Settlement was housed in a disused warehouse in a narrow street near the docks and with the exception of the

Superintendent, who was paid a salary from some church fund, I gathered, it was served entirely by volunteers. The lodging-house and soup-kitchen sections were open twenty-four hours a day and manned mostly by church workers and students who were members of the Student Christian Movement, but the clinic, small, unhygienic and ill-equipped, was open only in the evenings from six until ten in theory but on Friday and Saturday evenings the doctor was fortunate if he could close the door at midnight. These doctors were men in practice in the city who gave to the clinic as many evenings of their time as they could and they were assisted by a number of medical students like myself.

In the course of my walks and tramcar rides around the streets of Glasgow I thought I had seen something of the slums of the city, something of the difference between the solid offices and villas of the merchants and stockbrokers and the rickety tenements of the back streets, something of the chasm between the exclusive stores of Sauchiehall Street and the pubs and pawnshops of the slums, but I did not look into the human face of poverty until I went to the clinic, had no idea of the distortions, physical and mental, that poverty could work upon human kind.

There were rickety children, children crippled in backyard accidents, children crippled at birth. There were women crippled by child-bearing, men crippled at work, men and women rotted by venereal disease. There were the attempted escapists, their minds crippled by alcohol or some hell-fire religion of hatred, but the saddest crippled of all were those who had, mentally, been beaten down into a grey squalor, their minds anaesthetised by misery, their eyes and faces dull and vacant. Sometimes a last straw of misery would act like an injection, piercing through the anaesthesia to the core of life that remained and a husband would throw his wife down the tenement stairs and as if this were the spark starting the fire, all the occupants of the seething tenement would flare into a blazing riot and the clinic would be inundated by the injured brought in by the police.

The constant enemy that the clinic fought was, of course, dirt and the consequences of dirt. We students often referred to the place as the 'Louse Patch' and we all became very proficient, men and women, at the bathing and cleansing of young children and at the treatment of such diseases as scabies.

Doctor Mason was in his forties and a bachelor who gave more evenings to the clinic than any other one of the volunteers. He used to arrive with a half-bottle of whisky in his overcoat pocket which he drank, mixed with water, in a white enamel mug in the course of the evening. He was a native of the city, could speak the dialect and his mind was of a cast similar to that of his friend Doctor Gill. The statement which he made more often than any other about our patients was: 'Nothing wrong with any o' them that money wouldn't cure,' and there was the reverse of this statement: 'Money – other folks' money – made them what they are,' which meant the same thing. These statements were like the two sides of a penny. The patterns on the two sides of the coin differed but the coin was still a penny and I soon came to learn that, for another reason, our child patients called Doctor Mason 'the Penny Doctor'. He would examine the weals on the back of a child, weals inflicted by a drunk father, dress them, give the child a penny and say: 'Now, then, don't spend it all in the one shop.'

At the end of my second month at the clinic, I was bankrupt, all my spare cash for the month distributed in small sums among our patients. I still had some savings in the bank but my allowance, which had hitherto seemed so ample, was finished, the next instalment not due until the morrow and I had to walk to the station to catch the train home because I had not the penny for the tram fare. The next day, it was macabre to call at the solid offices of the bank to draw some of my allowance and remember the clinic where I had parted with my last penny the evening before and it was even more macabre to come home to Laurelbank and pass Lord Mammon in his temple on my way from the back door to my bedroom. I seemed to live in two incompatible worlds and I began to hate the clinic but I could not stay away from it and often went to it because my conscience would not let me go home to the warm wealth of Laurelbank.

In the meantime, the uneventful calendar of the aunts' days unfolded. Mr Guthrie and the piano-tuner came and went, the burglar money was hidden on the last Saturdays of each month and Treasure and I held musicales in the early mornings and in the afternoons at the weekends but although we went into the drawing-room, where I sat on the piano stool and Treasure sat on the hearth-rug and although we called our meetings musicales, we did not play or sing as much as formerly. I might give the 'Green Eye' and Treasure might give 'A Lost Chord' but in the main I talked mostly about the clinic and Treasure listened, but when I say that she listened I do not mean that she merely let me talk, for this was not so. She did not permit me to run away into emotional nonsense.

'You keep going on about misery, Mr Charles,' she said one Sunday afternoon. 'These youngsters are not as miserable as you think, I'll bet my boots. Oh, I'll grant you they are not very happy sometimes when they've just had a leathering or when they've got impetigo or something but a big lot of the time they have great fun. Youngsters do and nobody can stop them. You do what you can for their scabs and their lice but don't worry yourself about them being miserable because they're not.'

On another Sunday afternoon, Treasure said something which I have since recognised as a factor that changed the course of my work and my life. I had gone upstairs to fetch a book and had heard the sound of snoring on the landing as Aunt Bessie slept off her far too large and heavy lunch.

'The aunts are up there snoring like pigs,' I fulminated with, of course, the grey half-starved faces of the clinic at the back of my mind. 'It is a wonder they don't die of over-eating.'

'You and your over-eating and under-nourishment and your microbes and bacilli,' said Treasure. 'If you ask me, folk get sick as much through their minds as through their bodies. I never had enough to eat until I came here to Laurelbank but no whooping-cough bacilli ever landed on *me* because my mother said that whooping-cough was vulgar and I was too bloody frightened to let the bacilli land on me. And you can laugh and say that's rubbish if you like but people being well or sick isn't all eating and microbes. The ladies are not going to die of over-eating because they believe they are eating to keep up their strength and if you believe you are keeping up your strength you are not going to die of what keeps it up, are you?'

I laughed at her energetic although incoherent expression of a point of view new to me as, indeed, were many of Treasure's views and said: 'And what are they going to die of, Doctor Robertson?'

'Don't you get all sarky and try to cod *me*, Mr Charles. The ladies will die when their time comes like everybody else and of something that's *in* them, likely. The doctor said my granny died o' the 'flu but I've thought since that ever since my father got killed at the war my granny was just waiting to get the 'flu or something that would give her an excuse for dying.'

In this way, Treasure halted my ruthless march towards pure science and war on malnutrition and microbes as a cure for all the ills of the world. She kept the complex nature of human life constantly before me and reminded me that the physical mechanism contained and was animated by the inexplicable thing which we called 'the mind', but it was only when the Frenchman, Émile Coué, came to some international notice with his theory of auto-suggestion and his slogan 'Every day and in every way I am getting better and better' that I began to take serious notice of Treasure's thought and to take an interest in the mysteries of the mind.

Throughout my first year in medicine, the clinic near the docks was my main practical interest, while my dreams hovered round the distant goddess, Isabel Adair. I found my university work straightforward and all the unplanned but extensive reading I had done ever since I left school stood me in good stead. Treasure, of course, was a constant encouragement and her comments from over my shoulder while I was reading had a helpful habit of popping back into my mind during examinations, such as: 'So that's typhoid fever? Gyad, the ugly wee bugger!' which was how she described the illustrations of the bacillus.

When the drunken orgy that heralded the dawn of 1925 was over, we had what was called a party for the women and children at the Settlement, but it was more of a super-soup-kitchen, with an unending line of cold, wet hungry people filing past the counter to be served with plates full of greasy stew and boiled potatoes. After I had served the first half-dozen, I found their thanks and their attempts at cheerfulness unbearable and I had spent the rest of the afternoon washing-up greasy plates at the chipped sink. When it was over, I caught the five-five train and it seemed to me to be the last straw of depression when Mary Lawrie stumbled into my compartment at the first station up-the-line and allowed her untidy face to fall completely apart while heavy tears began to roll down over her putty-coloured cheeks. She was repulsive and pathetic all at once and I wanted to change to another compartment but, instead, I asked her what was the matter. I had imagined that there must have been a lovers' tiff but this was not so. Mary had failed her end of winter-term examinations and was almost afraid to go home.

'My father'll be so angry,' she sobbed, 'and so will my

mother but I can't do these subjects. I've tried and tried and studied and studied and I just can't. And I don't want to be a secretary anyway.'

'Then you must tell your people so,' I said but this led only to another flood of tears and more fears of the rage of her father. Was there no moderation in the world, I thought with exasperation? Either parents did not care at all about their offspring, it seemed, or they were over-ambitious for them. By the time the train reached Lochfoot she had stopped crying and was less convinced that the world had ended for, as I pointed out, it was the early summer examinations which were really important and I suggested that, during our train journeys in the spring, I would coach her in so far as I could, try to explain the subjects that she found so incomprehensible.

That evening, when I told Treasure of this, she said: 'You don't know what you've taken on, Mr Charles. Mary Lawrie is as thick in the head as shit in a bottle,' which made me laugh away all the dreariness of the long grey day.

I still paid my Saturday forenoon visits to the morning-room while Treasure went out shopping and in my stupid over-enthusiasm, I had the absurd idea of trying to interest the aunts in the Settlement. I think I was launched on this foolish course by a sepia print that hung behind Aunt Bessie's chair, just round the corner of the room from the portrait of old Snake-eyes. This picture showed a great deal of woolly cloud in the centre of which was a lady angel with huge wings and her left forefinger pointing upwards, presumably to Heaven. Approaching her in full flight from the left-hand side were two more female angels but more of the servant class, with less splendid robes and less dramatic wings and between them they bore through the air a child dressed in a nightgown. Underneath this picture was written:

Lo that night from out the alley did a child's soul pass away,
From dirt and sin and misery to where God's children play.

The night after our New Year's party at the Settlement, a woman had come into the clinic with a baby wrapped in a dirty grey shawl. Doctor Mason took the bundle from her, unwrapped the shawl and found that the baby was dead. Standing beside him, I saw the little puny face before he drew the shawl back over it. I had seen the dead face of my father but I had never even imagined a dead child. It was on the Saturday forenoon after this happened that I told the aunts about the clinic. Engrossed in what I was saying, my eyes on the angel picture on the wall, I became unaware of the aunts as I relived the scene in the clinic and when I fell silent I discovered that they were both on their feet on the hearth-rug, their faces distorted with horror, their bony hands shaking.

'Charles,' said Aunt Bessie, 'how dare you waste your time at that shocking place? We are paying your fees that you may pursue your studies, not waste your time in the slums of Glasgow.'

Both aunts said a great deal more of a similar kind and I quickly realised that I, far from arousing any charitable impulse in them, had merely prejudiced my allowance and study fees. I lied my way out of the situation by telling them that Mr Guthrie, Doctor Gill and my professors had all advised me to gain experience by attending the Settlement and in the end they subsided but on the protest that it seemed 'most peculiar to encourage young men of good family to go into such places'. I then made my escape from the morning-room, feeling that there had been a bad moment which was now over, but it was not over.

'Mr Charles,' said Treasure over lunch, 'you have gone and upset the ladies. Why did you go and tell them about that Louse Patch?'

'I thought I might get a contribution out of them, I suppose,' I said. 'For pity's sake, don't *you* start making a fuss next.'

'I am not making a fuss, Mr Charles, but I wish you could understand the ladies better. You have made them real upset and nervous.'

'Nervous? What about?'

'It's hard to explain. It's as if they're frightened that these poor folk at the clinic will come down here and steal all their money. They asked me if I was being sure to put the bolts on all the windows at nights.'

'Their own consciences are upsetting them,' I said, 'and I hope they go on upsetting them. Lo that night from out the alley did a child's soul pass away! It's enough to give ye the boke!'

And now Treasure was on her feet at the opposite side of the table, glaring at me. 'Speak proper, you!' she commanded me sternly. 'Me and that Louse Patch is no help to you in the way of speaking but you're not going to speak vulgar like us if I can help it. You've got the ladies into a proper tirravee, so you have, you and your Louse Patch. I'm not to go down-the-line to the public library the-day because they're frightened to be alone in the house.'

'Oh, heavens, Treasure, I'm sorry. Look, go to the library. I'll stay in.'

'Leave *you* here alone with the ladies? That Louse Patch might come marchin' in through the front door. No. *You'll* have to do the library and a fine goat you'll look taking love stories off the shelf and serve you right. Mr Charles, will you *never* learn about the ladies? You are nearly as hard to teach as wee Sammy was. I tried my best to teach him how things were but he never learned. You'll do the library, Mr Charles? They'll be more upset than ever with no nice love stories for Sunday.'

'They should have thought of that before they told you to stay in, but never mind. I'll go.'

Treasure and I did not recognise it at the time but this crisis marked a further withdrawal into their cocoon on the part of the aunts for, after this, there was always a fuss if they were to be left alone in the house. At first, Treasure would have been a constant prisoner, so nervous were they of myself but, at the same time, they did not trust me to do the shopping or to go to the bank so that, trapped by their own distrust, they had to have me as their protector while Treasure went out and their fear of the aura of the clinic which they seemed to see around me made our conversation more ludicrously stilted than ever.

I made the journey to the public library after the crisis that I had precipitated and took over this chore as one of my own. The library stayed open late on Friday evenings and I used to drop off the train on my way home, spend half-an-hour there and catch the next train up-the-line.

I had known for some time that Treasure derived some income from burglar money hidden in library books but it seemed that, after I scared the aunts so much over the clinic, they hid more and more money in the books which they kept in the morning-room, being too nervous to venture as far as the staircase or upper landing as they used to do during the monthly Saturday ceremonial. Now that I was doing the public library chore, Treasure insisted that burglar money found in library books was mine and one morning very soon after the crisis I held a novel by its spine over the pantry table and shook a five-pound note out of it.

'A fiver!' she said. 'Lucky you.'

'Halvers,' I said.

'No. Keep it for your Louse Patch. I've got three quid in the biscuit barrel in the dining-room that'll be ripe on Thursday. What was that fiver in? *Flames of Passion*?'

I looked at the title of the book. 'No. *Love Came at Last*.'

'They must have liked that one. Mind on it and get it out for them again in three months or so,' she advised me, teaching me the tricks of this new trade. 'And you'd better get them *The Sheik* again today. They haven't had it for a while and it's often good for a quid or two.'

'They read the same novels over and over again then?'

'Aye, their favourite ones. How often have I told you that the ladies don't like change? Mind you, a new one is a good thing now and again if they happen to take a fancy to it. That *Love Came at Last* is new but it seems they liked it. You can bring that one again before too long. And they are very partial to *The Way of an Eagle*. Listen – ' she went off at a tangent ' – I had an idea last night. Three of the Murphy lassies are working in the shirt factory now and Mrs Murphy's not too bad off. I've still got most of that side of bacon and two boxes of tangerines and a tin of biscuits that came with the Discounts. Would you like them for your Louse Patch, Mr Charles?'

'Would I not?' I said. 'Thank you, Treasure.'

'I thought the bairns might like the tangerines. Pity there isn't a hundred of them instead of a couple of dozen. But how will you get the stuff up there, Mr Charles?'

'I'll get it there, don't worry,' I told her, which was how it came about that I arrived at the Settlement with a side of bacon in an old Gladstone bag which I had found in the attic.

After I had carried the Discounts to the Settlement, the bag found repose in the bottom of a cupboard in the pantry and Treasure would put into it tins of corned beef and packets of tea which she had managed to 'look after the Louse Patch with' on the household grocery bills. At intervals of about a month, she would say: 'Bag's full, Mr Charles. Are you going to the Louse Patch tonight?' and I would set out with my burden, casting a triumphant glance at Lord Mammon in the hall as I turned down the basement stairs.

The children at the clinic came to recognise the bag, which must once have belonged to my grandfather or my uncle for it bore on its side the large black initials 'C.S.' and I used to walk self-consciously down the street, like an unwilling Pied

Piper, followed by a troupe of little urchins who shouted: 'Doctor Charlie and his bag! Doctor Charlie and his bag!' Doctor Mason said that some of the women obligingly blacked one another's eyes on the days that the bag came down the street so that they would have a legitimate excuse to call at the clinic, and certainly one drunken old crone named Maggie invariably appeared on the heels of myself and the bag, repeating her refrain: 'I'll give ye me oath, Doctor, not a bite has passed me lips since Tuesday!' It did not matter whether the day was Wednesday or Saturday, Maggie had never had a bite since Tuesday.

My attempts to coach Mary Lawrie in the train between Lochfoot and Glasgow began at the start of the new term and at the end of the first journey it was obvious that Treasure's description of the 'thickness' of Mary's head was very apt. After a very short time I was at a loss to understand how the girl had achieved the standard to enter college in the first place and if she had crammed for the entrance examination all she had learned had already drained away from her. She had no concentration, no ability and she was not even interested in the work. With exasperation, I would find that while I was patiently showing her the rudiments of book-keeping as described in her primer on the subject she was gazing out of the window, unseeing, withdrawn and as remote from the matter in hand as the factory chimneys that belched smoke into the sky.

'It is ridiculous,' I told Treasure. 'The girl shouldn't be at college at all. Why can't she tell her parents that she can't do the thing? She admits that she can't.'

'Old Boney Lawrie is no Mr Adair,' Treasure said. 'It's harder for Mary than it was for Colin. Old Lawrie thinks that if he pays the fees, the college should make a secretary out of her, like himself putting odds and ends into his machine and turning out sausages.'

'But that is just mad.'

'Mad or not, that is how he is and there is nothing anybody can do about it. Don't you go worrying your head and wasting your time on Mary Lawrie, Mr Charles.'

I took Treasure's advice. The attempts to coach Mary died a natural death but I continued to see her on the train, plain, pathetic, listless except after her assignations with her young man. It was pitiful to see the life drain out of her after she had left him and as the train came nearer to Lochfoot, when she resembled an animal that had glimpsed freedom resigning itself once more to the bars of the cage.

On a Friday afternoon towards the end of that spring term I went into the Sutherland as usual shortly after four o'clock. I had with me a smaller Gladstone bag which I had found in the attic and in it were six of the aunts' romantic novels which I intended to change at the library on my way home. I stopped short in the doorway of the teashop for, sitting at the table which the Adairs and I had made practically our own, was not only David but Isabel, while Mary Lawrie, like a grey shade, was sitting at another table in a far corner.

'Hello, Charles,' Isabel greeted me. 'Why the bag? Don't tell me you are carrying instruments already?'

I felt myself blush with shame, as if the goddess had the power to see through the leather and black initials of the bag and read the pulsing words of *Strong Silent Lover*.

'Books,' I managed to say. 'I am dropping off at the library down-the-line' and I stuffed the bag under the table.

David got to his feet. 'I've got to go. I'm meeting a chap,' he said and Isabel too rose from the table.

I gathered all my courage and addressed her. 'Can't you stay and have a cup of tea with me?'

She turned her eyes upon me, blinding me. 'Why not?' I heard her say out of the flame-shot darkness. 'Yes. Thank you very much, Charles.'

I do not remember a word that was said – it is probable that I did not speak at all – until the grey shade that was

Mary Lawrie passed our table and went out into the street.

'That is Mary Lawrie from Lochfoot, isn't it?' Isabel asked, looking after the lumpish figure.

'Yes.'

'She is just the same old lump she was at school.'

I closed my mind to the thought of Mary Lawrie, concentrated all my powers on the beauty across the table. Isabel had taken off her felt hat, and her bobbed hair, thick and dark and gleaming with auburn lights, sprang with a life of its own above her high white forehead.

'I didn't know she was married.'

She meant Mary Lawrie. 'I don't think she is,' I said.

'Then she should be,' said the goddess. 'She is pregnant. Well, Charles, it is time for your train.'

I did not want to catch a train. I wanted to stay with Isabel for ever and ever but the goddess had spoken and I left her on the pavement and went into the station. The train was about to move away as I reached the ticket barrier and heard her call my name: 'Charles!' Treasure and I had been mistaken, I thought in a split second, when we laughed at our musicales at Tennyson's 'Maud' for it was true that—

My dust would hear her and beat,
Had I lain for a century dead;
Would start and tremble under her feet,
And blossom in purple and red.

I looked in the direction of the voice and stood tranced as she ran towards me, dodging through the crowd, the shining hair flying about her head. She ran like an athlete, rhythmically, economically, effortlessly and my breath stopped as she came towards me, her face bright with laughter, eager, urgent.

'Your bag,' she said, thrusting the thing at me. 'Scoot! The train's moving!'

At the command, I snatched the bag, ran on to the platform and hurled myself into the nearest compartment.

When I regained normal consciousness, I became aware of Mary Lawrie sitting in the opposite corner. The complete contrast to the Atalanta with the bag, she was sitting humped disconsolately, as if she were in the last compartment not because she was too late for the train as I had been but because she had not had the energy, physical or mental, to walk further up the platform. I said hello to her and then sat silent, hating her. When the train stopped at the station where she met her young man she did not get out. She merely looked at the spot where they used to meet, sighed and then misery seemed to exude from her, spreading in wavering grey swathes about the compartment. I thought of what Isabel had said, tried to picture her as she spoke, but the goddess was elusive. There was no mind picture of her now, only a vibration of light and energy somewhere in the far distance and a few feet away sat the grey, solid insistent lump that was Mary Lawrie.

CHAPTER TEN

There is but one
With whom she has heart to be gay.
'Maud,' by Lord Tennyson.

WHEN I look back, I can only describe this period after I met Isabel Adair as a time of dark enchantment. I was not happy but, at the same time, I did not want to break free of the spell that held me. I could liken my attitude to that of the alcoholic who, during his periods of remorse, despises himself and hates the drug that has dominion over him, swearing that he will use it no more but who, immediately he thinks of the bottle, remembers the smell, visualises the place where it can be procured, forgets his remorse and his oaths and will lie or steal or in any way abase himself to obtain the means of his self-destruction.

I dreamed of Isabel all night and she dominated my mind all day, my desire to be near her circulating like a dark fury in my blood, like a heavy cloud darkening my mind, like a promise of freedom from my misery disappearing always over a sultry horizon and when I found myself in her presence, I was more unhappy still. She was as far away as a goddess, the air and light of the world between her and myself and I longed to be alone, free of her, to retreat into that darkness of the mind in which, it seemed now, she was nearer to me and might be possessed.

It was only in the depths of myself, of course, that the world stopped turning, that natural laws were suspended, that the wild music pulsed in the enchanted dark. Outside my physical body which was possessed by this black flame-shot magic, the mundane world went on as before and outwardly I went on with it, although doing some things which I had never done before, such as hanging about on the wet pavement outside the Casualty Entrance of the central city hospital to which Isabel had moved at Easter. Bleak with the shamed thought that I ought to be at the Settlement, I spent hours on that pavement in the fine grey rain, only to turn away, disconsolate and cold with misery, when I at last saw her come out in the company of the colleague who had shared duty with her and walk away with him in the opposite direction without, apparently, noticing my presence.

But if Isabel did not notice me, there was someone who did, a nurse called Teresa Riordan, a pretty little dark girl with deep blue Irish eyes. There was a diabolical contrariness, it seemed to me, in the fact that although everything in me cried out to Isabel, the cries were heard only by Teresa, but at the same time her gay yet deferential friendliness was soothing to my vanity and balm to my sore spirit.

Motivated by some vague idea of making Isabel 'sit up and take notice' as Teresa would have put it, I began to respond to Teresa's inviting glances from under her stiff white cap as she came off duty. In retrospect, I see that, physically, she had some of Treasure's lively charm but she had none of Treasure's incisive clarity and independence of mind. Teresa was romantic, sentimental and loved the Hollywood films of the time, in which sombre-eyed heroes and tigress-like heroines faded out in clouds of happy-ever-after after two hours of unlikely adventure. In the dark of the picture palace, Teresa would hold my hand and sigh and weep in sympathy with the shadows on the screen while I sighed and wept, inwardly, over Isabel. When we emerged into the lights of the street, however, drizzly grey reality would break through and when I had put Teresa on a tramcar for her lodgings and had taken myself to the station, I would despise myself for giving Teresa a false impression and hate Isabel for forcing me into this situation. As the train rattled me back towards Lochfoot I would swear never to go to the Casualty Entrance again, to get on with my work, to think no more of Isabel and the resolve would stand firm until I left the train, but the evening-clouded sky, the spring-budded trees, the wind in the reeds at the lochside and the tangle of the back garden, where Pan stood hidden with his pipes in one hand and his bunch of grapes in the other all worked together on the side of the enchantment and by the time I came into the house I was in the grip of another night of sultry lightning-shot dreams.

One morning during the Easter vacation I came downstairs feeling lackadaisical and sullen as I so often felt now and Treasure came out of the pantry to meet me in the hall. The light was dim, the sky was weeping grey rain as it seemed to do all the time now and the flakes of light from the stained glass were sombre on the walls and furniture. Treasure pointed to Lord Mammon.

'Mr Charles,' she said, 'I wish you would not do that.'

'What?' Peevishly, it seemed to me that there was no justice in the world, that I came downstairs, lovelorn and unappreciated by the goddess, to be met with nagging about some unimportant household trifle.

'Hang your mackintosh on his axe.'

Oh, God, who was I to be gnat-bitten by trivia like mackintoshes and axes?

'I've taken it off there three times this week. Please take it off and don't hang it there again, Mr Charles. It worries me,' said Treasure and went back into the pantry.

Her voice was unsteady as she spoke the final sentence and this pierced my misery with a different misery, a misery born of the awareness that I had done something to hurt Treasure.

Lord Mammon's halberd had a flat blade with a curved edge at the front of the shaft and a six-inch-long spike at the back and it was on this that I had hung my coat the night before. I now removed the coat, fetched a cloth from the pantry and mopped up the pool of water on the rug and the floor.

'I am sorry, Treasure,' I said, squeezing the cloth at the pantry sink. 'I won't do it again.'

'It's all right, Mr Charles, but the ladies wouldn't like it.'

She wanted me to forget her admission of 'It worries me' and now transferred her reason to the aunts, I noticed.

'Come and have your breakfast. Are you going down-the-line today?'

Momentarily, I wanted to answer that I was not, that it was the Easter vacation, that we would have a musicale that afternoon, but the spell was upon me again and I said: 'Yes. I am going to do some reading at the library and I'll probably go to the Louse Patch at night. Will you leave me some sandwiches?'

'You don't think you are spending too much time at that Louse Patch, Mr Charles? Shouldn't you take a holiday?'

I was not going to the Settlement, I was lying to her and this enraged me but I spent the rage on Treasure, not on myself.

'What for? To keep up my strength? You'll have me drinking Abernethy's Tonic Wine next,' I said nastily, was at once ashamed of myself and retreated into my black pall of gloom. Naturally, I thought that I was isolated in my misery, that I was the only man who had ever suffered like this, that even Abelard had never known such pangs as mine and I think I would have been horrified rather than relieved to discover that there were dozens of young men in situations very similar to my own, young men torn by passionate tensions and all keeping them secret, just as I was.

But there is an obscure law of life that dictates that like will reach out to like and there is also an obscure law of history that dictates that the moment has come for concerted action. One of these moments came now. A few of the more advanced medical students who did volunteer work at the Settlement rose in wrath when a backyard wall collapsed, killing three children and injuring five more. The collapsing wall was only the spark to the tinder and the tinder did not burn purely with rage at the victimisation of the poor by the slum landlords. 'Down with the Slums!' were the words of the battle-cry but every student involved in the movement that arose had a secret battle-cry of his own. I think mine was 'For love of Isabel!'

In every generation a greater or lesser number of university students rise in rebellion and make an attempt to set their world to rights. In the late sixteenth century, a fair number rose in the cause of religion at Cambridge and in the late eighteenth century a handful of Cambridge and Oxford men rose against British society and conceived the idea of the Susquehanna Pantisocracy. These small rebellions are remembered by some as little by-ways of social history, which is all they were, but when some fifty of us at Glasgow rose against the conditions in the dockland slums in the spring of 1925, an onlooker might have been forgiven for thinking that the planet had ceased to turn on its axis, so great was the local uproar.

The attitude was that we must on no account be given a hearing but be silenced at once, not because entrenched society felt that we were in any way dangerous but because our loud expression of our views was so impolite, so indecorous, so much as if dockers from a slum public-house had invaded a suburban drawing-room. The outraged attitude was, now, that we were behaving like 'navvies' instead of 'students', then, that we were children who had forgotten that the child should be seen and not heard. It was now that I noticed a basic difference between Glasgow University and the universities of Oxford and Cambridge, a difference of words, those straws that indicate the direction of the wind of opinion. At the latter seats of learning young males were called 'men' or 'undergraduates'; at Glasgow we were called 'students' and by most of the populace the 'Yooni' as it was commonly called was regarded as a slight extension of high school. Students ranged in age from seventeen to twenty-five years, with a few eccentrics of between forty and sixty who now had the opportunity to attend classes that they could not afford in their earlier days and there was the apocryphal story of the monied man of sixty-three who had been a student since he was eighteen, who systematically failed every examination but enrolled again year after year because this was his chosen way of life.

None of the worthy citizenry, including the parents of students, seemed to recognise that, between the ages of seventeen and twenty-five, blood flows at high pressure and must have an outlet for the energy and exuberance that it generates. Many of the students were the sons and daughters of a rural society, of people who lived by the land, where early marriage was the rule and nobody recognised that this group suffered the pressures which a first break from a long family and race tradition entails. The Adairs belonged to this group. Isabel was a fanatical student of medicine and continued to find full satisfaction in it after she was qualified; Colin was of a contented conforming nature and now that he had found the course that he wanted to pursue he pursued it quietly and diligently but David was the wildest and most loud-voiced of rebels. He was twenty-four and deeply in love with a girl in the Arts faculty. Marriage, for students, was out of the question for the degree had to be taken, the sound appointment found, society decreed, before a man could marry and set up house. David, the son of a man who had married at twenty and was a father at twenty-two, turned his repressed urges, as I did, to the betterment of the world, or that part of it that lay immediately around the Settlement.

We held a great number of meetings of our own where we voiced our indignation about many things; we invaded meetings held by various city bodies and heckled the speakers until we were forcibly ejected by the police; we were summoned before the university authorities and threatened with rustication; we expended a great deal of energy but achieved no concrete results except, perhaps, the release of some of our own frustrations.

With the coming of the summer vacation, the students dispersed and the movement died a natural death, leaving behind it in my own life a curiously muddled aftermath. I, along with several others, had been taken to court and fined forty shillings for breach of the peace, an incident which was reported in the *Glasgow Herald*. The first reaction came from Treasure.

'Mr Charles, what *have* you been up to? I've torn the page out of the *Herald* and I don't think the ladies will notice it but for goodness' sake watch your eye, Mr Charles.'

Next came Mr Guthrie, who invited me to lunch at his club, remonstrated with me for a long time in a benign fatherly way before admitting: 'I know that things are far from being perfect, lad, but you could build your Utopia tomorrow, move your Settlement folk into it and they would make a slum of it inside a month. The answer is not in uproar but in education and education is a long tedious process – ' his eyes twinkled with understanding ' – as you yourself well know. Slum landlords, as you call them, are not monsters. A lot of them are decent, good-living people, like your aunts.'

I felt a sudden distaste for my food. 'Are you implying that the aunts own slum property, sir?' I asked.

'Nearly everybody who owns property in Glasgow owns some slums. It is a city and a people that breed slums and a damned poor investment they are, with the tenants tearing up the floorboards to make their fires and throwing their empty whisky bottles through the windows.' I had nothing to say and he concluded: 'You'll do more good in the long run, lad, by teaching one bairn at your Settlement to keep itself free from lice than by setting fire to the City Chambers and burning down all the villas in Kelvinside.'

But it was Isabel who chastened me completely, who made

me grovel, mentally, at her feet. She commanded her brother David and myself to appear before her at Dunn Square, while commanding Colin and Ian to take themselves off to the pictures and keep out of the way. Isabel spoke to us from a shabby wooden chair as from a throne, a distant throne in the cold altitude of Olympus. 'Your job is medicine,' she told us, 'not social economics. That whole uproar at the City Chambers was very ill-conceived and in very bad taste. It does the profession no good at all for a lot of embryo doctors to behave like hooligans.'

By the time she had finished, I felt so diminished that, the next Saturday, I had to bolster up my ego and I upset the ladies by telling them that I was about to set out on a walking tour of the Highlands. I did not mean to upset the ladies. I was going on the walking tour to demonstrate my independence of Isabel, but my announcement in the morning-room caused such an uproar that, at the instigation of Treasure, I had to fetch Mr Guthrie from Glasgow to assure the aunts that this was a most normal thing for students to do, that it was a cheap way of taking a holiday and that the Highlands were not noted for gambling dens or other haunts of vice.

'Honestly, Mr Charles,' Treasure said when Mr Guthrie had gone away, 'I don't see how you can be so clever in other ways and so stupid about the ladies. It was real silly of you, so it was, to go and upset them like that instead of getting Mr Guthrie to tell them in the first of it.'

I stayed away for three weeks, but all the time I walked northwards through Glencoe and on to Oban I could feel the attraction of Isabel behind me in an almost physical way, as if a magnet were exerting its influence on a vertebra between my shoulder-blades. With determination I walked on, up by the side of Loch Ness to Inverness with the magnetic point throbbing in the biceps of my right arm and then on again on the main road by the coasts of Ross and Sutherland to Wick in Caithness, the throb as strong as ever in the middle of my back now. At Wick, I spent a long dull day sitting on a deserted beach looking out over a grey North Sea and then I turned for home. At last I accepted the fact that, if I wanted to win Isabel, the way to go about it was to concentrate on my work, qualify, achieve the position that society demanded of a man before he could satisfy his inner desires. And, society apart, I saw now, Isabel herself would demand success of me. Young, recently qualified as she was, she was already marked among the hospitals of the city as one of those with the stamp of distinction upon her and she did not countenance second-rate people. Some of the Olympian dazzle fell away from her as I walked southward towards her and I began to see her and myself more clearly, to make meaning of words she had spoken instead of remembering only her voice as magically maddening music.

At a point on Loch Lomondside on the second-last day of my tour, I looked over the wall by the road into a bed of reeds at the edge of the water. In the sunlit wind, they whispered the archaic music of Pan, but Isabel was not of that archaic world and did not hear its music. Isabel belonged to the here and the now and if I were to win her I must become the master of my here and my now.

Throughout the rest of the vacation, I went to the library in Glasgow and read through my days, then on to the Settlement and worked through my evenings. I was duly rewarded. One Friday evening, Isabel descended upon the Sutherland and took my breath away by suggesting that I might assist her in her Casualty Ward on Saturday evenings. 'I am allowed to have student assistance,' she said casually, unaware of the signal honour that she was bestowing on her unworthy slave. 'You'll find it pretty rough, though, worse than the Dockland Settlement. We get the football fighters, the broken bottle stuff and the razor slashers.'

'It seems odd that they should put a woman in charge of that stuff,' I said.

There was a sudden gleam of cold hard steel between us. 'In Casualty,' she said, 'there are no men and women, only patients, doctors and nurses.'

'And students,' I added humbly.

The gleam on the steel died out. 'And students,' she agreed.

I received my baptism of blood and vomit in Casualty at the beginning of October, when the football season opened for the winter and even the staff agreed that I had elected to jump into this sordid pool at the deep end. In the midst of the cuts made with razors and broken bottles and the vomitings of the drunks which were the accepted norm, there was an adumbration of the future of all Casualty Departments when police and ambulance attendants deposited upon us four of the city's gilded youth who, in Saturday night exuberance, had driven their open sports car through a plate-glass shop window in Renfield Street. By the time we had dealt with them, the surgery was like a butcher's shop without benefit of sawdust on the floor, but at last there was a lull, broken by Isabel: 'Simpson, it's ten to. You'll miss the midnight train. Riordan, clean up that trolley before you go off.'

Simpson, Riordan, the slaves of the goddess in the white coat. Panting with rage more than with exertion, I ran through the streets towards the station and threw myself into the last compartment of the moving train. There, sitting in a corner, was Mary Lawrie, looking more miserable than ever, as if she were the very spirit of that dreary frustration which was the root cause of the sordid scene in the Casualty Ward, the very apotheosis of all the down-trodden Simpsons, Riordans, football-fighters and drunks.

'Hello, Mary,' I said.

'Hello,' she responded drearily and turned away to look at the blackness beyond the glass of the window.

I remembered how, in the spring, Isabel had said with such certainty that Mary was pregnant but now, although I did not wish to impugn Isabel's judgment, I thought that she must be mistaken. Surely Mary would be 'showing' more by now, but then, sitting slumped as she was, shoulders drooped forwards as always under the heavy tweed coat, she had no shape. She was a mere lump of flesh that exuded an inner misery. She did not speak or move during the journey and when we came out of the train at Lochfoot she did not respond to my goodnight but walked away heavily, as she always walked, towards the main street of the town, while I walked up by the loch and stopped as I always did above the rocks to deepen my gloom by staring down into the gloomy black water.

Why did it have to be Mary Lawrie who shared a compartment with me? Why could it not be Isabel? Why did it have to be the Irish eyes of Teresa that smiled at me over the instrument trolley while the eyes of Isabel remained as clinical and expressionless as her white coat? On this night I faced the fact, which I had been avoiding for some time, that I would have to take some definite action about Teresa, for she was growing too roguishly possessive to be borne and the knowledge that her behaviour was the outcome of my own spinelessness made it no easier to deal with the situation. Tired of the emotional muddle, I turned away along the lane and in through the gates of the back drive.

There was a light in the pantry which meant that Treasure was still up although it was one o'clock in the morning, but then, I reminded myself, Treasure would be interested to hear about Casualty, interested as she was in all my departures.

'What was it like, Mr Charles?' she asked as soon as I appeared. 'Worse than the Louse Patch?'

I felt at once as if I had come out of cloud into sunshine where everything was clearly outlined. 'In a way and not in another way,' I told her. 'At least there were no children, only fighting drunks and so on. I don't know why they go to watch football if all they can do is fight about it.'

'There comes a time,' Treasure said, 'when folk have to

fight and if there isn't a war to go to they will fight about football. Cocoa or milk, Mr Charles?'

'Cocoa, please. But do people *have* to fight, Treasure?'

'You should know. You were the one who fought about the slums.'

'That was different,' I defended myself.

'Not all that different,' she argued. 'The men that were fighting in Glasgow tonight went to the football to forget about the slums. Then they got drunk to forget a bit more, but the slums are aye there so they get to thinking that each other is the slums and fight with each other. It is something like that that it goes. Are you hungry? Like a slice of cold beef?'

'No, thank you.'

'It's not just the slums. It's all kinds of circumstances – their work, the same old thing every day and nothing to take an interest in, the feeling of not being *in* it with anybody or anything. Imagine Isabel Adair working in that place! I bet she makes a job of it.'

'Yes. She does.'

One of Treasure's most pleasing features to me at this time was her enthusiasm for Isabel. It was not too difficult for me to still the paeans of praise that filled my mind when Treasure was there to sing aloud on my behalf. My mind shifted from thought of Isabel, bright-eyed, decisive, fearless in her white coat as she controlled Casualty to Mary Lawrie, sullen-eyed, dull-edged and cowed as she slumped in the corner of the railway compartment. 'Mary Lawrie was on the late train tonight,' I said. 'She looked more miserable than ever.'

'She has every right,' said Treasure. 'Nobody could live in the same house as old Boney Lawrie and not look miserable and Mrs Lawrie's no better.'

'What sort of people are they?'

'Holy,' said Treasure succinctly. 'Old Boney is an elder in the kirk and Mrs L. runs the Band o' Hope. The lips that touch liquor will never touch mine,' she sang and then: 'as if anybody, liquor or no, would want to kiss that old pint o' vinegar.'

'Is Mary the only child?'

'Mr Charles, if I didn't know you to have a fair amount of sense, I might think you were sweet on that Mary Lawrie, the way you are for ever asking about her.' Her tone changed. 'No. She had a brother.' She giggled. 'Ye know what his name is? Paul, for the love o' goodness. Mary an' Paul – Bible, ye see. Paul – the Saint we all called him – fathered three bastards before he was twenty but the last one was on Beery-belly the police sergeant's Minnie so there was a bit of a shindy about that and the Saint cleared out in a hurry. Not that I'm saying any harm about the Saint. There was nothing wrong with him that a good clout on the ear wouldn't cure.'

'Did *you* ever clout him on the ear, Treasure?' I asked to discover whether I had read her face and tone aright.

'Now that you ask me, twice,' she replied. 'But that's neither here nor there. The Saint was all right. I don't go much on this thing of lads like the Saint being all bad and Beery-belly's Minnie being a poor wee thing. It takes two to make a bastard.'

'True enough,' I agreed. 'Where did Paul go?'

'London. He did all right for himself. He got a job down there and married the boss's daughter, so folk said. Anyway, he was back here on a visit last year with a wife and their two youngsters, drivin' a motorcar and everything and Mrs L. had her nose stuck in the air with pride like a cat carryin' a stinkin' herrin'.'

The next day was a cold wet Sunday and I began to look forward to an afternoon musicale in the drawing-room, something we had hardly indulged in, except at Christmas, since I had met Isabel for, in my first fevered state, if I could not be with Isabel, I had preferred to be alone. I was disappointed in my hopes, however, because at breakfast Treasure asked me if I would stay at home and let her go out.

'I'll leave tea ready to take into the morning-room and I'll be back to serve dinner,' she said.

I agreed at once and willingly, for Treasure was virtually a prisoner in the house and she had been especially so, I remembered with shame, during those black months of my all-consuming passion when I was hardly in the house in day-light at all, except for the grudging hour spent with the aunts on Saturday forenoons.

That afternoon, while Treasure was out, I made a fire in my room upstairs and sat there reading but it was the face of Treasure that came more frequently to my mind, distracting me from my book, than the familiar ill-defined vision of Isabel. I remembered the cold aloofness with which Isabel had rebuked me for my part in the 'Down with the Slums' campaign. Treasure had not rebuked me. She had merely torn the page from the newspaper that my aunts might not know of my misdemeanour. I remembered how Isabel had trodden me underfoot when she said that there were no men or women, only patients, doctors and nurses in her Casualty Ward. Treasure had never trodden me underfoot. She had always bolstered me up, adjured me to 'think more' of myself. What was this thing in the blood that rose to Isabel as if in response to a clarion call and remained unmoved by the music of Treasure's personality which was as fresh and natural as bird-song? I tried to be harshly logical. Was my genteel early background exerting an influence here? Did Treasure, despite my knowledge of her, still bear the stigma of the 'skivvies' at school to whom the 'young gentlemen' did not speak? I pushed aside these ugly ideas and chose to accept the more pleasing concept that I was attracted to Isabel basically because she was attracted to me. It was a biological fact that the insect is attracted to the flower because of reciprocal need, the insect's need for food and the flower's need for fertilisation. Thinking in these terms, I contrived to assure myself that Isabel, although she did not know it, was as much attracted to me as I was to her. If this was not so, why had she asked me to join her in Casualty when she had often expressed her preference for women students? The women, she said, were given fewer opportunities than the men; prejudice was still rife in the profession and as soon as she was in a position to have student assistance, she would give the preference to women. And she had been true to her word with one exception, myself. This could mean only one thing.

At the end of this exercise in doubtful logic, I was in such an exalted state that, as soon as Treasure returned, I went out into the windy rain and took my bliss for a long walk across the moors.

It was about nine o'clock in the evening when I turned back towards the town and it would take me about an hour to descend by the winding road through the folds of the moors that would bring me to the end of the Crescent. About half-way back, I stopped at a bend in the unfenced road and looked down towards the town in its Sunday evening silence. It was an evening of gusty wind, with a white half-moon that was blotted from sight now and then by the grey clouds that blew across the darker grey sky and under this turbulence the black earth and the black water of the loch seemed to sleep, the town hiding under its smoky blankets with a nightlight flickering here and there from an unblinded window or from a street lamp. From here, Lochview Crescent looked like a lasso thrown from a giant hand out from the town to the hillside, the houses of the Crescent held in darkness inside a loop of lights made by the lamps at the roadsides. Either end of the Crescent could be approached from the town, one end by turning left off the main street, as I had done on my first day on the instructions of the old man in the Village and the other end by the road that ran up the lochside from the railway station. The downhill road from the moors on which I was walking now divided when the woodland of the Crescent began, the right hand of the fork going to the station, the left leading to the main street. Laurelbank was situated at about the middle of the Crescent and I always found a childish pleasure in deciding whether I would approach the back lane from the town or from the lochside. Tonight, I chose the loch, which would be romantically Gothic under the uncertain moon and as I stood by the roadside looking across the black rocks at the silver-rippled black water, thinking of my Isabel, the ghosts of the romance-ridden Carlo and Kittenpuss should have arisen to haunt me but they did not. The trees of the Crescent gardens tossed their boughs, the reeds down the hill from the rocks swayed to silver and back to black, the water slapped against the rocks and the dark figure rose against the grey sky, stood wind-blown for a second on the peak of the low cliff and then jumped. I vaulted over the fence, burst through some hawthorns, dropped my mackintosh, pulled off my shoes and jumped down in pursuit. As I struck the water, I remembered how, one day when it was too cold to swim, a bigger boy had pushed me off the pier of the seaside resort near the school. I saw something surface as the water closed over me and when I came up again I saw a hand a few yards away, clutching frantically at the air and it was not very long before I had a shapeless bundle on tow down towards the reed-beds beyond the rocks. Gasping, the reeds moaning around my head, I recognised by the light of the moon the grey terrified face of Mary Lawrie. She did not speak when I had got her to her feet and began to propel her through the reeds towards the road. I helped her over the fence and still she did not speak but when I tried to turn her in the direction of the town, she swung her clumsy body around so that she faced uphill. We were both shivering, the stones of the road were cutting into my feet. It seemed easier to lead or, rather, to push and propel her towards Laurelbank.

Treasure had gone to bed. There was not a light to be seen

in the house except a small blue jet that burned in the passage inside the back door. I took Mary in, set her down in a heap on the back stairs and locked the door in case she might be inspired to return to the loch, although she looked so inert that the possibility was remote. I then tiptoed up the back stairs and tapped on the door. 'Treasure!'

'Mr Charles! Come in. What's wrong? Is it the ladies?'

I opened the door to find Treasure disposing of her book with one hand while putting a slipper on her foot with the other and then: 'Mr Charles, you're dripping wet! You'll catch your death. What have you been up to?'

'It's Mary Lawrie. She's downstairs. She jumped into the loch.'

'Mary—' Treasure's eyes stared, seemed to grow dark, then to gleam with understanding. 'Oh, the bloody fool!' and she was off downstairs.

I stood, dripping, in the middle of Treasure's floor after we had brought Mary up and set her down on a chair with a pool forming around her. I came to full consciousness only when Treasure opened a drawer and took out a white nightdress and with the consciousness, rage at Mary Lawrie rushed upon me.

'*She* can't get into anything of yours!' I said, pointing at the inert lump on the chair. 'I'll get her a suit of my pyjamas.'

'Maybe you're right.' Treasure dropped the nightdress. 'Get out of your own clothes while you're at it and put a kettle on in the pantry and a pan of milk. Here's some matches. Watch your eye now and don't disturb the ladies.' She turned to Mary: 'Now then, you, get these wet clothes off.'

Cursing the aunts' 'waste-not-want-not' as we called it, that decreed that every light be turned out when they retired to their bedrooms, I lit the gas in the pantry, my shaking hands endangering the mantle, and put the kettle and the pan of milk on the gas cooker. The light from the pantry saw me safely round Lord Mammon and up the staircase but the upper landing was as dark as the pit. As a rule, when I came in late, I could find my way in the dark but the guilt of having a stranger in the house made me fearful. Having listened to the snores beyond the heavy doors which were, I knew, curtained inside with plush to exclude draughts, I struck a match, lit both mantles of a gas bracket on the wall and defiantly turned both lights up full. I felt like Lady Macbeth crying 'More light! More light!' as I shivered on the snore-sounding landing and then lit the bracket in my bathroom and two more in my bedroom.

I stripped off my clothes, got into pyjamas and dressing-gown, found pyjamas for Mary and ran back to the pantry where I filled a hot water bottle and made a jug of cocoa.

When I went back to the attic, Mary was sitting in Treasure's bed with a woollen cardigan buttoned round her shoulders, her flat moon face looking sullen and once again fury exploded inside my chest. How dare she sit there in that bed, waiting for the next thing to happen to her? Treasure took the pyjamas which were over my arm.

'Thanks, Mr Charles. Put the tray over there. Did you bring some biscuits?'

'No. I'll get some.'

When I came back again, Mary was wearing my pyjamas, which was less offensive but she was still a grey lump in the white bed.

'Right, Mary, drink this cocoa. It's Pat McPhee's, isn't it?' and Treasure looked at the lump under the sheet. 'Ach, never heed Mr Charles, ye bloody fool. He's a *doctor*, for the lord's sake. It's Pat's, isn't it?'

'Aye.'

'And where is Pat now?'

'I don't know.'

'As far away as he can get, likely. And so your old man showed you the door? When?'

'When he came home from the kirk. All of a sudden, he

noticed and then—' She moved her heavy shoulders, shrugging events away, nullifying them under the weight of her inertia.

'And so then you come up here and chuck yourself in the loch?' Treasure pursued. Mary did not reply. She chewed on a mouthful of biscuit and swallowed some cocoa. 'Well, Mr Charles pulled you out and if you try that again I'll report you to Beery-belly so what are you going to do now?'

'I don't know.'

'Have you any money?'

'No.'

'Where is Paul?' There was no response. 'Here, you, wake up! In the name o' the Kingdom o' Heaven, ye've got a nerve, Mary Lawrie! Ye nearly get Mr Charles his death an' then ye come in here an' go to sleep. Listen, where's Paul your brother?'

'Twenty-two Bright Street, London S.E.9.'

'If you go to London, will Paul take you in?'

'I don't know.'

'Well you'll have to try. You can't stop here.'

'No money,' said Mary and yawned, as if bored with the entire discussion.

'Ah help my Jimmie Johnson,' said Treasure, 'she's hopeless. Mary, ye're goin' to London on the night train tomorrow!'

'All right,' said Mary and slumped down into sleep, spilling dregs of cocoa on the sheet.

Treasure stood looking down at her. 'In the name o' the kingdom,' she said, 'I could murder her. Aye and you as well, Mr Charles. Just think o' the how-d'ye-do in Lochfoot if this gets out. They'll say the bastard is *yours*!'

'Well, it isn't,' I said. 'Let's go down to the pantry. It will be warmer.'

Seated at the pantry table, with a second brew of cocoa between us, Treasure said: 'All right, Mr Charles. Halvers. How much will it take to get her to London and a bit extra just in case? I think the Saint will take her in though. He's all right at heart. It's the rest o' him that's the bother but that won't bother Mary.'

'You are not *in* this, Treasure,' I said. 'I got her out of the loch and I'll get her to London.'

I spoke with all the decision I could command but I hoped that Treasure would not hear the echo from the pit of uncertainty inside me. What with the 'Down with the Slums' campaign, my walking tour, the Settlement and taking Teresa out, my savings had dwindled away for my allowance was not staying the distance from a month's beginning to the end. I had now only some fifty pounds left in my savings account and if I gave thirty of this to Mary Lawrie I would be in very serious case. Yet, the girl must have at least thirty pounds, to allow some margin in case the doubtful Saint proved to be a true son of his father.

'After all,' I said now, 'do we have to send her to London? If I go down tomorrow and see her father and tell him how—'

'Mr Charles,' said Treasure sadly, 'sometimes I think you are too innocent for this world, honest I do. Old Boney would jump to it right away that the bairn was yours.'

'Oh, rubbish!'

'Mr Charles, ye can't mix with the crows without getting shot at. One thing follows another. I told you long ago that I don't trust doing good turns to folk. Oh, I know you jumped into the loch after Mary without stopping to think but start thinking *now* for the lord's sake.'

'Oh, all right. I'll take her up to town tomorrow and put her on the night train. We'll have to catch the one-thirty. The bank closes at three.'

Treasure sprang up in exasperation. 'Finish that cocoa and get off to your bed,' she told me, 'and try and get your brain cleared before the morning. I think you've got some o' the loch water in it. Imagine you parading down to the station with Mary Lawrie and that bundle under her belt! You'll go down-the-line in the forenoon as usual and I'll send Mary to the eight o'clock train at night, after it's dark. It will take me till then to get her clothes dried anyway and a bonnie ticket she will look but it won't matter for she was never an oil painting. And you'll meet her in Glasgow, buy her ticket and put her on the London train. Have you got that into your thick head?'

'Yes, Treasure.'

'Well, get off to your bed for goodness' sake.' As I got to my feet, her mood changed and her face became thoughtful. 'I wonder what possessed Mary Lawrie to get herself into this mess for Pat McPhee of all men?' she said. 'She must have known all the time that he would never marry her. Tinkers like their own kind.'

At the thought of the intimacy between Mary and her lover, the thought of Isabel possessed my mind suddenly and I felt blood rushing hot to my head and face. To cover my confusion, I turned away and said: 'I suppose she heard the Pipes of Pan one night when the moon was full and the wind was whispering in the reeds.'

There was a vibrant silence which made me look back from the doorway at Treasure by the table. Her eyes were very large and blue above the blue dressing-gown she wore and her little face had the age-old wisdom of the street urchin's face. 'The pipes o' Pat McPhee ye mean,' she said scathingly. 'Goodnight.'

I went up to bed but I could not sleep, probably through nervous reaction to all the excitement but it took the form of a niggling uncertainty about my financial situation which led me to more and more resentment of Mary Lawrie. If fate had to elect me to rescue a damsel in distress, I felt, it should have provided me with a more delectable damsel than that suety lump now sleeping in Treasure's room, seeming to imbue the place so private with something of her sordid ill-arranged life.

While the wind moaned out-of-doors around the grey block

that was the house and indoors the furniture creaked forth its night sounds, it became nightmarishly grotesque to think of the aunts, two old women snoring inside their cocoon of wealth while, in another part of the house, there was a young woman, pregnant, with no money and no armour against the winds of the world. I heard the big clock down in the hall strike four, thought of Lord Mammon guarding the temple and as I hovered at last on the edge of sleep, I thought of three pounds weight of solid silver, tortured into the hideous form of two snakes and a vulture, lying in the darkness of the mahogany coal-box in the strong-room down below. Last of all, I thought of Isabel, tried to picture her, but the only pictures that came were of Treasure in a blue dressing-gown saying 'The pipes o' Pat McPhee' and of Mary Lawrie, in Treasure's bed, wearing my pyjamas. Isabel took the form of a flame in the blood, a sharp tingling of the nerves but there was no mental picture.

I was awakened, within moments of going to sleep, it seemed, by a heavy pounding on the panels of my door but even although this was unusual, I had time for the thought that that nightmare idea of 'pinching the snake inkstand', as Treasure would put it, just went to show how distorted one's mind could become in the small sleepless hours.

'Charles!' came the furious voice of Aunt Bessie. 'Charles, come out here this moment!'

I remembered Mary Lawrie and a sweat of terror broke on the back of my neck to be followed by the thought that to be terrified was ridiculous. Aunt Bessie could not kill me. People were not killed for pulling people out of lochs. Treasure would be furious at this upset but this time I would give Aunt Bessie a piece of my mind and ask her for the money to send Mary Lawrie to London into the bargain. I hauled on my dressing-gown, wrenched the door wide open and there was Aunt Bessie, like some primitive priestess in a long grey woollen robe.

'Charles, how dare you? Do you want us all to end up in the work-house? Look at these lights! Just look at them! And still asleep when you should be at your lessons. Really, it is disgraceful!'

'What is it, Bessie?' Aunt Jessie enquired from her doorway.

'Nine o'clock in the morning and every light in the house ablaze! It is enough to make dear papa turn in his grave. Charles, get dressed this instant!'

She turned off the lights on the landing, swept into her room and both doors closed before Treasure, her eyes huge, appeared round the corner of the stairs. 'Holy jumpin' cats,' she whispered, 'I thought they'd found out about Mary!'

'Me too,' I said and retired, deflated, to my room, cursing my double stupidity of forgetting the lights and then oversleeping. But, by the time I had washed and dressed, my mood had changed. The work-house indeed! My *lessons* forsooth! I was twenty years old and those two stupid old women did not seem to understand that I could take them one in each hand and crack their silly heads together. Why should I forgo cups of tea at the Sutherland with Isabel and the cinema with Teresa to help somebody that they could help without even knowing that they had helped her? I took the smaller Gladstone bag from the bottom of the wardrobe. It closed and no more over the snake inkstand from the strong-room. Leaving the bag at the bottom of the back stairs, I went up to Treasure's room and finalised our arrangement with her and Mary. I sold the inkstand in a back-street pawnshop near the Settlement for forty pounds. I met Mary, bought her ticket, gave her all the money that was left and watched gladly as the London train steamed out.

I then came home to Laurelbank but I did not tell Treasure what I had done. Treasure had introduced me to her theory of 'Laurelbank honesty' but I had carried the theory a little further, I thought, than Treasure would approve. According to Treasure, one had to give value by the lights of the ladies for what one took and the ladies would not regard the attempted rescue of Mary Lawrie as value for their silver ink-stand. It irked me, though, that the lumpish Mary Lawrie should have been the cause of the first Laurelbank secret that I had ever kept from Treasure.

CHAPTER ELEVEN

Stitch! Stitch! Stitch!
In poverty, hunger and dirt,
And still with a voice of dolourous pitch,
She sang the 'Song of the Shirt'.
'Song of the Shirt,' by Thomas Hood.

WHAT Treasure called 'the Mary Lawrie set-to' left its mark on the household for some time. The lights found burning on the landing when Aunt Bessie arose to go to the bathroom at nine in the morning took several weeks before they were totally extinguished.

When I returned in the evening after despatching Mary Lawrie to London, Treasure said: 'I've been had into the morning-room, Mr Charles. We'll have to watch our eyes for a bit. The ladies are upset enough to pop out to make sure you are sober when you come home from Glasgow.'

'Sober?'

'They think you came in drunk last night and lit the lights full up after I had turned them off and then forgot about them.'

'As long as they don't think that *you* forgot about them, that is all right,' I said.

'Well, I've lied myself black and blue so you'd better stick to the same story for there's sure to be another Battle o' the Boyne when you go in there on Saturday forenoon. I said you came in at exactly twenty past nine and went upstairs and I went up behind you and put out the lights. I said that you told me this morning that you had dropped a half-crown on the landing and that I believed you, because I had kicked something at the top of the stairs when I went up to do the lights. After you got undressed, when you counted your money, you missed the half-crown.'

'Don't be ridiculous, Treasure! As if I would do anything so silly as stand around half-naked counting loose change!'

'Dear papa,' she said in the voice of Aunt Bessie, 'counted the money from his pockets last thing every night and put it in two piles on top of the chest of drawers, the silver in one pile, the copper in the other. His wallet, of course, he locked in his desk.' She changed to her own voice: 'Listen to *me*, Mr Charles Simpson, do you want to get the upper hand of this Mary Lawrie set-to or not?'

'Oh, all right. I counted the bloody money.'

'So you came out and lit the gas full up to look for the half-crown and you found it away at the back of the Discounts table where I must have kicked it, see?'

'I see. All right, but they'll have calmed down by Saturday. But, Treasure, if you look all this straight in the face, it is silly. Why don't I simply tell the aunts about Mary Lawrie and the loch and that I forgot about the lights?'

'And get me the sack?'

'Don't be silly. They'd never sack *you*.'

'Maybe that's true,' she admitted, 'but they wouldn't like to know about Mary jumping in the loch and you getting her out. They would think things about you like old Boney Lawrie would, Mr Charles. And then there's us having Mary up the back stairs and everything. It would all upset them. Jumping into the loch is disgraceful. Your Uncle Charlie jumped into the loch and the ladies have never got over it. Och, no, Mr Charles, it would never do to tell them all that. They wouldn't like it, but they'll *like* the story about you counting your money and missing the half-crown. You'll see for yourself that they do.'

The next Saturday forenoon, I did indeed see for myself

that the aunts approved of my counting my loose change every night as a ceremonial before sleep, as followers of another religion might say prayers.

'Look after the pennies, dear papa used to say and the pounds will look after themselves,' said Aunt Bessie.

But in this house, where we looked after the pennies, the pounds lay forgotten under door mats until Treasure 'looked after' them.

'But dear papa, your – er – grandpapa is no longer with us to provide for us, Charles. We are living on capital.'

They were not. I knew from Mr Guthrie that they were living on interest and from my own observation of them I knew that they did not know the difference between capital and interest. 'There is nothing coming in, nothing at all, so we have to be careful and in future you must remember the gas. Jeanie assures us that you were not the worse for liquor that night which was the only reason we could think of for such carelessness.'

By the time Treasure came back from the shops, I was in a raging temper. What would Isabel think if she had heard me being lectured like that? If I had the guts of a louse, I would tell the aunts what to do with their money and clear out. Only a bounder would take money made out of slum property anyway.

'Now then, Mr Charles, sit down before you bust your boiler,' said Treasure. 'That old rascal Guthrie is real fond o' you and if he gets his way, the ladies' money won't all go to the Cat an' Dog Home after all. 'Smatter of fact, I think some of it is down for foreign missions so that they can buy bibles for the poor heathens. I would rather see *you* get the money and leave the heathens in peace.'

'You are off your head! The aunts would never—'

'Damn the fear of me being off my head. My head was screwed on real tight long ago. The last time old Guthrie was here, he had a big lump of hard rustly paper with him and he came out o' the morning-room looking like a dog wi' two tails. Mr Guthrie doesn't go on the Cat and Dog Home or the heathens any more than I do and I bet you he's knocking off quite a nice bit on the side for himself out o' the ladies. He deserves it. He can get them to swallow things like this new pantry and you coming to live here without upsetting them a bit.'

Treasure, that artist of a liar when minimising the amount of 'upset to the ladies' was incapable of telling a lie about her views of the world and its people. There was a stark truth about the aunts in the manner in which she spoke of myself and the new pantry in relation to them in the same breath for this, I was convinced, was how the aunts saw me. I was an upset, like the installation of the pantry but, unlike the pantry, I was a continuous upset. Treasure was correct too in her estimate of Mr Guthrie. The old man was genuinely fond of me, considered me not such a 'cissie' after all following the Down with the Slums campaign and I could see for myself that he was a realist, with little sympathy for cat and dog homes and bibles for the heathen. He had, too, the Victorian respect for wealth, although he knew too much about it and its uses to fear it as a mysterious god in the way that the aunts did and he had told me in so many words the very first time I had met him that he liked what he called 'continuity'. If he could persuade the aunts to leave me some money, I could buy a good practice and Isabel and I—

'So you turn your pride down low like the gas on the landing, Mr Charles,' Treasure advised me, 'and save these poor heathens from the bibles and use the money to build yourself a new clinic at the Louse Patch, if you like. You could have a delouser in it. Somebody has invented one. I read about it in the paper.'

And so, with a few more Saturday forenoon lectures about the gas and the evils of liquor, the Mary Lawrie set-to slipped into the past, its final note being an ill-written postcard to

Treasure which told us that Mary was having a nice time with Paul and his wife and sent me her kind regards.

Christmas came along and Treasure and I celebrated it very much as we had done the year before. I gave her a large red-bound volume of the complete works of Shakespeare, for I had discovered that she was addicted to the sonnets and she gave me a gold-mounted fountain pen with the little letters 'CS/TR' engraved on the band.

'Fancy me thinking you could write cough mixtures in pencil,' she said. 'They have to be in ink. It just shows I didn't think at all. I got into the habit of not thinking when I was at the school and sometimes it comes over me still. The schoolmaster was Mr Cockburn. He's dead now, poor old brute. Old Cock, we called him. You are not-a here to think, he used to say. You are-a here to learn-a the ten-a command-a-ments.'

She dropped the character of Old Cock and became herself in her graver mood. 'Mr Charles, schools should teach things and not thoughts. School sickened me of the ten commandments for life.'

'Things and not thoughts?' I repeated.

'Aye, things like 1314-Battle-o'-Bannockburn are all right for folk that want to know about history. But what's the good o' teaching thoughts like honour-thy-father-and-thy-mother to folk that's got fathers and mothers that get drunk every night and leather them black and blue like a lot o' the folk that was at the school with me? The Battle o' Bannockburn happened in 1314 and there's damn all you can do about that but folk don't have to *think* what folk thought in 1314 for gyad's sake.'

'I see what you mean,' I said lamely.

'Still, I'm glad I went to the school although it was pretty good purgat'ry at the time, because I learned to read. Reading, you can learn other folks' thoughts if you want them and throw away the ones that are no good to you.'

'Have you thrown away any thoughts lately, Treasure?'

'Are you not the funny man? Come on, let's give Christmas Day in the Workhouse. Where's the Gyarland? There are so many dirty words to that thing, I can never remember the real ones without the book.'

I enjoyed spending Christmas Day with Treasure for it was peaceful, comfortable and familiar but I thought a great deal about Isabel, as I did every day and wondered what it would be like to spend hours alone with her like this. I did not speak of Isabel to Treasure any more than I spoke of Treasure to Isabel. Both were private areas of thought of which I spoke to no other person but at times when the thoughts of Isabel became too dominant, I would speak to Treasure of her brothers, especially my medical fellows, David and Ian for I saw very little of Colin nowadays.

The Adair brothers, of course, had gone home to Perthshire for the Christmas vacation and Isabel had gone with them, on four days' leave from the Casualty Ward. Perthshire seemed to me to be a hundred thousand miles away, although in the summer I had walked past the boundaries of the estate where the Adairs lived. This feeling of distance, however, had the effect of cooling my fever somewhat, so that I could see matters in less delirious terms and I began to be aware that my position in relation to Isabel was not only false but verged upon the absurd.

She was four years older than I was and this, along with my chance resemblance to her brothers – strong in relation to Colin, less so in relation to David and Ian – made her attitude to me big-sisterly and the fact that I was a student, working under her in the Casualty Ward, stressed the senior-to-junior slant. Then, in the early days of my friendship with Colin, I had given him the impression that the aunts were in straitened circumstances, an impression that had been unwillingly strengthened by Treasure on the day that we met him at the teashop. Colin remembered the days when 'seven were kept' in the houses of the Crescent and in his eyes, no doubt, the diminutive Treasure must have looked like a serious reduction in circumstances.

Whatever the reasons, Isabel regarded me as one more student on limited pocket-money and extended a cool friendship towards me because I was a friend of her brothers. I, on the other hand, longed to court her, to spend my allowance on taking her to dinner and the theatre as often as she would come, instead of holding hands with Teresa in picture houses. But if Isabel had known of my allowance, generous in the eyes of all students other than those of a small gilded clique, I feared that the old Lochview Crescent-Lochfoot cleavage would have come into operation so that Isabel probably would not even have me in her Casualty Ward.

'Colin Adair told me once that when he was at school you all thought that all the people in the Crescent here were millionaires,' I said to Treasure in the course of our musicale.

'So we did,' she confirmed. 'I used to think that God lived at the Castle and that the Crescent folk were the archangels or something.'

'But it's ridiculous,' I protested. 'People are just people.'

'No, they're not,' she told me firmly. 'They've all got a set of circumstances around them like an iron railing or the Castle wall and there's no good thinking you can do away with them, because you can't. They pull people together and they pull them apart and there's damnall you can do about it or not much. Talking about circumstances, the ladies are bothering me a bit. They read in the *Leader* about somebody breaking into the chocolate machine at the station and it has brought back that fright you gave them when you told them about the Louse Patch. When I go out on Wednesdays, they ask me how soon I'll be back and when you will be in.'

'It is a lot of nonsense, Treasure,' I told her. 'Don't take any notice of them. If you give way, they will leave you with no free time at all.'

'That is just what I was thinking. Quite often, before, I

never bothered to go out on Wednesday or on my monthly Sunday, but I go out now for all my off time, so as not to get the ladies into bad habits. But it's funny how contrary things are. It's sort of unreasonable.'

'It is the aunts who are unreasonable and you pay far too much attention to them.'

'I don't like to see them upset,' she said quietly, 'but they don't understand that there's other folk in the world besides them and you have to draw the line somewhere. What about another song?'

From long practice, we knew every sentimental ballad in the music stand and every piece of bad verse in the Garland of Gems. In the latter, however, there were three pieces that we ignored by mutual consent. My father had been wont to reduce his audiences to tears with his recitation of 'The Burial of Sir John Moore at Corunna' but I considered this poem to be too sincere for our burlesque treatment and another of my father's recitations had been 'Sennacherib' which we both felt to be in the same category. Of this last, Treasure said: 'It's good but I don't like it. It makes me think of Mr Adair's lambs long ago and the Assyrian coming down on them like a wolf on the fold.' The third piece of verse that we ignored was Hood's 'Song of the Shirt', also because Treasure did not like it, although she was less forthcoming about the reason for her dislike than she was about 'Sennacherib'. 'I just don't like it,' she said, her small face closed and unusually sullen.

'It is too bad to like or dislike,' I said.

'I still don't like it,' she repeated.

It was another demonstration of the attitude she had to Lord Mammon, a shuddering revulsion that she could not or would not explain.

When we had performed another ballad or two, Treasure sat down on the hearthrug and said: 'It was nice of Mary Lawrie to send us that Christmas card but imagine her putting Miss Jean Robertson and Mr Charles Simpson on the envelope like that, the bloody fool! If the ladies had seen it, they'd have bust their boilers.'

'I know but then Mary was always as thick in the head as sh—'

'That's enough, you! None of that vulgar talk, Mr Charles. I suppose we'll have to write her a letter. To tell the truth, I never even thought of sending her a card. I'd forgotten all 'bout her.'

'So had I.'

'I suppose we wanted to forget her,' said Treasure, firing dead centre on target as usual. 'After all, she's not what you would call a bee-eautiful memory.'

'Treasure,' I said suddenly, out of some confusion of thought about Mary Lawrie, Teresa, Isabel and myself, 'what do you intend to do with your life? You can't stay in this barrack of a house for ever.'

'I don't know,' she answered, with her wide-eyed look of solemn honesty. 'I've never wanted to do anything in partic'lar, like you wanting so much to be a doctor, Mr Charles. I suppose I'll just wait and see what turns up.'

'I suppose you will get married.'

'I don't know.' She wrinkled her brow. 'Most women like me get married to get a home of their own. Oh, they think they are in love and all that stuff,' she said scornfully, 'but it's the home o' their own that they're really after.'

Her scorn irritated me. 'So you don't believe in love?' I enquired in superior tones.

She ignored my superiority. 'I believe it can happen. It happened to Shakespeare.' She nodded at the book I had given her where it lay on the sofa. 'But I am not Shakespeare and if you think that's the greatest thought o' the present year, you should watch your eye. And I don't have to get married to get a home, because I've got a home already, Lilac Cottage, in the Village.'

'What if somebody came along with an estate of six thousand a year like in Jane Austen?'

'If he had six thousand a year, he wouldn't want *me*,' she said. 'Money goes to money. And even if he did think he wanted me, I would likely tell him to shove it because a man with six thousand a year wouldn't *need* me. My granny was my grandfather's second wife. He was left a widower with my father no more than a baby. My granny married him because he needed her and so did the baby. I don't know much about love, Mr Charles, but I know about being needed and not needed. I would rather stay here where the ladies need me than get married just for the sake of getting married, like so many folk do.'

'But what about children, Treasure? Wouldn't you like to have a family?'

She was thoughtful. 'I don't know. I might be like my mother and *your* mother too – I might not like them after I had them. Besides, there's too many bairns in the world already – look at that Louse Patch o' yours – and Mary Lawrie is having another one. No. I think I'll give getting married a bye. I can't see anybody needing me enough.'

I thought of Isabel, wondered if she needed me as I needed her and could not conceive of Isabel 'needing' anyone or anything.

'And you don't need anybody?' I asked Treasure, envious of her serenity and contentment.

'No. I am doing fine, thanks. Give me one more performance o' the "Yellow God", Mr Charles and then I'll have to go and see to the ladies' dinner.'

For the rest of the vacation until the spring term at the university opened, the weather was very wet and I went out very little and to Glasgow not at all. I was tempted to go to the Casualty Ward on the Saturday evenings but I was huffy with Isabel for retiring into the bosom of her family over Christmas as if I did not exist and I also wanted to avoid

Teresa. I was beginning to feel too guilty for comfort about Teresa. With the grey weather beyond the walls and Treasure singing in the pantry, the fantasy world which had come into being in the house encircled me again and Isabel and the world outside became very remote.

On a day between Christmas and the New Year, Treasure went down to the Village during the afternoon to pay her annual call on her tenants and I carried the tea tray, which she had left prepared, into the morning-room. The Mary Lawrie set-to was now well behind us but the aunts did not like the small difference in routine of my arriving with the tray, although Treasure had pre-arranged it with them. When I went into the room, they were sitting tensely upright in their chairs, their hands idle, their spectacles nowhere in sight, as if ever since they had arisen from their lie-down they had been steeling themselves for my arrival. I put the tray beside Aunt Bessie and got out of the room as quickly as I could but, even so, their edginess had affected me and in the hall, with its turned-down glimmer of gaslight, I paused and looked up, feeling the weight of the house above and all around me. At that moment, the lamp-lighter came along the road outside with his flame on the end of its long pole and applied it to the lamp on the pavement at the front gate. The first bright flare of light struck the stained glass windows of the hall and filtered through on to Lord Mammon, turning him to a brilliant amber colour all over, except for one spot of bright green on the front of his helmet. 'The green-eyed yellow god!' I had time to think before the light from the street lamp dulled to a steady white glow and Lord Mammon lost colour and merged into the dimness again. Hastily, I drew the hall curtains which I should have drawn earlier. But it had been a nasty moment which made me wonder how Treasure had borne with the aunts and with this house for so long, especially during the time before my arrival when, for long days on end, she had seen and talked to nobody. I went into the cheerful pantry, despising myself. Even nowadays, when I was in Glasgow, Treasure spent long hours alone in this place which was causing my own nerves to jump at the end of a single hour.

I tried to read but could not concentrate and was glad when six o'clock came when Treasure's notes began. '6 p.m. Please turn oven on medium. 6.15 Put in pie.' After that, there was something to be done every fifteen minutes as I followed her careful programme and then I remembered that I had not taken out the tea tray, which I fetched an hour and a half late to the accompaniment of sad sighs from the aunts. 'Studying to be a doctor and he cannot even serve tea!' When seven o'clock came, I began to open the baize door at the top of the basement stairs and listen for Treasure's return and then I began to go down to the back door and peer into the darkness of the drive. Next I left the back door open altogether and listened every two minutes at the top of the stairs. At last, I was sure I heard a sound and opened the green baize door to hear Treasure's voice: 'If I am not there at five, you will know that I can't manage. Goodnight,' and a male voice said: 'Goodnight.' I let the green door close quietly and ran up the stairs to my room. I did not know whether I was jealous or angry or merely afraid but I was certainly what Treasure would call 'upset' and I stood in the middle of the floor in my dark bedroom, trying desperately to regain control of myself for she would think it odd if I were not at my post in the pantry. Hitherto, on her infrequent outings, I had been meticulous in my attention to her instructions. I ran downstairs.

'Oh, you are back, Treasure! I must have left the door of my room open. It was banging. I think the dinner's all right. Did you have a nice visit?'

'Yes, thanks, but that poor young Mr Gilmour is awful sick. It must be terrible for his mother, watching him get sicker every day. He can't lift his teacup now. They have to help him.'

But there had been someone at the back door who was not 'awful sick' and she said nothing about *him*. She merely checked the pans on the stove, looked at the pie in the oven and said: 'Thank you, Mr Charles' before going up to her room to change into her uniform.

Nor did Treasure even mention who had come to the back door with her but during the ensuing week she asked me if I could be at home on the following Sunday evening so that she might go out. I agreed and after that she went out on most Sundays but only for an hour or two on most occasions. She usually brought the tea tray out before she went and returned in time to serve dinner for she was still true to her rule that the ladies must not be upset.

The year had turned again. After tea on New Year's day, we once more had the ceremony of the Discounts and once more the ham from the butcher was smaller than ever and when the spring term began, I went to Glasgow with my larger Gladstone bag, carrying the side of bacon to the Settlement.

Now that I was back at work and, more important, back in the ambience of Isabel, I became more reasonable and tolerant about Treasure's 'follower' as I thought of him, in the parlance of the aunts. There was a subtle fleeting resemblance between Treasure and the girls at the shirt factory with some of whom she had gone to school but I could not imagine Treasure indulging in the raucous giggling, pushing and shoving which was the form that courtship seemed to take between Maisie and her colleagues and the railway porters, vanmen and lorry drivers. I did not realise, of course, that I could not imagine Treasure at all except as seen by my own eyes against the background of Laurelbank and that I did not know her except in relation to that world which, in self-defence against its monstrous quality, we had peopled with fantasies.

And in the early part of 1926, Laurelbank itself lost some

of its significance in my mind for things were afoot in the world that might put even its solidity in jeopardy. The spring before, a few of us had caused a local uproar with our Down with the Slums campaign but this spring it was not only a few 'student hot-heads' who became restive, but the entire working-class population of the country until the injustices and frustrations, the social evils and the blind greed that underlay them exploded into the General Strike of the month of May, a strike that paralysed the country.

The university population split into three factions over the Strike. There was the large majority who, like Colin Adair, went on with their studies while complaining about the transport difficulties; there was a fair number made up mainly of men of wealthier background who regarded the affair as a lark that gave them the opportunity to drive for no pay the trains and trams that the workers had been underpaid for driving and there was an even smaller number, including myself, who ranged themselves on the side of the strikers, sympathising with them, although we could give little practical help.

Indeed, when the Strike became general and the trains ceased to run, all I could do was to try not to blame the striking railwaymen for separating me from Isabel and I prowled about the moors above the Crescent, fulminating at my own uselessness, cursing the aunts who ate and slept their days away as usual, refusing even to be conscious of the crisis and the misery beyond the walls of the house.

On about the third day of national stand-still, I came down from the moors in the late afternoon by the lochside road that joined the main street near the station and found that, here, the nation was far from standing still. In the street, there was nobody other than myself but in the yard of the shirt factory there was a furious shouting mob of girls and women and at the centre of it the redoubtable Maisie, who seemed to be threatening grievous bodily harm to her red-faced employer.

He was backing away from the building, trying to reach the gate in the fence and the safety of the road but he was impeded by the mob of women who swarmed round him like wasps.

'Get the police!' he shouted at me. 'The police!'

I opened the gate, went into the yard, caught one of the girls by the arm and asked her what was the matter.

'It's Maisie. She's worked here ever since she left the school and now he's sacked her, the dirty bugger!'

The screams rose in volume and somebody clawed the man's red face from behind, leaving three red weals down his cheek.

'Don't!' I shouted. 'Don't fight! Don't assault him! Strike!'

Maisie turned her back on the man, thrust the crowd of women away on either side of her and strode towards me, her arms akimbo, her eyes glaring through her tousled hair. 'What the hell you doin' here, Prince Charlie?'

'The whole country is on strike,' I said, waving my hand at the silent station, at the empty tramcar standing at the terminus. 'You people shouldn't be working either.'

'Jesus,' said Maisie, 'who's for Prince Charlie?' She turned to the red-faced man, spat on the gravel at his feet. 'Ye can take ma machine an' ye ken where ye can put it. Ye've got plenty o' room for it up that hole, ye big bladder o' lard. I'm on *strike*!'

'Strike!' the others began to shout and forgetting about me and their employer who was slinking towards the empty factory, they went streaming out of the gate and up the main street of the town, their shrill voices tearing the air of the spring evening to ribbons.

The railways and tramcars had begun to operate again before the shirt factory girls went back to work. During the period of full nation-wide stoppage, I used to walk through the town each day and usually met Maisie and one or two of the others. They were defiant. They were not going back to work unless the 'factory takes back Maisie and gives us our thruppence', for I learned that Maisie had been threatened with the sack when she had asked for an extra threepence on the nine-hour day for herself and the senior workers and an extra twopence for the younger girls.

The thing that appalled me most about these women was their ignorance about their social rights. They were unaware of having any rights and I had to explain to Maisie that the police could not imprison her for refusing to work, but that she could be severely punished if she caused bodily injury to her employer or did any damage to his property.

When the train service was restored, I began to travel to Glasgow again but I maintained contact with the factory women and by the middle of the third week of idleness, their faces began to look pinched and some of them were abandoning all hope that they would win their 'thruppence'. At this stage, I did not want to see them fail and one evening, as I travelled home on the train, I thought of how I would probably meet some of their pinched faces, for the women stood around the outside of the factory fence for most of the day and in the next moment I thought of that miser's hoard of silver at Laurelbank. I would sell some more of it and keep these women on strike for six months if need be, I decided and let them return to work only when I had found a negotiator who would obtain their 'thruppence' for them.

When I came out of the station, Maisie and some of the others were by the fence and I called her aside. 'Maisie,' I said, 'you must be getting short of money.' I took out my wallet. 'Look—'

'Ye dirty brute!' she interrupted me. 'If ye're lookin' for a cheap lay, Maggie Gordon up the Back Lane'll oblige ye. She takes a shillin' a time.' She was turning away but she checked suddenly, seemed to sense the sickness I felt at the gulf of distrust between us. Her sharp eyes glared at me from under her tousled hair. 'Ye mean ye'd help us wi' *money*, money for *nothin'*?' she asked, with shrill stress on the final word.

'Yes, Maisie.'

'Ye must be daft. Naebody pays money for nothin'. Awa' an' bile yer can. We can manage. We're goin' to win. Auld Arse'ole – Mr Hassall to you – is down-the-line seein' the bosses the day. He's askin' them for our thruppence. We'll get it, ye'll see. He'll be back on the next train, likely.'

The next morning, when I went to the station, there was a line of women inside the factory fence and I crossed the station yard to raucous cries of: 'Three cheers, Prince Charlie, we got our thruppence!' Maisie came out through the gate and stopped me.

'Jist you watch your eye roon' aboot here, Prince Charlie,' she told me mock sternly. 'I'm the new fore-wumman!' and she dealt me a rousing slap between the shoulder blades.

All day, I felt extremely pleased with myself, felt that I had struck a small blow for the have-nots like myself and went home in the evening in high spirits. Treasure was not in the pantry but spread on the table was a copy of the *Lochfoot Leader*, the local weekly newspaper which was back in print after a two-week lapse. On the front page was the black headline: 'Prince Charlie marches again! Strike at the O.K. Shirt Factory.'

I was reading the exaggerated report when Treasure came into the room and looked at me across the table before her eyes filled with tears that spilled over and ran down her cheeks. 'Oh, Mr Charles,' she said, 'why did you do it? Oh, *why* did you do it?'

'Oh, lord, have the aunts seen this?'

'No. It's not that.' She sniffed, mopped her eyes. 'But *why* did you do it? That place of all places?'

'Treasure, I don't understand. If the aunts haven't seen this—'

'Ach, that!' Passionately, she seized the newspaper, screwed it into a bundle and pushed it into the small rubbish bin beside the sink. She then looked up at me. 'No. You don't understand. Mr Charles, you're *that* innocent and it's all my fault. I should have told you but I didn't want you even to *know* about him, didn't want you to be *in* it with him even as much as knowing his name.'

'But, Treasure, who?'

'That man on the train that you call the Pauper. That's old Pillans. That's the man my mother married and he's bad, Mr Charles. He's real bad, *pure* badness all the way through. And he *owns* the shirt factory.'

'Well, he has to pay the girls threepence a day more now,' I said. 'Why are you so worried, Treasure? He can afford it.'

'Afford it? He could buy and sell half Lochfoot but he's a miser, a *real* miser and *real* bad. He'll get back at you for this, Mr Charles. He'll get back at you!'

'Nonsense. Sit down. What can old Whatsisname do to *me*?'

'I don't know.' Weakly, she sat down. 'But I'm frightened, Mr Charles.'

'Then don't be. If he tries to hit me at the station, I am bigger than he is.'

'He'll not do that. He fights dirty, not clean. I wish you hadn't done it, Mr Charles.'

'Well, I did it and that's the end of it.'

She shook her head slowly from side to side. 'With Pillans, nothing ever ends,' she said.

I did not understand why she was so worried and she could not explain further than she had already tried to do. She seemed to have an irrational horror of the man, Pillans, similar to the horror she had of Lord Mammon and the snake-bodied dragons on the scrolls in the drawing-room and now I remembered that moment when the lamplighter's torch had turned the bronze figure in the hall into a green-eyed yellow monster. My own moment of terror then had been irrational too and I felt that if this house could render myself irrational in the space of an hour or two, it was little wonder that my latest thoughtless escapade which might 'upset the ladies' had made Treasure, whose nerves were probably over-taut already, nearly hysterical when the newspaper headlines glared up at her.

'You have got yourself all upset like the ladies, Treasure,' I told her, 'and you must get out more. What about Sunday? Tell the aunts that I'll serve tea and dinner and have a good long time off for once.'

'All right, Mr Charles.' Her eyes, unusually sad and docile, looked up at me out of the wan fragile little face and although I still thought that she had allowed herself to become hysterical, I felt a stab of pain that I should have been the cause of the dulling of that bright spirit.

During the remainder of the summer term, she seemed to be less gay than she used to be, more turned in upon herself, her mind less alert for the outside world, more concentrated upon her inner life but when the summer examinations came along, she suddenly broke out of her silence and became once more the Treasure of the musicales. As the examination results began to appear in the newspaper, she watched the columns for the names of the Adairs, myself and other friends I had told her about and her pleasure in our success was unbounded although of myself she said: 'Mr Charles, you are just plain monotonous. I know now that you've passed before I look up the paper. Do you not find any of the exams hard?'

'Not really. I am what is called a glib examinee, on paper, that is. Where I am going to come unstuck is in the practical way. With a chief watching me, I am liable to strangle a patient with my stethoscope.'

'Get away for gyad's sake! You never have enough confidence in yourself. You'll roll 'em in the aisles when it comes to it!'

To her acute disappointment, David Adair came down in one of his finals, which did not surprise me for he had been more of a militant strike-leader than a medical student during the spring and summer terms.

'But why was he making speeches instead of doing his work?' Treasure asked and this annoyed me. Isabel had been saying the same thing all through the strike crisis which had annoyed me too, but I did not want to annoy Isabel by showing that I was annoyed. I did not mind, however, being my annoyed and ugly self with Treasure and said: 'You simply don't understand and you have no right to express opinions.'

'I am not expressing opinions,' she pointed out imperturbably. 'And I *don't* understand and that is why I am asking.'

'David wants to be a doctor more than anything in the world but there are other things as well.'

'What other things?'

When Treasure wished to understand something, she was persistent. It was as well to be frank. 'Ida Mackintosh for one thing. She is a girl in the Arts faculty and he is dotty about her and her face probably got between him and his exam paper.'

'Poor David,' said Treasure, capitulating at once and showing understanding as Isabel had never done although I did not admit this to myself. 'I should have thought of that. Only, I thought he was more like Isabel, caring for nothing but doctoring.'

'Is that what Isabel is like?' I asked carefully.

'Ach, I don't know. It's years since I knew Isabel. But at the school she was never in it with anybody. Although she was the Leader in the playground, she was always on her own like. Poor David. You know what I think, Mr Charles? If the country wants doctors and schoolmasters and the like, it should pay the folk to study so that they can get married if they like while they're learning. *That* would stop their girls' faces getting between them and their exam papers. Maybe folk will see that one o' these days.'

I had a momentary vision of Paradise, of Isabel and myself together at the end of our day's work. The vision exploded in a red flash. 'When pigs can fly!' I said scornfully.

'As dear papa used to say,' said Treasure, glaring back at me with a scorn the equal of my own before she added in parody of one of our ballads: 'Papa is dead and gone to glory, so are the things he used to say. Pigs can fly *now*. Anybody can put a pig in an aeroplane.'

Unable to think of a retort, I flung out of the pantry and the house in a pet and walked on the moors in a cloud of pity for myself, caught as I was in the toils of this monstrous regiment of women, the aunts who had the money and the power at home, Isabel who had the position and the power at Casualty. Then there was Teresa with her roguish possessiveness and now here was Treasure growing far too clever by half.

There was no doubt that Treasure was different of late, that she had grown away from me during these last months, as if she had opened up some mental territory away beyond the fantasy world we had shared and into which I could not follow her because she did not want me there.

Indeed, although all these women seemed to exert power over me, none of them wanted me, except Teresa whom I did not want, I told myself bitterly when, at the beginning of August, Isabel took her leave and went off to Vienna – Vienna, mark you. She was to be allowed to attend a Medical Congress and hear papers read by the leading doctors of the world, an honour she had achieved by wheedling and lick-spittling round old Professor Hamilton, the chief of her hospital, old Have-It-Out Hamilton, whose idea of medicine was that the whole world had acute appendicitis. I was not only furious with Isabel for going off blithely to Vienna, not caring who she left behind, I was also so jealous of her that I seemed to carry red-hot coals inside me, while my feelings were further complicated by the guilty knowledge that if old Have-It-Out had chosen myself to go with him to Vienna, I would have gone just as blithely and uncaringly as Isabel had. I was glad she was out of the way, I told myself savagely, out of sight so that the muscles of my abdomen would not tie themselves in knots every time somebody in a white coat came through one of the doorways of Casualty.

The day after she left for Vienna, I left Lochfoot to go walking in the Highlands and I would stay away, I told myself, until the winter term began. She could do without me in Casualty for a time after she came back. Let her see how she liked it, without me to fetch and carry for her and snip with the scissors when she was stitching. I looked firmly away from the coiled snake of suspicion in the dark corner of my mind, the suspicion that Isabel would like Casualty without me as much as she had ever liked it and that there were plenty of other people to fetch, carry and snip for her. And, of course, on the first Saturday after her return, I was waiting in Casualty, my scissors ready in my hand.

In September, David re-sat and passed with ease the final that he had ploughed in the summer but Colin Adair, who had been pursuing his quiet way, astounded us all. He had taken three subjects at degree standard in May and now, in September, he took another two and after a graduation ceremony early in November, he emerged as a Bachelor of Science (Agricultural). Isabel was as amazed as the rest of us that Colin had done this in two years, although the subjects that he had taken to degree level in his year in the medical faculty had been of help in his science degree, but Isabel was not impressed. Isabel could not be impressed by any achievement other than in the field of medicine, but I was impressed by Colin's single-mindedness when I realised that, unobserved by all of us, he had been spending his vacations on farms, that while David and I were wasting our time on useless rebellion, Colin had been working as steadily, as unaffected by his surface surroundings, as some process of growth deep in the earth.

And in addition to being impressed, I was jealous of Colin, who had achieved the status of the qualified man, who had something to offer to the world and to an Isabel and when, at the beginning of December, he left home to undertake a probation period of three months as under-factor on a ducal estate in the Border country, my jealousy flared higher than ever.

In my unreasoning mental state, I could visualise Isabel only in relation to myself. I did not look at her in the singleness of her own identity, so that the thought that Isabel would not want to be carried off from Casualty to a country farmhouse in the Borders did not occur to me. What I saw in my fevered jealous dreams was that if Colin achieved this appointment at the end of the three months and I had no doubt that he would achieve it, he would have an income, a house, a bedroom – I could see the curtains at the windows, the furniture and feel the carpet of the stairs under my feet and the feet of Isabel. And when I came out of the dreams, I was twenty-one years old and a medical student finishing the first term of my third year. Time, like a limitless desert, dotted with the prickly cacti of frustration, stretched ahead for ever and I hid from it inside the hair shirt of my misery.

CHAPTER TWELVE

The Assyrian came down like a wolf on the fold
'Sennacherib,' by Lord Byron.

WHEN the Christmas vacation began, Isabel, in her cool Olympian way, swept aside my last shreds of earthly comfort and also infuriated me by informing me that Casualty had no more to teach me but that, if I would like it, she would 'speak for me' to Mr Duff, the chief surgeon who sometimes permitted a student or two to enter his operating theatre. I wanted at one and the same time to grovel at her feet, asking her to keep me in Casualty and to strike her down for the tact and influence she could exert and which would certainly see me through the sacred portals of Duff's theatre, but I had learned through experience that Isabel did not like displays of what she called 'temperament'. Anger, fear, emotion of any kind, Isabel described as 'temperament' in a judicial voice as cold and clinical as her white coat so, for the moment, I did not speak at all.

'I have had enough of Casualty myself,' she said next. 'I have applied for a post in a midder home in Edinburgh.'

Edinburgh! Fifty miles away! Train fares. Isabel fifty miles away. Well, there it was.

'Thanks, Isabel,' I said, 'if you think Duff will have me.'

'I think he will,' she said with a cool certainty and just as coolly she went off to Edinburgh for her day or two of Christmas leave, to find out what she could at first hand about the maternity home, the staff of which she wished to join.

Amid the grey snow of the winter city, after my last class of the term, everyone except myself seemed to have gay plans ahead, friends to join, places to go and in my pity for myself I did not see that, by mooning after Isabel and wandering about alone, dreaming about her, I had played myself into this position of isolation.

But when I left the Union and came out through the gates of the college drive, my isolation was less complete than I had thought for Teresa Riordan was waiting there, pink-cheeked in the cold. I had been avoiding her of late and she was wearing a determined look. She had a few days' leave, she told me and she was going home to Ireland. She suggested that I should come too and meet her family. I knew enough of the conventions by which Teresa lived to recognise that acceptance of this invitation would place our relationship on a new plane. To go to stay with her family would be almost tantamount to announcing our engagement to marry. This outcome of my spineless dithering seemed to rush upon me like some angry beast, making me first panic-stricken and then angry, so that Teresa and I had an ugly quarrel, which ended with her saying: 'So it's that starchy bitch Adair, is it? Well, I wish you cold comfort of her for that's all you'll get.' She then turned about and walked away from me into the grey drizzly snow, while I looked at the back of her dark green coat, hating her for the misery I had caused her, hating my own misery out of which Teresa's misery had been born. I then began to walk downhill through the dreary streets to the Settlement, the best place for me, I told myself, one more of the abandoned and accursed, on my way to join my abandoned and accursed fellow-beings.

At twenty-one years old, however, a mood of high tragedy is difficult to maintain, no matter how hard one may try and after a night's sleep at Laurelbank, cheerfulness broke in. Here, the snow was white and not grey and here was Treasure who did not care that I had mooned and gloomed my way through the winter term and had forgotten all my grand promises of the time after the Strike to give her more opportunities to get out. When I came down to breakfast on the first morning of the vacation, she was drinking tea in the pantry with her copy of *Pride and Prejudice* propped in front of her and I thought with pleasure of the parcel in my wardrobe upstairs which contained all the novels of the Brontë sisters, ready for presentation on Christmas morning.

When Christmas Day came, it was on the surface exactly like the two others we had spent together, with a musicale in the early morning and another in the afternoon, but we did not play the piano or sing. In the early morning, Treasure looked through the books I had given her, caressing the bindings with her fingers and I admired the silver key-ring she had given me, with its dangling miniature label on which was engraved 'CS/TR'. I strung upon it the key of my newer suitcase and the key of the smaller Gladstone bag. The key of the larger one was lost. I wished I had more keys, more important keys. As I was wishing this, Treasure looked up from her books. 'You will have a lot of important keys one day, Mr Charles,' she said.

The quiet hours of the day floated by on the river of our contentment and it was six in the evening when Treasure said: 'This has been a funny musicale, Mr Charles, with no music.'

'It seems a pity in a way,' I said, 'but I have rather grown out of the Gyarland, I think.'

She nodded. 'I think I have too but it was great fun while it lasted. Would you give me the "Yellow God" though, just for auld lang syne, like?'

'The Yellow God', auld lang syne. I cast a glance towards the memory of my father and went to the piano.

There's a one-eyed yellow idol to the north of Khatmandu,
There's a little marble cross below the town;
There's a broken-hearted woman tends the grave of Mad Carew,
And the Yellow God forever gazes down.

At the end of the first verse, I stopped and closed the piano, for evidently there was enough of my father in me to make me recognise that I was giving a bad performance. 'I am sorry, Treasure,' I said. 'I don't seem to be able to do it any more.' She smiled, a gentle contented smile. 'It's all right, Mr Charles. I don't really seem to feel like being rolled in the aisles today anyway. Besides, lately I've been thinking that maybe it isn't the mackay to make fun of these songs and the poetry in the Gyarland. Folk believed in them long ago. Maybe you shouldn't laugh at things that folk once believed in.'

Snow did not last long at Lochfoot, for it shared the wet muggy climate of Glasgow and during Christmas night a storm of rain and wind came, moaning through the trees and howling round the house. The storm went on for days and I felt that the great solid house would have been like a beleaguered fortress if it had not been for the postman who trudged up the back drive every morning, delivering the Discounts. Come hell or high water, it seemed, the calendar of the aunts' year must complete its wealth-ordained cycle.

On the first day that the weather cleared a little, I went out, intending to go up to the moors but a branch of a tree had come down in the back drive and having cleared that to one side, I felt an urge to go into the wilderness which neither Treasure nor I had entered since October. In winter, Mrs Grey dried her washing in the old laundry in the basement.

As I neared the centre of the place, I halted with a sinking feeling of the heart. Many of the shrubs were bare of leaves now and ahead of me I could see a great gash in the crown of the weeping elm where the wind had torn away one of the drooping branches. I went towards it. The little Pan lay on his side on the ground, his head severed from his body. 'Great Pan is dead' the dying wind seemed to cry among the bare trees.

I did not go to the moors. Having made sure that Treasure was upstairs in her room, I fetched my bigger Gladstone bag from the pantry, put the two pieces of the statue into it and carried it down to the builders' yard in the town. The man was not interested in my request that it should be repaired as soon as possible. He humoured me as an absurd eccentric and at last said: 'We'll attend to it when we can, sir, but there's been a lot of *real* damage, serious damage, folk with chimneys down and half the roof torn off the Shirt Factory. It'll be a while before we can get round to that wee job, sir.' With this I had to be content. The shirt factory took precedence over the little god Pan and I could only hope that they would do the repair before Treasure made her first Wilderness journey of the year, to see if her snowdrops were coming up through the cold bare earth under the leafless trees.

On the last morning of the year, the back doorbell rang while Treasure had her hands deep in a bowl of flour and she said: 'It must be the Postie with another Discount. I thought they were all in.'

'I'll go,' I said and went downstairs.

The postman handed me a cube-shaped parcel and a letter for Treasure and back in the pantry, I held up the parcel. 'Feels like another tin of biscuits. The Settlement is going to do well this year. Letter for you Treasure. I'll take this up to the altar.'

When I had deposited the parcels beside the others that had come in during the week, I returned to the pantry to find Treasure sitting at the table, her bowl of flour pushed to one side, the single sheet of her letter in her hand. 'Mr Charles,' she said, 'you've got to help me.'

'Is something the matter?'

'Yes. No. Ach, in the name o' the Kingdom, I'm a stupid goat! The ladies are going to be *that* upset. I should have told them long before this but I kept putting it off.'

'Putting what off?'

She seemed to go off at a tangent, while she made exasperated gestures with her hands. 'Colin's got that job. They've decided at the end o' his first month that they want him and he's coming here tomorrow. Oh, Mr Charles, what am I going to do? The ladies—'

'Do about *what*, for God's sake?' I almost shouted at her.

'Not so loud, Mr Charles,' she cautioned me and then: 'About giving my notice and getting married to Colin,' she said as if this were something I ought already to know about.

'Getting married to Colin?' I repeated, stupefied.

'We've only been waiting till he had a job,' she said impatiently. 'What *will* the ladies—'

'When did all this start?' I asked and my voice seemed to come from far away, as if I were semi-anaesthetised. 'You and Colin, I mean. You've been damned secretive about it.'

'I didn't mean to be secretive with *you*, Mr Charles,' she said, her blue eyes wide and honest. 'In fact, you would have known about Colin and me quite natural if you hadn't been so in it with Isabel all the time that you could think of nothing else.'

How did *she* know that I had been thinking of Isabel all the time? I was furious and blazed out: 'Don't talk a lot of rubbish! I am not in it, as you call it, with Isabel Adair!'

Treasure ignored my rage and also my words. 'If I have been secretive,' she was saying, 'it is mostly because of Isabel. She doesn't like Colin liking me.'

'That's a lot of nonsense!' I had been bombarded too suddenly with too many ideas that were new and strange and my instinct to defend myself against further bombardment was to shout 'No!' to everything that was said.

'It isn't,' said Treasure quietly but inexorably. 'Colin took me to the digs in Dunn Square once and Isabel made it quite clear what she thought. I never went again. But since then I've kept quiet about Colin and me because I wanted him to be quite sure that I was what he wanted and not have a lot of circumstances of folk thinking about us and talking about us to bother him.'

'I think you are wrong about Isabel,' I said. This was untrue. I knew that Isabel was ambitious for her brothers and I also knew that in her mind people were separated into distinct social strata but the words I spoke were another 'No!', an avoidance of the main issue of Treasure and Colin.

'You can think what you like Mr Charles,' Treasure said in her firm way, 'and there is nothing that Isabel can do about Colin and me now, anyway. Colin has his job, he can do as he likes and so can I.'

At the last three words, a typical short statement by Treasure of the situation, a statement of her independence, her separateness, everything in me shrivelled away to a withered sense of helplessness.

'When did it all start, Colin and you, I mean?' I asked, trying to call her back from that separateness, to call her back towards myself.

'About a month after that time you took me to meet him at the Sutherland. He wrote to me,' she said. 'That was when it started. Mr Charles, what about the *ladies*?'

At the sight of her wide worried eyes, in the presence of her selflessness, this antithesis of my own self-love, I felt so shamed that I had to take refuge in anger. 'Oh, to hell with the ladies!' I said and went stamping away upstairs.

The underhand, cunning little bitch, I thought, carrying on with Colin all this time while I carried in the tea tray and put pies in the oven! Carrying on under my very nose when I - I - - I— When I what? I discovered that I was staring at the wall of the landing where the words on a brass plate under a picture swam into focus: 'A Lost Chord'. I had lost the chord of my anger for, when I looked for the reason for it, there was no reason to be found. 'I cannot be angry,' came the thought, 'because I have no right but how could she do this to me? Do what? She had done nothing to me. Yes, she had. She had hurt me. How could Treasure hurt me like this? But she had not done it deliberately, knowingly. How could she know that her being *in* it with Colin, as she would express it, would hurt me when I myself had not known, until this moment, that such a thing could hurt me?'

Very slowly, reason brought calm out of the chaos of shock and when I got up from the side of my bed, Treasure's happiness had emerged as more important to me than my own inexplicable misery. I had to go downstairs. She must be thinking, by now, that I was 'upset', as the ladies would be, at this threat of disruption to our household.

When I went down to the pantry, she turned round from the cooker to look at me. 'I am sorry if you are angry, Mr Charles. It is an upset, I know, but Colin needs me more than the ladies do, I think.'

'And do you need Colin, Treasure?' I asked.

She gave me a grateful little smile for not being angry with her after all. 'I think I do. When somebody needs you and wants you as much as Colin does, you get different. You begin to need them – him too.'

'It couldn't be that you love Colin?'

'I don't know much about love – I've told you that before – but, yes. I suppose when folk need each other and want each other, that's loving.' She looked down at the eggs she was frying. 'The trouble is that the ladies need me and want me too but only in a way they can pay money for and I don't need them or want their money any more. The ladies don't understand things. They are going to think I am selfish and disloyal, as they call it.'

'They have no right to think any such thing, Treasure.'

'It would be better for themselves if they didn't think like that but that is what they are going to think all the same. It's the money, you see. They will never see that with Colin and me money isn't *in* it. For them, always, money has been in everything. For them, it has *been* everything. They have had nothing else. You will help me to tell them, Mr Charles? Will you?'

'Of course I will, Treasure.'

'There they are, coming down now. I'll get the breakfast in. We'll let them have *it* in peace.'

When she went to the morning-room, I retired upstairs again. There is a near amnesiac state in which memory is not lost but submerged, so that the surface of the mind remains aware of it as, when standing by a grass plot in a graveyard, one is aware that a body lies under the ground. In this state, the mind deals with immediacies and can deal with them very efficiently as, in the graveyard, the sight absorbs the grass, the trees, the gravestones although the reason for the very existence of this place and these things, the body in the grave, is beneath the conscious surface of the mind.

Sitting on the edge of my bed again, I saw that the aunts must be told of Treasure's intention – I did not use the term 'marriage' for that thought and all that it entailed lay buried – Treasure's intention as soon as possible and this act, this 'upsetting of the ladies' was something that had been fretting her for a long time, something that, uncharacteristically, she had been postponing because she dreaded it. Why should Treasure be fretted and given over to dread because of two old women? Why should she be 'upset' by having to witness their 'upset'? I myself would tell them, take the first shock of their reaction. It was the least I could do for Treasure.

I knew the iron routine of the household to a split second. If I stayed in my room after they rang the bell for Treasure to clear breakfast, Treasure would decide that I was not going to help her to break the news and would put off the evil moment until she saw me again. She would wash up breakfast, go up to tidy her own room, then do the day's laundry in the basement down below. That would be my moment. When Treasure went down the back stairs, I would go to the morning-room.

The moment came. The green baize door swished shut and

I presented myself in the morning-room, walking in without knocking.

'Charles!' Aunt Bessie jerked clumsily to her feet, wrenching off her spectacles while her knitting fell to the hearthrug.

'Good morning, Aunt Bessie, Aunt Jessie. I came in to tell you something, something important.' Aunt Bessie, distrustful eyes staring at me, sank into her chair. 'Jeanie has given a month's notice.'

'Notice? Jeanie? Our *servant*? You must be out of your mind, Charles or – have you been drinking again?'

Again. 'I do *not* drink, Aunt Bessie. Will you look facts in the face for once? Jeanie is a pretty young girl and—'

'Charles Simpson, what do you mean? Have you been – been—'

'Don't be so damned filthy-minded!' I said, standing over her. I wanted to strike her ugly, suspicious furtive face but at last I felt that I had control of the situation. She cowered back in the horse-hair armchair. 'Jeanie is leaving to marry a young man from the Village. She was at school with him and has known him all her life. She gave her notice to me this morning because she did not want to upset you.'

'Jessie,' said Aunt Bessie, recovering somewhat and grasping at the clichés in which she thought, 'it is just as I have always said. There is no gratitude, no loyalty in any of them. They are all alike. To think of how we took her in here untrained, gave her a home—'

'—and that new pantry and everything—'

I felt that they might air these grievances that Treasure had predicted for ever so I broke in with: 'Shall I ask Mr Guthrie to arrange for new staff?'

'New staff? New *staff*? Really, it is too bad, this upset! Go away, Charles, this minute. Go away!'

I went straight to the basement and met Treasure coming down from her room. 'Well,' I said, 'I've told them, Treasure.'

'Told – told the *ladies*? Oh, Mr Charles.' She caught

her lower lip between her teeth. 'Are they very – upset?'

The bell on the staircase pealed. 'Very upset,' I said, 'but you have given a month's notice as of this morning and don't you go back on it.'

She looked up at the bell on the wall which was still swinging angrily. 'I can't go back on it. Colin will be here tomorrow.' She caught my arm between her hands and squeezed it hard. 'Oh, *thank* you, Mr Charles.' The bell rang again, jiggling as if in rage and she looked up at it, then at me and her left eyelid fell over the eye. 'Gyad, the bells o' hell are ringin' as if the Lord had left Ireland,' she said and ran upstairs.

I sat in the pantry and waited for a long time before she came out of the morning-room. Several times, I thought of going in there and fetching her out and it was only the thought that she might dislike the implication that she could not 'look after' herself that restrained me. At last she came, shut the pantry door, sat down and began to cry quietly and painfully.

'Treasure,' I said, 'don't let them hurt you like this. They have no right to make you cry.'

'I am not crying *at* the ladies, Mr Charles. I am crying *for* them,' she sobbed.

'They won't cry for *you*,' I said harshly and she looked up at me.

'Do ye not see, Mr Charles, that that's what's so sad? The ladies can't cry for anybody.'

I left the house and took to the road that wound and climbed its way over the moors. About twelve miles from Lochfoot, there was a little wayside inn which catered for char-à-banc tours from Glasgow in the summer but which, in winter, had no patrons except the shepherds from the remote cottages in the surrounding hills. Today, it had no patrons except myself but the landlord, who was feeding his sheep in a pen nearby, agreed to give me a bottle of beer, some bread and cold mutton. I remember the windy sky beyond the window and the brown of the winter moors but I do not think I thought about anything. I was conscious only of a hollow misery.

When I came back to Laurelbank, Treasure was serving dinner, as if the routine of this house were indestructible. 'How are they now?' I asked, jerking my head to indicate the morning-room.

'Quite the thing, Mr Charles. I don't think they're really taken it in. Will *you* see Mr Guthrie about staff? I don't think the ladies are going to do anything themselves. They've got out of the way of doing anything.'

The house was heavy with their inertia. 'Yes, I'll see to it, as soon as his office opens after the holiday.' I turned away to go upstairs.

'What would you like for your supper, Mr Charles?'

'I've had something, Treasure, thanks. Goodnight.'

The next morning, New Year's morning, was in routine like any other morning at Laurelbank but I found it unbearable to be in the presence of Treasure. She seemed to radiate a calm happiness that mocked at my own misery, threatening to expose it, red and raw and I did not want to spoil her joy as the aunts had done the day before. 'When will Colin arrive?' I asked at breakfast.

'The evening sometime. He's getting a lift by car. His boss is coming to Glasgow to catch the night train for London.'

'I'll be out for lunch, Treasure. I met a chap yesterday and we arranged to spend the day on the moors.'

'You are a great one for the moors, Mr Charles. I like them too. It's the all-aloneness, I think and the wandering noise the wind makes in the heather, like the Lost Chord.'

But as I walked away up the road, I thought that Treasure did not know about true 'all-aloneness'. Our *servant*, Aunt Bessie had said, stressing the word as if it denoted not a human being but some thing that could have no desires, no motivation, no self-determination, no single identity. But Aunt Bessie did not know the true quality of the servant that

Treasure, the perfect treasure, was. When she was all alone, as she was so much and liked to be, she was still serving all the time, thinking of us all and planning her service to us. The time and thought that she devoted to 'looking after' herself was minimal compared to what she gave to others. She was never all alone. Her mind was constantly peopled with those who needed her.

I had something to eat at the little inn again and tried to steel myself to the homeward journey, to the meeting with Colin Adair. I had the cowardly thought that I need not return until midnight or later and not see him at all but this was so ugly in its ungraciousness to Treasure that I hurriedly swallowed the last of my lunch and took to the road, walking faster than I had done on the outward journey, hoping now that I would reach the house before Colin arrived. Laurelbank, I felt now, had been ungracious and ungrateful enough without my own contribution of boorishness.

When I was inside the back door, I had the knowledge that Colin was already in the house. I can only account for this by saying that the air vibrated with the watchful, distrustful sullen resentment with which the house greeted any invader, even the harmless invited piano-tuner, from beyond the walls. I hesitated in the passage in the blue light of the low-turned gas jet and at that moment, I heard the voice of Aunt Bessie from above, shouting: 'Charles!' raucously, half-hysterically, as she had shouted on the morning of the Mary Lawrie set-to. What had I done this time? But Colin was in the house. Aunt Bessie must be silenced lest Colin thought we Simpsons were all mad. 'Charles!' the crazed voice shouted. 'Jeanie!'

I bounded up the stairs, butting the green door at the top ahead of me and Treasure and Colin were already out of the pantry and standing in the hall. In the dim waste-not-want-not light, I saw Aunt Bessie standing half-way down the stairs, with Aunt Jessie a few steps above her. Aunt Bessie now raised her right arm and pointed downwards with a long bony forefinger. 'Thief! Wastrel! Scoundrel! Thief!' she shouted and she was pointing at Colin. Sick with shame at this hysterical outburst against Treasure's sweetheart, which was how I interpreted the words, I ran towards the staircase, determined to silence her at any cost but as I reached the bottom step, her body stiffened, her spine arching like a bow and she came slumping forward and sideways. The heavy body thudded dully against Lord Mammon and with a hideous groan of tearing wood, the thing began to slew round on its base and then to fall. Treasure was nearest to me and I threw her clear, hard against the door of the dining-room but Colin went down, with the mass of metal on top of him and Aunt Bessie lay in a heap beside them both.

'A doctor! Nursing home at the corner,' I said to Treasure.

She had been standing as if frozen but when I spoke, life seemed to leap in her. She wrenched open the front door and ran away into the darkness, while I sprang at the gas bracket and turned the lights fully up. The crumpled heap that was Aunt Bessie I ignored and took a second or two to decide which was the surest way to lift the lump of metal from Colin's body without doing him further injury. I glanced at Aunt Jessie but there was no help there. She was sitting on the stairs, stupefied. I straddled the body of flesh, grasped the metal body by the shoulders, exerted all my strength and lifted. At this time, after my experience at the Settlement and in Casualty, I had seen something of the vulnerability of human flesh and since then I have experienced the ugliest war that history has ever known but nothing in my life has ever matched the horror of that moment. When I lifted the metal carcase, the head and shoulders of Colin began to rise with it. The long spike at the back of the axe-blade was driven deep through his temple and into his skull.

CHAPTER THIRTEEN

I do not know what I was playing
Or what I was dreaming then:
'A Lost Chord,' by Adelaide Anne Procter.

IN words that Treasure had used, we came into a time of things and not thoughts. It was not possible to think of what had happened and there were things that the doctor told me to do and I did them. Then, when Colin's body had been covered with a sheet and Aunt Bessie and Aunt Jessie had been carried upstairs, I remember the doctor telling me that he would have to call in the police, that this was a case of fatal accident. When the fat sergeant and his skinny constable arrived, my brain began to think again, to think that I must deal with this alone, try to save Treasure this pain. I also began to think that the sergeant was enjoying his position of importance at the centre of the most sensational event, probably, that had ever happened in Lochview Crescent. After strutting pompously around the hall for a time, he permitted Colin's body to be taken away. He then sat down at the large table under the stained glass windows, taking out his notebook and began to question me, while the skinny constable stood by the door, trying to look official. I now had one of the strangest, most distorted experiences of my life and I remember every detail.

It has been said that truth lies at the bottom of a well, that it peeps over a glass's rim when dinner's done, that it is the daughter of time and it has been described in many other ways. I now discovered that, where two or three people are gathered together, truth goes into hiding. There was a number of people in that hall, but truth went into hiding inside the carcase of Lord Mammon, which was lying close to the wall between the staircase and the pantry door.

'Mr Adair was a friend of yours, sir?' the sergeant asked.

'Yes.'

'At the Yooni together, weren't you?'

'Yes.'

'And he called at the house today?'

'Yes.'

'When?'

'I was out when he arrived. I came in shortly before five.'

'And he was waiting for you?'

'He and the maid were in the hall here.'

'He had just arrived likely. Go on, sir.'

'My aunt came down the stairs, calling my name. She sounded very angry.'

'Show me where you were standing, sir.'

I did as he asked and then indicated Lord Mammon. 'That – that statue stood at the bottom of the stairs here.' I went on to tell him the remainder of the story and he then said: 'What had made Miss Simpson so angry, sir?'

'I don't know.'

'Had you ever seen her so angry before?'

'Yes. Once, when I left the gas burning on the landing all night.'

'Poor lady. Upset about some domestic matter,' he said, writing in the notebook. 'I think that will be all, sir,' he said after I had answered a few more questions. 'Very painful, losing your friend like that but we have to get a true and detailed report, sir, you understand. The maid was a witness too?'

'Yes. She is upstairs with my aunts.'

'You can give me her name, sir?'

'Jean Robertson.'

'Thank you, sir. You have been very helpful.'

He went away with his henchman, satisfied that he knew the truth of what had happened, which was that Colin had come to the house to visit me and had been the unfortunate victim of an accident.

As I shut the door behind him and came back into the hall, I realised that the 'truth' as it had entered the sergeant's mind had been told to him more by the carcase of Lord Mammon than by myself. He had based the questions he had asked on certain assumptions that arose out of his class consciousness, so that he now believed that the young gentleman friend of the young gentleman of the house had met his death because one of the two old ladies of the house had been subject to fits of rage, the latest of which had brought on an apoplectic stroke, causing her to fall against a statue which, in turn, had fallen upon the young gentleman friend of the young gentleman of the house. A maid-servant named Jean Robertson had also been present at the time but this fact was of only minor importance.

Aunt Bessie died shortly after two in the morning, which was merely one more thing in the nightmare and my mind began to deal entirely with things again, not thoughts.

The doctor had telephoned to Mr Guthrie for me and he arrived with his two sons before nine o'clock in the morning. Once more the tale had to be told and I now let it stand as it had been accepted by the police sergeant and Mr Guthrie, too, accepted his own assumption that Colin had been calling on me. I had come to the belief that this assumption might ease matters a little for Treasure, with her privacies and her liking to be 'on her own' and if she wished Mr Guthrie to know of her relationship with Colin, she could tell him herself. I had not seen her since she had gone upstairs the night before for Aunt Jessie, the nurses told me, would not allow her to leave her bedside. Like the police sergeant, Mr Guthrie asked me if Aunt Bessie had indulged in a similar fit of rage before and I told him too of my leaving the landing lights on all night.

'The fuss went on for quite a long time,' I ended, 'several

weeks. She had made up her mind that I had been drunk when I came home.'

'Poor lady.' Mr Guthrie shook his head slowly from side to side. 'We can never know what goes on in another person's mind.'

Treasure can know, I thought, because she is more interested in the other persons than she is in herself. 'And you have no idea what misdemeanour you had committed this time, lad?' Mr Guthrie asked.

'No, sir. I can't think of anything.'

'Some trifle more than likely. Well, we'll never know now.'

'Unless Aunt Jessie knows?' I suggested.

'It is of no importance, lad. Maybe it is better not to know what annoyed her, especially if it was some trifle like a few extra pence on the gas bill. This business is tragic enough without bringing the ridiculous into it. The best thing you can do now is to go and pack your stuff, Charles. This house has never been the right place for you and you must want to see the back of it for good now. Besides, wee Jeanie has enough on her hands with Miss Jessie. You go up and get your things together.'

I did what he told me, gathering my things together into two suitcases, the two Gladstone bags and filling an old trunk from the attic with my books. We then loaded it all into the car and Jim Guthrie drove it to the station, put it on the train.

The three Guthries were very busy making arrangements for the funeral, Treasure and the nurse were in Aunt Jessie's room and I wandered about the house like, as Treasure would once have said, a Lost Chord. The mahogany altar on the landing was an untidy mess of opened and unopened parcels, paper and pieces of string. Of course, yesterday, centuries ago, had been New Year's day and the ladies had been opening the Discounts, as their calendar had dictated, when the routine of years had exploded into tragedy. Looking at the untidy table, I tried to imagine what had happened, what thought had suddenly entered Aunt Bessie's mind to send her shouting across the landing and down the stairs. The door of Aunt Jessie's room opened and Treasure came out. Her face was very pale and strangely still under the white cap but she was steady.

'Treasure!' The gas-lit landing was like a continent between us, a flat waste of silence. 'How is Aunt Jessie?'

'She will be all right, Mr Charles. She is sleeping. There is something here that you ought to see.' She was efficient, distant, the household servant who was dependable in a crisis, the perfect treasure.

She went to the mahogany altar, lifted some shavings out of a cardboard box and gestured that I should look inside. The box contained the inkstand made of silver snakes and a vulture that I had sold for forty pounds in the pawnshop near the Settlement. I looked from it to her still face, feeling that this tortured nightmare had no end.

'Last night,' she said quietly, 'while the nurse looked after Miss Jessie, I was undressing Miss Bessie. This was in her hand, along with her specs.' She put her hand under her apron and drew from the pocket of her dress a crumpled sheet of paper. Holding it, she said: 'Can we go into your room, Mr Charles?'

Behind the closed door, she handed me the paper. It was a letter with no heading, no date. 'Dear Madam, The piece herewith was sold to a member of my staff by a young man with the initials C.S. I have reason to believe that the article is your property and may have been sold without your knowledge. If you wish to re-imburse the purchase price of sixty pounds, I will be grateful, but I leave this to your conscience. Yrs. respectfully, P. Pillans, Secondhand Shop, Lochfoot.'

The first thing for which I could find words was the concrete fact of the profit factor. The letter gave the purchase price as sixty instead of forty pounds. 'But it was only forty pounds I got for it!' I said.

'When did you sell it, Mr Charles?'

'At the time of the Mary Lawrie set-to. I bought her ticket and gave her the rest of the money.'

Treasure took the letter from me, took the matches from the mantel and, kneeling on the hearthrug, burned the sheet of paper in the grate. Still kneeling, she looked up at me. 'Nothing is your fault, Mr Charles. We are all in it – old Pillans, my mother – she must have told him where that ink-stand came from – and me, especially me. I should have told you about old Pillans and his terrible badness but I did not see any way he could harm you, Mr Charles, and I did not want you to have the thought of him inside you. Then you got in it with the strike at the shirt factory and it was too late.'

I held out my hand and she took it and rose to her feet. 'Treasure, I—' but there was nothing that I wanted to say that she would want to hear and I repeated her name, 'Treasure.'

'I have to go back to Miss Jessie, Mr Charles. If she wakes up, she will need me. She doesn't know what happened last night.' She indicated the black shreds in the grate. 'She doesn't know what made Miss Bessie so angry. Nobody knows except you and me. And nobody knows about Colin and me except Miss Jessie and you, Mr Charles. Miss Jessie won't tell and I am asking you not to tell either. I don't want folk being sorry for me.'

'I won't tell anybody,' I promised her and she turned away. 'I must go now,' she said.

'Wait a minute, Treasure. I am to go to Glasgow to stay with the Guthries and then go into lodgings.'

'That will be best,' she said quietly and finally.

'But may I come back to see you?'

'Not soon, Mr Charles. Not for a long time. I am not angry, Mr Charles. Nothing was your fault. We are all in it, like I said but – ' her hands moved laterally through the air, palms downwards and fell still by her sides ' – it is all over now.'

She went to the door, paused and turned round. 'There is one thing, Mr Charles, I would be very thankful if you would do before you go.'

'What, Treasure?'

'Will you please take that – the inkstand down to the Killection and put it on the writing-table where it was before? You know where the key of the Killection is.'

'Yes, I know where the key is and I shall put the inkstand back.'

'Thank you, Mr Charles,' she said and went away.

When the door closed between us I felt a sharp pang of grievous loss but what I had lost I could not identify. I wished that she had accused me, blamed me and it was some time before I came to understand that my loss was that Treasure, in her own phrase, was no longer 'in it' with me. In that instant, when Lord Mammon, with a rending of wood and a groaning of three rusty screws began to slew round and fall, in that instant when I pushed Treasure away from me and towards the door of the dining-room, the world that we had shared had been shattered. In the world we had made together we had turned the outside world around us into a legend, a comedy, in the way that men down the ages have turned Pontius Pilate and Judas Iscariot into the Punch and Judy show. We had hated the gods that the world around us worshipped, so we had laughed at them as Lord Mammon and his Discounts Altar and at our musicales we had made mock of the verses that were the hymns of praise to these gods in which we did not believe. The mistake we had made was in thinking that gods which we believed to be false were powerless to harm us, that our fragile private world was proof against the gods we were mocking. Our little world had been destroyed in the end by the realities on which its myths were based, the Ladies, the Pauper, Lord Mammon and the Discounts Altar. Little Pan, the stone figure of the Wilderness, had been the victim of an ill wind of chance but Treasure and I were the victims of ourselves and of one another.

During the bleak month of January, I avoided all my friends, gave not a thought to Isabel. I had last seen her at Colin's funeral, when she had looked upon me with more kindness than she had ever shown before. The doctor and the police had given the Adairs their version of the accident and again I let it stand. Isabel had put it behind her, did not want to talk about it, spoke some formal words of sympathy about the death of Aunt Bessie and went away. I watched her go and felt nothing.

Walking the grey wet streets of Glasgow, I remembered how, long ago, in the rooms in Islington, I had longed to be on my own, knowing nobody, being known by nobody but I had never imagined this desolation of isolation. At that time in Islington, I had been on my own in the solitude of one who had never known a human bond. Since that time, I had found a whole world and now I had lost it.

I began to write to Treasure in an attempt to reclaim that lost world, to bring life back to the deadness that lay between us. I would not have cared what form her reaction might take, would not have cared were she angry, grieved or accusatory, if only something between us could be revived. But she did not reply to any of my letters and when February came, I made a plan. I would go to Laurelbank and present myself at the front door at precisely three o'clock on the anniversary of my first call there.

The blank wood of the door faced me as it had faced me that other day, as I pulled on the bell and heard it tinkle in the distance. The door did not open. The silent house brooded beyond the low-drawn blinds. I pulled on the bell again and now one of the blinds at the bay window of the dining-room was pulled aside and behind the glass I saw the face of Treasure. Under the frilly white cap, it was pale and still, the eyes not looking at me but past me into some infinite distance. Looking at her, I pulled on the bell a third time. She shook her head slowly from side to side and the blind was released and came between the face and the glass. As the tinkling of the bell in the distance became faint, then was lost in the silence, I turned about and walked away.